Mavericks

Mavericks

Walt Coburn

THORNDIKE
CHIVERS

This Large Print edition is published by Thorndike Press®, Waterville, Maine USA and by BBC Audiobooks Ltd, Bath, England.

Published in 2006 in the U.S. by arrangement with Golden West Literary Agency.

Published in 2006 in the U.K. by arrangement with Golden West Literary Agency.

U.S. Hardcover   0-7862-8531-1 (Western)
U.K. Hardcover   10: 1-4056-3743-9   (Chivers Large Print)
U.K. Hardcover   13: 978-1-405-63743-5
U.K. Softcover   10: 1-4056-3744-7   (Camden Large Print)
U.K. Softcover   13: 978-1-405-63744-2

The text of this Large Print edition is unabridged.
Other aspects of the book may vary from the original edition.

Set in 16 pt. Plantin by Al Chase.

Printed in the United States on permanent paper.

British Library Cataloguing-in-Publication Data available

Library of Congress Cataloging-in-Publication Data

Coburn, Walt, 1889–1971.
    Mavericks / by Walt Coburn.
        p. cm. — (Thorndike Press large print westerns)
    ISBN 0-7862-8531-1 (lg. print : hc : alk. paper)
    1. Large type books.   I. Title.   II. Thorndike Press large print Western series.
PS3505.O153M38 2006
813'.52—dc22   2006001543

Mavericks

Chapter I

The adjuster for the life-insurance company called it suicide. It was a brutal sort of statement to make in front of Lance Mansfield, the dead man's seventeen-year-old son; brutal, and not altogether discreet, considering the fact that Lance was an inch under six feet and had the shoulder muscles of a prize-fighter. The boy stiffened, white-lipped.

"Damn you for a lying —"

Lance finished the sentence after his uppercut had lifted the insurance man from his feet and landed him on the floor.

"Don't kick 'im, son," warned old Judge Truman, who had grown white-haired in frontier towns where men fought by no rules whatsoever.

"I won't, sir." The boy smiled and the judge was startled at the resemblance he bore to the dead man who lay in the bedroom with a British flag across his coffin. It was Tom Mansfield's smile that had made so many enemies; oddly enough, the same smile that had won the stanch friendship of Judge Truman, who came from Virginia and who understood.

"I'd advise, suh," said the judge, as the insurance man got to his feet, "that you let mattahs stand as they are. Thomas Mansfield was accidentally killed while cleaning his gun."

There being no proof to the contrary, the adjuster dropped the suicide subject and drove back to town in his hired top-buggy. When the man had gone, Lance Mansfield faced the old judge squarely. The boy looked younger, now that the glint was gone from his blue eyes. He stood stiff-backed, heels together — a habit that came from years spent at America's smartest military academy. He still wore the blue-gray uniform of the school, for he had come directly upon receipt of Judge Truman's night letter that told of his father's tragic death. "Sit down, boy," smiled the judge. "You ain't in school now."

"That — that damned coyote said Dad committed suicide! I'd like to know the truth, sir. What cause had he to hint at that?"

"The man's a confounded whippersnapper, son. Don't let it rile you, suh. Not for a second. He'd hint that if there was a shade of chance to prove it, for if Tom Mansfield had killed himself, you'd get no insurance. I'm inclined to think that the man is quite convinced." The judge chuckled softly. "Quite convinced."

"And do you share that conviction, sir?"

"Eh? How's that? Share the conviction?" Judge Truman poured a drink from the decanter on the library table. The question, put so squarely, was a facer. For, deep in his heart, Judge Truman knew that Tom Mansfield had carefully planned and executed his own death. But now, braced by a jolt of twenty-year-old Bourbon, he lied like the gentleman he was.

"Share hell, suh. I was your father's attorney and his friend. You saved me the trouble of taking a blacksnake to that rascal. Now, my boy, sit down. I want to talk to you."

Lance took a chair. Back of his stiff bearing, behind the brave light of his eyes was hidden the grief that ripped his boy's heart. For Tom Mansfield had been his hero as well as his father. And because Tom Mansfield knew of that hero-worship he had never let the boy see that side of his nature by which the cow country judged and condemned the man who owned the Circle Seven outfit on upper Beaver Creek. So when the tin-horn gamblers had stripped him of his last dollar, he had made his plans with characteristic thoroughness and had died. And Lance would collect one hundred thousand dollars, retain respect for his dead father, and be well guided by the sage advice of Judge Truman, who would understand.

It had been Tom Mansfield's final gesture in his life of folly — the final curtain to the bitter drama of his life. There had been a faint smile on his cold lips when they found his body in the gun-room.

Judge Truman had understood this Britisher with his pride and his smile and his vices. There had been some admirable qualities in the tall Englishman who bought the Circle Seven, stocked it with blooded cattle and horses and sheep, and had gone broke. This huge log house with its plumbing, its hardwood floors, its well-stocked cellar, was part of the British folly. The splendid barns and corrals, the paddock and quarter-mile track where blue-blooded horses were tried out — the debts and notes that had stripped the stables — the guests that had robbed Tom Mansfield at poker. And even when his credit was gone and he paid off his Chinamen servants and cooked his own meals, Tom Mansfield had dressed for dinner every evening. Now Judge Truman saw the crooked, wistful, stubborn smile on Lance Mansfield's mouth and knew that he

10

was dealing with Tom's true son.

"We can turn over the Circle Seven at a decent figure, Lance. That money, together with the hundred thousand life-insurance, will set you up nicely in whatever business you later care to go into. Meanwhile it will give you the balance of your education. How many more years have you to go?"

"I'm through now, sir. I'll have my roommate send me my stuff. I'll carry on where father left off."

Judge Truman reached again for the decanter. He needed fortification for the coming battle. To carry on where Tom Mansfield left off! Good gad! a show place — fifty thousand acres of land, with a hundred head of cattle scattered to the devil over it. There were some brood-mares, polo and racing stock, a five-thousand-dollar stud; some game-cocks. Good gad! And he perspired for two hours, explaining the stark idiocy of any attempt to make something of the Circle Seven.

"It takes a cow-man to make a living at the business in Montana."

"I've spent my summers here, Judge. I can ride. I know the range conditions. I can read brands."

"Can you pitch hay?"

"I can learn, sir."

"Ever lost in a blizzard?"

"No, sir. But I've stood at attention while my ears and nose froze stiff."

"Attention, hell!" exploded Judge Truman.

"Yes, sir." Lance smiled again. The judge poured himself another drink and rose.

"I'll be back in the evening. Funeral will be held here in the morning. I'll stay with you to-night."

"You needn't, sir. I'll not be scared. And for to-night, the last night he'll be here in the house, I'd rather it would be just he and I together, sir."

"Yes, yes. To be sure, my boy. Quite so." And Judge Truman drove back to town, muttering to himself. Clearly, Lance Mansfield had inherited all his father's stubborn pride. The judge hoped to God that the boy's heritage did not include his father's weakness for whisky and cards.

Chapter II

Lance Mansfield was alone with his dead father. He sat in the bedroom, tear-filmed eyes fixed on the dead man's face. A handsome face, clean-cut, firm-jawed, a smile on the lips under the close-cropped white mustache. The hair above the high forehead was white as freshly fallen snow. Across the dead man's chest and legs was the British flag that Lance had never before seen. The flag had been put there by Judge Truman in accordance with a wish expressed by Tom Mansfield one night as the two played chess.

Vaguely, Lance felt an underlying tragedy in the life of the man who had been his father. For one thing, father and son had seldom spoken of the boy's mother. He had no memory of her. His father never mentioned her name and had given the boy the impression that it was a subject taboo. The boy in him now hungered for the softness of a mother's comfort. He felt horribly alone — alone with the ache of his grief, his mind whirling with countless memories of the living Tom Mansfield. . . . Days under the blue sky, when they followed the pack of staghounds after a coyote or wolf. . . . Lazy afternoons when they lay stretched out in hammocks on the huge veranda, watching leggy colts playing in the paddock — his father talking dreamily of India and army life. . . . Tales of those colorful years when Tom Mansfield had held a major's rank in the British army — years of soldiering and polo and dances, and leave spent at the country place in Sussex. . . . Months of hunting big game in Africa.

The ranch-house was filled with rare trophies of those hunts. Now and then there had been dropped the vague hint of a family back in England — all those times when the elder Mansfield had lowered the whisky decanter at his elbow. Lance gained the vague impression that, if enough older brothers or uncles were to die, there would be a title waiting.

Memories! The boy's under lip quivered a little and he bit it till the blood came. He felt that his father would not wish any girlish grief. Yet it was hard — damned hard — sitting there alone in the quiet house. The afternoon sun slanted across the room, bathing the bright colors of the flag where it lay across the dead mm. No curtains were drawn in that room of death. Tom Mansfield had always hated dark rooms.

14

Hard! A sob choked the boy's throat and he loosened the tight collar of his blouse. Then when the grief in his heart could no longer be checked, he walked out into the next room and threw himself on a couch, his hot face buried in the lion skin that covered it.

He did not hear the hoof-beats of a horse outside. Nor was he aware of anyone standing outside the screen door. The door opened softly and a girl in shabby riding-clothes came into the room. She was a leggy, rather ungainly youngster of about fifteen — tanned, wide-eyed with awe and fright, tiptoeing across the room with a pair of spurs in her hand. She stood there uncertainly, listening to the terrible sobbing of the boy in blue-gray uniform.

"Lance!" she called timidly. Then almost ran as the boy swung up to a sitting posture, pulling a sleeve across his eyes.

"Damn it, I wasn't bawling," he said fiercely. "I suppose you'll tell your brothers I was."

"Nobody said you were bawling, did they?" she flared like some kitten that faces a hound pup — spitting at the half-grown and rather harmless dog that barks at her.

"Well, I was bawling," he admitted stubbornly, "and you caught me at it. But I

15

don't reckon you'll tell." He buttoned his blouse collar and sniffed. "No, you won't tell on me, Teton Kirby. You're a good kid, even if Bob and Dick are rotters."

"They're not!" She defended her brothers hotly. "Because they're not dudes, and don't go away to school, you think they're not good enough. Maybe I ain't, either, so I'm not fit to be here, I guess, even if I did fetch you lunch because I heard Judge Truman tell Dad that God knew what you'd find to eat except cheese in the house — that you couldn't fry a egg if you met one face to face — and who the hell was goin' to feed the dogs and you, because you was goin' to stay alone here. . . . Say, you ain't, honest?"

"Ain't what?"

"Goin' to stay here alone? With spooks?"

"Well, I am," he said, his grief momentarily driven away. He'd somehow never thought about how dark and lonely that night would be. "I ain't any more scared of a ghost than I am of — of Bob Kirby."

"I fetched a lunch, Lance. A whole pie an' doughnuts an' grub for the dogs. Mother fixed it, too. She said to say you was welcome to come over to our place for the night. Buck an' Slim could set up with your father. Dad told Judge Truman them two'd set with the devil if they had a bottle."

"Well, they won't," said Lance. "Let's go see the dogs." He cast a quick look toward the bedroom. "Father'll be all right. Colleen has six pups. Three of 'em are marked like old Sparticus. I bet they'll catch a wolf plenty quick. Don's got some porcupine quills in his nose that we'll have to pull out. They all kinda smell skunky. They're not lookin' good, either."

"How could they, with nobody to —"

She broke off, looking a little frightened. She was repeating things she'd heard her brothers saying, and Lance hated the Kirby boys. "What was that?" asked Lance, who was leading the way outside.

"Well, Ah Hell quit your father last week, so I guess there wasn't a cook to feed 'em, that's all."

The boy and girl were at the kennels now, surrounded by some fifteen staghounds and wolfhounds that ate wolfishly of the inadequate food Teton Kirby had brought in her saddle pocket.

"Gosh," said Lance, "they're sure enough hungry. We'll kill a sheep for 'em." He went to the meathouse and returned with a butcher knife. He had helped butcher sheep and beef. Over his uniform he wore blood-smeared overalls and jumper. They cornered a wether and Lance killed it while the

17

circle of dogs watched. Colleen, the Irish wolfhound, had brought her roly-poly family along, to Teton's vast delight. Lance ripped off the sheep pelt and with surprising skill quartered and divided the carcass. Half an hour later the two sat in the shade and partook hungrily of the lunch Mrs. Kirby had sent over. They were finishing the lunch, when two riders came through the gateway. Two tall young men, each riding a half-broken gelding that wore the Bench-K brand.

"Bob and Dick said they was comin," announced Teton. Lance's eyes hardened.

"What for?" he grunted, rising.

"Don't be a — a dude, Lance," whispered the little girl. The "dude" was a word gleaned from the cowland's resentful opinion of the Mansfield clan. The word was usually accompanied by profane coloring. In a way it typified Tom Mansfield's standing among his neighbors, the Kirbys, Crawfords, and so on — cow outfits and horse outfits. Even the gamblers who won from him did so under Mansfield's smile of cold contempt. They cursed him behind his back even as they smoked his imported cigars and cigarettes and drank his excellent whisky.

"Dude, eh?" retorted Lance as he eyed

18

the riders, who pulled up their horses and swung to the ground.

The Kirby boys were a few years older than Lance Mansfield. They had gone, together with other ranchers' youngsters, to the little log school over on Cottonwood — riding ten or fifteen miles through rain or snow. They were ranch kids, cow-hands while still in the fifth reader — fighting broncs before they went to high school at Helena or Great Falls. They were men at sixteen — learning the ways of cows and horses and poker and whisky, riding mean horses, doing the work of men. They were old before their time, yet would retain youth till time whitened their hair and sent rheumatic pains into broken joints. Cowpunchers in the making, hard as rawhide, carefully hiding any sentiment as being sissyfied, yet in their way, after their own code, lovers of the sentimental. Hard for the tenderfoot to understand, for they are a hard breed to meet and comprehend from the Eastern viewpoint.

"Howdy, Lance." They shook hands limply, embarrassedly. For cowboys loathe even that slight show of sentiment and almost invariably offer a half-hearted, limp hand in greeting.

Lance, tutored in such manners, gripped

hard, then dropped each hand as if he wished to get the formality over and done with.

"We was right sorry to hear your dad was killed," Bob Kirby lied politely. "Rode over to see what we could do. Like as not you'll be busy with other things fer a few days. Me'n Dick'll look after the stock. Reckon it's about time us boys was buryin' the hatchet, eh, Lance?"

"Thanks, I'll get along all right," replied Lance stiffly, now horribly fearful that traces of his recent grief showed. He saw their keen glances of appraisal, the hint of a derisive smile at his trim uniform, a quiet sort of inner mirth at what they had once called his "monkey jacket an' dude britches."

Teton Kirby, with feminine intuition, sensed the attitude of her brothers and of Lance Mansfield. She stood there pulling Colleen's shaggy ears, hoping in her little heart that they would not fight as they usually fought when they met.

"The old man was sayin' you'd better saddle up an' come on over to our place," Dick Kirby added.

"He's sendin' Buck an' Slim over to set up with the corpse."

"I'm staying here," said Lance, a stubborn bulge to his jaw, "alone. Buck and Slim'd put in the night in the cellar where the booze is."

"Make it easy on yourse'f, kid," said Bob Kirby stiffly. "It's your funeral."

"His old man's funeral," corrected Dick, with a crude attempt at humor. "Let's go, Bob. We ain't no more welcome at the Circle Seven than we ever was."

"Damn fools fer takin' a fifteen mile ride here," muttered Bob, the older brother, as he checked his bronc and swung into the saddle. "You be home fer supper, Tonnie," he warned his little sister. Tonnie, running true to form, stuck out her tongue at Bob, whose horse was showing signs of wanting to pitch.

"Only that this knot-head colt's about tuh come apart," growled Bob Kirby, "I'd git off an' tan your hide. Come on, Dick."

The Kirby boys rode away. Outside the gate, Bob gave the bronc its head and rode the bucking animal as if he enjoyed it.

"Showin' off," snapped Teton. "Smart Aleck."

"Bob's right," muttered Lance, watching the two riders disappear in a cloud of swift-moving dust. "You better be going home, Tonnie. It'll be past sundown when you get there."

"I'm not going home," came the defiant reply.

"You're what?"

"Well, I'm not. I'll turn Rabbit in the meadow an' stay. You can't sit up all by yourself. You needn't think you can make me go, Lance Mansfield — you or Bob or anybody. I reckon I can take care of myself."

"You heard somebody say that," said Lance. "You can, too — that is, pretty good for a kid. But this is different. You just can't stay."

"Can't I, now?" she flared. "Who'll hold me?"

"Hold you?" he mocked. "Nobody. Hold you! Huh, that's good."

"You know what I mean, Lance Mansfield." She stamped a shabby little riding-boot, her face hot under the boy's teasing.

"Now don't go and begin bawlin'," he remonstrated, reading well-known signs of tears. "I won't tease you. But you just can't be staying here. Gosh, what'd folks say?" At school he had surreptitiously read a few books that dealt with such compromising situations. "Why, I'd have to sleep in the barn."

But the sophisticated reasoning of seven-

22

teen passed serenely over the small head of the girl. She began unsaddling.

"Sleep? Ain't we goin' to set on the corpse, Lance?"

"Not on it, silly; just — just —" The boy, again remembering the dead man under the brave colors of the flag, turned and went in the house. At the closing of the screen door, Teton looked up from the business of untying the latigo strap on her little full-stamped saddle. But the boy had gone inside and somehow the little girl knew that he wanted to be left alone. She turned Rabbit, a fuzzy, gray, fat pony, into the meadow. The hounds followed her solemnly — Bridget, Don, Sparticus, Fly, Blue, King, Lady, Rags, Spot, and big Brin; Brin, part Dane and part staghound, who could kill a wolf all by himself. Behind trailed Colleen with her family. The sun was dropping under the rim of blue hills. The little girl felt a bit frightened and lonely. She was suffering because Lance Mansfield was suffering, and that boy in his uniform was her hero.

To seventeen, fifteen is a mere child, once removed from swaddling-clothes. He tolerated Teton's company, rather liked her frank idolatry, and called her a good kid. She had trailed in his wake since she could remember. The Kirby outfit was the Circle Seven's closest neighbor and Teton's father, big Jim Kirby, was a frequent visitor. Big Jim had always been swayed between dislike and admiration for the tall Englishman.

"Well, Jim," Tom Mansfield had a way of greeting his visitor, "come over to rag me again, eh?"

"Just about the size of it, Tom. Why the hell don't you keep them cows of yourn outa the bog? Buck pulled two Circle Seven critters out yesterday." Or, "Put in the mornin' fixin' your fence. You owe me half a day's work. Ever work half a day at a stretch, John Bull?"

And because big Jim Kirby worshiped the little daughter whom he had named after the Teton Mountain, where he first settled in '74, he always brought her along on his visits — at first, in the saddle in front of him; later on, when her legs grew longer, on Rabbit.

"Lance, ride herd on Tonnie," he would say. And the two men would chuckle over their Bourbon as the boy and girl headed for the kennels or stables or the corrals.

It was big Jim Kirby who guessed that Tom Mansfield drank and gambled in vain hopes of obliterating some tragedy in his past life.

"Women in it somewheres," he confided

to Judge Truman. "I'd make a guess that his wife turned out bad er somethin'. He's a woman-hater if ever I laid eyes on one. Anyhow, he's got the guts tuh keep his mouth shet. Never unloads his troubles. Game cuss!"

Teton, who had the heritage of her mother's understanding heart, felt in a vague way what terrible grief now burdened the heart of her hero. She was willing to face any manner of punishment rather than desert him in his hour of need. She looked at the closed door of the big log house and felt hurt and shut out.

There was something prophetic about that door — Lance Mansfield beyond, with his dry-eyed grief — the girl shut out, unable to quite comprehend, yet willing to make any manner of sacrifice, in face of any opposition. There was to be another door, steel barred — another terrible test of her woman's loyalty; another sunset to come when Lance Mansfield would be alone, staring with hard eyes into the coming dusk.

Teton sat down on the veranda steps and waited. Presently Lance came out to her and they sat there in silence, her tanned little hand gripping his, their eyes, the eyes of youth, clouded with the shadow of their first real sorrow.

Chapter III

"You can tell Dad I'm staying," she told Buck and Slim. Lance was inside when the two cow-punchers rode up out of the dusk.

"What'll yore folks say about you bein' away from home?"

"I'm staying." The little girl's voice was firm. "Lance wants to be alone with his corpse. Can't you boneheads savvy?"

The two cow-punchers rode off, grinning but uncertain.

"Come dark," said Buck, "them two kids'll git spooky an' shore quit the flats, hell-a-kitin'. We'll mope on back later."

"I cud stand a swaller uh good licker about dark," agreed Slim. And they rode into a coulée, where they dismounted and squatted on their heels, smoking. Then they rubbed out the coals of their cigarette stubs and stretched out. They had been in the saddle since daybreak and sleep came quickly. So they did not see two other riders that kept clear of the main road and came with an air of furtive uneasiness through the gateway that led to the Circle Seven ranch.

Lance and Teton were in the huge living-room. A silence had fallen and they sat uneasily, listening to the small sounds that fill a house with the coming of night; little sounds, magnified in the silence; sounds that took on weird meanings because of what lay in the adjoining room where the candles burned eerily.

The clump of boot-heels on the veranda brought a gasp from Teton. Lance, startled and white, was on his feet, his heart pounding in his throat, making him inarticulate. Then two unshaven, overalled men stalked into the room without knocking.

"Evenin', young 'uns," leered one of them, a lanky man whose black whiskers held a sprinkling of gray. A black patch over one eye gave him a villainous aspect. The other, a short, bowlegged man of stocky build, glared about the room with a pair of steel-gray eyes. Both wore guns and filled cartridge belts. The short man was chewing tobacco.

Relief filled Lance's eyes. Teton eyed the visitors keenly. They were strangers to her and to Lance.

"Where's Mansfield?" growled the man with the patch.

"We're lookin' fer Tom Mansfield," grunted the short one, and spat in the general direction of the fireplace.

"Tom Mansfield is dead," said Lance steadily.

"Me an' my pardner here," said the tall man, "ain't in the habit uh bein' lied to. Where's Mansfield?" His tone was belligerent. Lance took an instinctive step backward. Teton huddled in a lump on the couch, her wide eyes on the men.

"I'm not a liar," said Lance. "My father's in there —" he pointed to the open door that led to the bedroom — "in there, dead."

"Take a look, Zack," growled the tall man. The short fellow obeyed quickly, his hand on his gun. A moment later he was back.

"The kid's right. He's deader 'n hell. Is that licker in the glass jug?" And he answered his own question by sniffing, then tipping up the decanter. In grinning silence he passed it to the tall man.

"Dead, eh? Now ain't that jest too bad! Orter drink to him, eh, Zack? Here's at him. May his hide-bound, dude carcass scorch in hell." And he hurled the decanter.

Lance, white-lipped, shaking, sprang like some animal. The decanter crashed on the floor. Lance and the tall man were on the floor and the boy was sobbing as he pounded at the startled face. Then Zack stepped over. He kicked the boy squarely in the ribs — kicked a second time, and the spurred heel caught Lance under the point of the jaw. Teton screamed shrilly.

"Buck! Slim! Help!"

"Come on, Lon," grunted Zack. "We gotta drag it. These yearlin's ain't alone here. Come on, yuh fool!"

"I'll tromp the guts outa the young —"

Zack pulled his taller partner away from Lance, who lay in a quiet, pitiful heap at the edge of the couch. Teton sprang to her feet and stood shrilling for help.

"Choke the young idiot, Zack."

"Choke nothin'. That's Kirby's kid. I ain't fond uh hangin'. Come on. Mansfield's dead. That's enough, ain't it? Damn it, come on," and he dragged the one-eyed man toward the door. They rode off at a run.

Lance stirred, moaning a little. Teton was sobbing when he opened his eyes. Zack's spur had ripped open the boy's cheek from lip to ear. His ribs pained terribly. But he did not whimper.

"Where are they?" he gasped.

"Gone. I yelled an' they beat it. Oh, Lance, you're bleedin'!"

"I'm all right." He got to his feet and went to the gunroom, wincing from the pain of each movement, but his lips were smiling crookedly. He came back with a carbine and a handful of cartridges. Loading the gun, he laid it on the table. Then he went into the bathroom to wash the blood from his torn cheek. The little girl followed in frightened meekness — another terror to add to her child's fright. But she helped bandage the cheek with gauze and adhesive. Lance, sick from the pain of his bruised ribs, sat on a chair and stared, hard-eyed, at nothing. When the cheek was bandaged, they went back and Lance lay on the couch, gasping with every breath. The carbine lay beside him and he never took his eyes from the door.

So it was that when, some hours later, a horseman pulled to a halt and swung to the ground, Lance Mansfield's carbine covered him when he stumped on high-heeled boots to the door.

"Whoa, there, son! Hold yore fire," boomed a big voice that became the bulk coming through the doorway. "What's the idee in gunnin' folks?"

"Pecos!" cried Lance, joy and relief in his tone.

"Pecos hisse'f, boy," and the big cowpuncher barged his way into the room — a giant of fifty-five or sixty, grizzled, grinning, covered with dust. He poked a finger into

Lance's ribs, picked up Teton and rubbed his stubble beard against her cheek, then took the carbine and laid it on the mantel.

"Now, kid, who cut yore face?" he growled, setting Teton down.

"Two men," said Teton quickly. "One chewed and spit right on the floor and busted Lance's ribs, I reckon, while Lance purty near killed the big one with a black hoodus on his eye and give him a bloody nose. I swep' up the glass, but it still smells, an' Lance was goin' to kill 'em next time an' let the hogs eat 'em, because their meat'd poison the hounds. Lance said so."

"Clear as the Colorado at high-water time. A man spit on Lance's ribs an' busted 'em while Lance hit him in the eye with a black hoodus. Say, what kinda spooks has you kids bin seein' here, anyhow? An' how come you two young 'uns is alone here?"

Pecos Hall lowered his voice. He had heard the news of Tom Mansfield's death and had ridden a hundred miles to get there. Time had been when Pecos was foreman of the Circle Seven. A year or so ago he and Mansfield had, as Pecos put it, pawed dirt in one another's faces an' the Circle Seven spread had gone tuh hell without him. Now he had come back to pay his last respects to his former employer. Since he could re-

31

member, Lance had worshiped Pecos. The big cow-puncher was his ideal; his ideal, that is, next to his own father. He put his father on a different sort of pedestal.

When Lance had any dark secrets that must needs be shared, it was the understanding Pecos who had shared them. It was Pecos who took Teton and Lance on strange expeditions. . . . A bear cave, where they lay hidden on a rim-rock for a long time and watched two cinnamon cubs wrestle and box. . . . A kit-fox den where a litter of tiny foxes were watched through Pecos's glasses. . . . An Indian graveyard; beaver slides; curlew nests. . . . And on many an afternoon, when during the slack summer months Pecos had plenty of time on his hands, he would take them to the huge prairie-dog town on Alkali Flats and the two youngsters would double up with glee as Pecos named the prairie-dogs after different cow-punchers.

"Yonder goes Buck, huntin' grub," he would say. "Always eatin'! There comes Slim now, a-sparkin' of the widder Smith — her a-entertainin' the preecher an' high-tonin' pore Slim. That pussy-lookin' feller's Judge Truman, holdin' court on them Bear Paw pool boys as shot up the town last night. Yonder's that brockle-faced schoolmarm, runnin' off at the head; hear her a mile with the wind agin' her. Yippy-yappin'!" And because Pecos picked apt comparisons with a native shrewdness, the children loved him. And while the big cow-puncher always spent his last dollar every shipping time, he never failed to have a sack of gumdrops or horehound candy stored away in his chaps or saddle pocket.

So bit by bit he got the story of the two strangers. He nodded, scowling.

"Askin' fer Tom, eh?" he mused aloud. "Zack Tanner an' Lon Jimson. Hmmm. Come a long ways tuh ask; plumb from Hell Crick, acrost the Missouri — a plumb long ride. Yeah!"

"Wish I'd had a gun when they came," said Lance.

"Jest as well yuh didn't have a iron, kid," smiled Pecos. "Them two slings fast lead. Kinda part uh their business, yuh might say. I was at Rocky Point when Lon shot the 'breed that gouged out that off eye uh hisn — twelve-fifteen years ago. Zack done time fer killin' three greasers down in the Pan-handle country. If they'd bin white men, Zack 'ud uh bin hung. Yeah, they're right handy with a hog-laig, them jaspers. Gotta be, in their business."

"What business is that, Pecos?"

"Swingin' a hungry loop, mostly. Rustlin' hosses, maverickin' calves — some says they bin mixed up in road-agent work. . . . Good men tuh let be. Dunno why they rid here — dunno. Goshamighty, Lance, yuh done growed since I seen yuh. Bigger'n Sukie's bull yearlin'. Them tin sojer clothes shore fits yuh right soon, eh? Do they teach boxin' or rasslin' at that dude school?"

"Sure," smiled Lance. "Football and rowing and all the rest." He did not announce the fact that he had been middleweight champion of the school and the pride of the boxing teacher's tough heart. Also he was captain of the football team and sergeant of the crack cavalry troop that had won the "Bully!" of our Rough Rider President, as they escorted the smiling hero on parade in Washington. Lance had Tom Mansfield's British conservative modesty to its very fault.

"An' Teton gittin' purty as a pitcher," chuckled Pecos. "Soon be doin' her hair up an' makin' eyes at the cowboys; dancin' the quadrille an' polka — the boys a-trompin' one another fer the next set; takin' pianner lessons an' fergittin' how tuh stalk a herd uh sage-hens er a cottontail. Ladies can't go crawlin' aroun' on their bell— stummicks after prairie-dogs, eh? But I see yuh ain't outgrowed them boots I measured yuh fer."

Pecos talked on, making no mention of the dead man in the next room. Pecos, who had a way with horses and wild things and kids, rambled on in his Texan's soft drawl that soon had Teton asleep against his big shoulder. Lance nodded occasionally and let Pecos talk him into going to bed finally.

When Buck and Slim rode up, Pecos sat alone in the dim-lit living-room.

"Take off yore boots, oxes," he whispered.

"Where's the kids?"

"Layin' quiet on the bed ground. What the hell's Jim thinkin' of, lettin' them two young 'uns stay here by their se'ves?" And he told them of the coming of Zack Tanner and Lon Jimson. Buck and Slim traded glances but said nothing. Pecos, seeing that swift exchange of meaning looks, said nothing more. But presently he went on sock feet to the cellar and came back with a quart of whisky.

"Corpse herdin' usually calls fer refreshments. Hit 'er easy, fer it's all yuh git."

And toward daylight, when the two Bench-K punchers were mellow of mood and fluent of speech, Pecos again mentioned the two rustlers.

"Between you an' us, Pecos," said Buck, glancing around, "it ain't the first time them two skunks has bin seen on the Circle Seven range. Me'n Slim cut their sign two-three times the past ten months. Ask me, an' I'll tell a man there's somethin' damn queer about it."

Pecos swallowed some hot retort at the insinuation. He was aware that Tom Mansfield had never been popular. As Mansfield's foreman he had bucked that cow country antagonism for fifteen years — almost since the first day the Englishman set foot on his newly acquired ranch.

"What yuh gettin' at, Buck?"

"Gettin' at some queer brandin' that goes on, now an' then. I ain't sayin' nothin' I can't prove." Buck reached for the bottle and scowled at the open door that led to the bedroom. Then he drank.

"Don't be blackguardin' no corpse in his own house," cautioned Slim. "Bad luck."

"I never said nothin' ag'in' Mansfield," said Buck. "Hell, he never run a iron ever on his own stock. . . . Left that to his hired hands. But what I'm claimin' is that doves don't herd with buzzards — ner rabbits with coyotes."

"Showin' that you shore know animals, Buck," grinned Pecos; "but meanin' just what an' whyfor?"

"Meanin', Pecos, that Zack Tanner an' Lon Jimson is damn thieves. They bin doin' some brand changin' along the river. An' twicet that I know about they stayed overnight here at the Circle Seven. Make what you kin outa that. If Tom Mansfield was so high an' mighty, how come he's throwin' in with rustlers?"

"Tom bein' dead," said Pecos, "he can't do no talkin' fer hisself. Whose cattle was them two skunks brandin'?"

"Quarter-Circle Z stuff from over in the Larbe hills. They makes a Circle outa the Quarter-Circle, drawin' 'er so's the under bar uh the Z makes the under side uh the Circle. When it's done, it looks like some careless brander has drawed the shank uh the figger Seven a might far so's it touches the under side uh the Circle. Easy pickin's! Only that me'n Slim happens tuh see them two rustlers a-workin', we'd never uh ketched on. We was huntin' horses an' picks up the play with our glasses. When they turned the critter loose, an' rides off, we taken a look at the yearlin' they bin workin' on. A month later they delivers ten head uh these new-made Circle Seven mavericks over to Tom Mansfield. He's buyin' stolen cattle, plain as the strawberry mark on Slim's briskit."

Pecos made no reply, but sat there smoking thoughtfully. Buck and Slim had no reason to lie about the situation. And Tom Mansfield, as Pecos had before announced, was dead and could not clear his name of the black mark against it. No use antagonizing the two Bench-K riders, who believed what their eyes had seen. As Pecos afterward put it, he didn't have nothin' to say, so he kep' on sayin' jest nothin'.

He did not know that this silence was shattering a boy's idol; that Lance Mansfield, awakened by voices, had heard his father being called a rustler while Pecos sat there and said nothing, sharing their condemnation of Tom Mansfield.

Lance lay there, shaking as if chilled, though his face was hot and his heart pounded feverishly. Pecos, who in the boy's eyes stood for all that was loyal and splendid, had lifted no hand or spoken no word in defense of a friend who lay dead in the next room. Pecos Hall had done that.

A sob choked the boy's throat and he swallowed hard. His father dead, Pecos, his idol, lacked the nerve to defend Tom Mansfield's name. In the space of a few days his two gods were gone — one dead, the other worse than dead. And he, Lance, stood alone.

He slipped softly from his bed and into some clothes. But he did not go into the living-room to tell those men that he had heard, for his heart was too hurt for that just now. He felt almost physically sick from the shock of disillusion. The bathroom separated his bedroom from his father's. So the three cow-punchers did not see Lance slip into his father's room and sit down by the coffin. But Pecos found him there, wide awake and haggard looking, when the sun rose.

Chapter IV

"Take a third of the hundred thousand," advised Judge Truman, "and salt it down. I know where you can pick up an outfit at a bargain — cattle, remuda, a small mare bunch, sixteen mules, and round-up equipment. They're over on the Rosebud. . . . No dogie stuff, Lance — native cattle that can rustle. A good buy, and you've got feed galore; hay rotting in the stacks — plenty more to be had for the cutting. All you need is a few good men."

"Yes, sir." Lance sat in Judge Truman's office. Judge Truman was also the banker and moreover the boy's appointed guardian. The judge had already put in Pecos as foreman and had contracted the haying to some half-breeds.

Lance no longer wore his uniform. He had on faded overalls and a sweat-streaked cotton shirt slightly ripped across the shoulder seams. His boots were rusty and when he moved, his silver-mounted spurs tinkled. Tanned, clear-eyed, a smile now and then lighting up the boy's rather serious face, he sat there listening to the older man's advice. Pecos squatted on his heels by the door, ignoring another chair.

"Never kin git chair broke," he explained.

Tom Mansfield had been dead two months. The summer rains had made the grave behind the ranch-house green and restful looking.

"How about selling Sultan, Judge?" asked Pecos. Sultan was the big black stud that had sired some of the colts that never were quite fast enough to amount to anything on the track — too hot-blooded for polo stock afterward. "He's eatin' his head off an' fetchin' in no dimes."

"Hmmm. I'd hang on to him, Pecos. Those range mares we're getting are good-sized and well-picked range stock. Sultan's colts out of those mares should make good cow-ponies — plenty of bottom and speed to boot. Hang on to Sultan. But turn that damn track into a feed yard and burn the sulkies and racing-stable equipment, or you'll go belly-up on race-horses that run fast enough to lose your money."

"When kin we take over this outfit on the Rosebud, Judge?"

"I'll close the deal this week. You can trail the outfit cheaper than you can ship. It'll give Lance a vacation from hay-shoveling. Eh, boy?"

Lance grinned. "Yes, sir."

"He makes a right good hay hand, Judge. He kin out-shovel big Ole in the field er on the stack. Had him workin' a bronc on the mower yesterday. But he eats enough, gosh knows."

So Lance went with Pecos to trail over the new outfit from the Rosebud. He learned a lot on that long trip; pointing a herd, night guards, swimming cattle, bedding them down in the evening, shoeing his own horses, and helping load and unload wagons. Riding from dawn till dusk — sometimes wet from the rain; sometimes choking with dust — learning cow-work; learning men and horses. Taking secret pride in the fact that this was his own outfit.

But he no longer looked at Pecos through hero-worshiping eyes. And he did not share his confidence with the big foreman. When they camped near Hell Creek, Lance got his gun from his bedroll and wore it in his chaps pocket. But it was Pecos Hall who rode into camp one noon to find Zack Tanner and Lon Jimson sipping coffee and talking to the cook. Pecos knew that Lance was carrying a gun. He had not asked the boy why, but he knew.

"How, Pecos," they greeted him. "Long time no see yuh."

"Yeah." Pecos looked down at them from his horse.

"They tell me Tom Mansfield's kid taken over the Circle Seven," leered Zack Tanner.

"He has. I'm kinda jiggerin' the spread fer him, lookin' out after his interests. You gents'll be late eatin' if yuh don't git on yore way. Must be twenty mile tuh yore place."

Lon Jimson's one bloodshot eye stared hard at Pecos. Then he laughed harshly.

"Meanin' that me an' Zack ain't invited fer dinner here, eh?"

"That about sizes up the idee, Jimson."

"Tom an' us was right good friends," put in Zack.

"So I've heard," said Pecos. "Likewise I've heard how tough you boys are in a ruckus. Yo're both needed now. My gun's in my bed. But that don't keep me from tellin' you two gents that you ain't eatin' Circle Seven grub to-day ner any time. The trail that leads outa camp is open. Hit it — an' keep off our range."

"Goin' kinda strong, ain't yuh, big feller?" sneered Lon, tossing his cup into the dishpan.

"I'm lookin' after the kid's interests, that's all."

The cook was an old Texan too crippled to ride any more. He might have been deaf for all the attention he paid to the conversation. He was mixing up a tallow pudding that is cow-land's pet delicacy, and is lovingly and profanely known as a son-of-a-—————-in-the-sack. He whistled tunelessly as he poked into the mess box, fishing out various ingredients.

Zack Tanner sniffed meaningly and winked at Lon.

"Now I dunno as we'd orter be movin' on, Lonnie, with that swell grub a-comin' up. Cook, are yuh gonna have a son-of-a-————— fer dinner?"

"Two of 'em, by the talk you're makin'." And Lon, leaping to his feet at the insult, looked into the black hole of the old cook's long-barreled Colt's. The gun was also covering Zack.

"If yuh figger this ol' hawg-laig is too rusty tuh bark, gents," the old fellow snarled, "crook a finger. No man kin come into my kitchen an' win no hell of a lot. Git, er I'll scald yuh with hot lead."

"You lousy ol' mossback, I'll —"

Pecos jumped his horse squarely into the crouching Lon, who had spoken. Then swinging to the ground, the big foreman towered over both the unwelcome visitors.

"Git, both uh you skunks," he growled, and with a swift move, collared them and

44

cracked their heads together several times, then kicked them. He handled them with ease and without a show of temper. And when they were sent sprawling, much of the fight was taken out of their systems. Their heads seemed splitting with pain and they stumbled on unsteady legs to their horses. They snarled something as they rode off.

"I'm obliged, Tex," Pecos thanked the cook, who had resumed his work.

"What fer? Damn a man that won't fight fer the spread he works fer."

And that seemed to end the incident. But Pecos knew he had made two bad enemies. As neither he nor the cook mentioned the incident, Lance was wholly ignorant of the visit paid by the two men.

They crossed the Missouri next day and trailed the cattle up the long ridge out of the Bad Lands. Pecos and Lance rode ahead to shove aside any cattle that were ahead and so prevent a mix-up that meant delay. It was almost dusk when Pecos rode up on Lance, who had a yearling tied down and a pitch fire going. Beyond, staring in half-fright, stood a cow and a calf.

"Hold up, kid," grinned Pecos, seeing a horseshoe heating in the fire. "What yuh doin'?"

"I'm crossing out the Circle Seven on this yearlin', that's all. He's following a Quarter-Circle Z cow. Some fool made a mistake." Lance reached for the red-hot horseshoe with two sticks.

"Hold on, son. Kick out that fire. We need beef at camp. I was gonna butcher this evenin'. Run a tally bar on the yearlin's thigh. Then we'll th'ow him into the herd an' eat 'im. I'll drop the Z outfit a line about it. We'll save the hide fer 'em. Saves any mix-up when, two-three years from now, that beef 'ud be goin' to Chicago. Savvy? Brand inspectors don't like a critter with a hide full uh crossed-out brands. The bar on the thigh is a tally brand."

Lance noticed that Pecos did the butchering with the aid of one of the Rosebud men who had come with the outfit. Save for Lance and Pecos, the men belonged over on the Rosebud. They had worked for this Figure Eight outfit there. That was the iron Lance had bought. So Pecos, with the shrewd caution of the old-time cow-man, had his witness. He saved the upper skull with the ears. For the only discrepancy in the job of making over that Quarter-Circle Z yearling into a Circle Seven, was the changing of the earmarks.

The Quarter-Circle Z mark was underbit

the left and swallow-fork the right ear. The Circle Seven mark was underslope the left, crop the right. And that person who had done the earmark changing had left a small portion of the slit in the right ear — the slit that made a crop into a swallow-fork, the latter being a cropped ear with a slit in it.

Next, Pecos sought out the Crow Indian boy who wrangled the horses. "Ever tan a hide, Walk-Slow?"

"My old woman, he tan 'em." Walk-Slow was in his twenties and father of four children.

"Reckon you could tan that yearlin' hide, leavin' on the ears?"

"Squaw work," Walk-Slow grinned and shook his head.

"For two dollars?"

"Hell! Sure, I tan 'em, Pecos."

So the hide was duly tanned and later sacked and put in the bed wagon. And the flesh side of the hide now plainly showed the tampered brand.

Since Lance now owned the Figure Eight iron, there was no need of putting any vent and Circle Seven on the newly acquired stock. They paid off the men and Pecos put a couple of punchers out in a line camp to throw back any of the cattle that were obsessed with the desire to return to their home range.

The hills became brown, a chill crept into the wind, and October brought the first snow-storm.

"Time a man shed his hen-skin underwear," said Pecos that evening. "Winter's done come."

Chapter V

Lance rode into his first blizzard and froze one ear. They were combing the range for poor cattle.

"Them Circle Seven cows is scattered like a mad woman's thoughts," complained Pecos one night as they came home cold and hungry from an all-day ride. "There's a hundred of 'em an' each cow taken a different direction to head fer. Tom musta shore let 'em scatter."

Lance nodded. He was beginning to realize, in spite of that stubborn loyalty to his dead father, that Tom Mansfield had let things slide from his grip. And he caught bits of careless conversation regarding Tom's drinking and gambling.

Now and then he met the Kirby boys or big Jim and Teton. Bob and Dick were a little jealous of Lance. Or at least that was the impression Lance got from their blunt greetings.

"H'are yuh, Lance? How's the cow-man?"

"Not so worse. Cold, ain't it?"

"Hadn't noticed. But us boys's used to it." And with a hint of patronage in their manner, they rode on.

But they did not smile the night that Lance Mansfield rode into the Bench-K ranch with his coonskin coat wrapped around Teton, who whimpered through set teeth — that night when the worst blizzard of the year swept Montana.

"Found her just before dark," Lance said; "underneath her pony. He'd stepped in a badger hole. I think her leg's broken. I had tuh shoot Rabbit. He'd broke a fore leg. Don't tell her I shot him."

"When she didn't come home, we thought she'd stayed with the Rawlins folks," said Bob Kirby. "Who'd thought she'd try to come home in a storm like this? Dammit, Dick, don't stand there like a cow waitin' to be milked. Go after Doc King. Now where *you* goin', Lance?"

"Home." Lance, shivering in the lee of the barn, was pulling on his overcoat while Bob Kirby wrapped the unconscious Teton in a blanket and started for the house.

"Home? In this blizzard? After you saved Tonnie from — damn you, Lance Mansfield, not if I have to knock you on the head. Quit actin' the fool. You're half-froze as it is. Hey, Jim! Jim!" The Kirby boys always called their father by his given name.

The elder Kirby, with a long buffalo coat

50

over his night-shirt, was coming with a lantern. Lance's horse had brought its double burden to the barn, and Lance had gone to the bunk-house rather than wake Mrs. Kirby. The boys slept there; and he had shaken Bob into wakefulness and told him that Teton was at the stable, hurt.

The white-faced old cattleman carried the girl to the house and Bob followed with Lance. Dick rode into the bitter night across thirty miles of blizzard-swept hills after the doctor.

"Lawzee!" cried Mrs. Kirby, and then went to work with dry-eyed efficiency. She and her husband got Teton's cold little body between hot blankets. Her leg was broken, but the break was not a bad one.

"Doc'll have 'er dancin' jigs in a month," said Jim Kirby. "There, there, honey, don't be scairt!"

For Teton had opened her eyes, stared about, then screamed terribly. "Don't! Don't! Don't!" She fought off her father's arms, terror in her eyes.

"Easy, honey!" he crooned, his big voice shaking. "God, the kid's outa her head. An' no wonder. . . . There, there, Tonnie."

Teton's fists were clenched and she stared with wide, unseeing eyes at the face of her father.

"Lay a hand on me an' my dad'll kill you!" she said. "Dad! Lance! God! Help!" And she screamed, fists beating against her father's big chest.

It was then that the elder Kirby saw Lance standing by the stove. The boy was terribly white and his eyes were hard as glass.

"She was like — like that when I found her — screaming and calling for help." Lance's voice was a hoarse whisper. Mrs. Kirby was in the kitchen, heating towels.

Jim Kirby, as he eased the now quiet child back on her pillows, saw blue marks on her little shoulder — plain, unmistakable, the black and blue marks where a man's hand had gripped. "Keep this between us, Lance," said Jim Kirby in a voice that was terrible in its calm.

"Yes, sir. Of course."

"Did you see anybody?"

"No. It was dark by the time I'd put Rabbit out of his misery and got her leg free from under him. I brought her straight here."

"When she gits her right senses," said Jim Kirby quietly, "she kin tell us who it was. Then —" He did not finish the sentence. Just stood there, his big hands clenched, staring at nothing. But Lance knew that big Jim Kirby meant to hunt down the man who had put the mark on Teton's shoulder and, when he found him, to shoot him as a man shoots a rattlesnake.

"Between you an' me it is, boy. Not even Bob er Dick is to know."

Lance nodded, inwardly proud that the grizzled old cattleman so trusted his manhood and discretion.

And in the gray, snow-filled morning, Doc King and Dick came in, half-frozen, caked with fine snow, their eyes swollen almost shut. Teton was conscious and trying gamely not to cry. She clung to Lance and her father with pitiful little hands. But when the three were alone in the room and big Jim put cautious questions, it was plainly evident that terror or perhaps the merciful hand of God had wiped away all memory of any encounter with a man. It had been snowing some when she left school for home. The storm had grown heavier. Beyond that she recalled nothing. Jim Kirby was a little disappointed, was nevertheless immensely relieved. There would not be that terrible memory to haunt her.

Lance and Jim Kirby now shared a secret — a terrible, sinister secret. The father's eyes bound the boy to silence.

Doc King warmed his hands briefly, gulped down a cup of scalding coffee, and opened his case. Lance got his first glimpse of cow-country surgery. He and Bob and Dick and big Jim helped the doctor administer ether. The break was mended; reducing the fracture, as Doc King put it. Lance, a little giddy, left the room later with a mingled impression of sickening ether odor, plaster of Paris, and stale tobacco smoke.

"You'll ride over often, Lance?" begged Mrs. Kirby, who, once the ordeal had passed, had dropped in a chair and sobbed heavily. "Teton will be laid up for a spell and she'll be wantin' you to come and see her."

Lance promised, blushing furiously as the good woman kissed him. He left the Bench-K loaded down with a sack of doughnuts, apples, and cake. His hand felt limp from big Jim Kirby's parting grip.

Bob and Dick Kirby had been awkwardly grateful.

"So long, Lance, old trapper."

"*Adios,* old kid. Don't wait till somebody busts their neck before yuh ride this way again."

"Thanks, boys. You want to drop in when you ride my direction." And he rode away. But he did not go directly home. Instead, he bent his course for the flat where Rabbit lay half-buried in the snow. His eyes filled as he looked at the dead pony. Then he spent the next few hours riding about, rather uncertain what he was searching for. Finding nothing and meeting no one, he rode toward home.

The storm had settled to a bitter cold wind that seared one's eyeballs and bit through overshoes and clothing. He rode with head down, into the wind. He thought he heard sounds of shooting. Then it suddenly dawned upon him that Pecos and the boys would be worried and no doubt were hunting him. He found his gun and emptied it into the sky. And presently Pecos and two cow-punchers rode out of the leaden snow-filled world ahead.

"Gawd a'mighty, kid!" growled Pecos. "You shore th'owed a scare inta me! Where the hell yuh bin?" And in the big fellow's growl was real affection. Lance read it in the big puncher's eyes and felt horribly ashamed of his mistrust of Pecos. Somehow, Lance got the impression that it was more than the blizzard that Pecos feared.

"Knowed that horse uh yourn 'ud take yuh either home er tuh Kirby's, if yuh had the brains tuh give 'im his head."

"But you had everybody but Ah Hell hunting me?"

"The boys needed exercise. They bin round-sidin' in the bunk-house, playin' cooncan an' monte an' smokin' till a man's gotta shoot a hole in the air tuh talk through."

Chapter VI

A few days later Lance rode over to the Bench-K ranch, leading a black three-year-old gelding.

"For Tonnie," he told Jim Kirby, "in place of Rabbit."

"But Tom turned down five hundred bucks fer that geldin', Lance!" gasped Kirby. "Best colt Sultan ever sired. A gaited show-hoss."

"Sure," grinned Lance. "Tonnie always liked Midnight. He'll make her a good mount."

"Out of an Arabian mare that set Tom back a heap uh money. Too good fer a kid."

"Not for Tonnie," defended Lance stubbornly. "She's feelin' pretty tough about Rabbit, I reckon."

"Bawled her eyes out. I told her Rabbit busted his own neck."

Lance had his reward when Teton's bed was moved to the window and Slim led Midnight past with her saddle on his black back. She threw her arms around Lance and kissed him, laughing and crying a little.

Jim Kirby made no mention of the secret he shared with Lance. Only when the boy

left for home after dinner he mentioned that
Teton was going to a girls' school in Helena
when her leg got well.

"Gonna make a lady outa her," grinned
Jim. "She'll come home with a lot uh la-de-
da airs, droppin' her 'r's' like that Boston
preecher at Chinook. She'll be high-tonin'
us, Lance — callin' Buck and Slim cow-ser-
vants, like as not."

But Lance knew that Jim Kirby had another motive in sending the girl away. It had
occurred to the cow-man that Teton, whose
active life in the open had matured her
beyond her years, was almost blooming into
womanhood. She was no longer a little girl.

Lance also realized this as he rode homeward. It occurred to him for the first time
that Teton Kirby had looked more than
beautiful as she kissed him. The delicate
oval of her face, with the firm chin, her well-
shaped mouth, her large gray eyes, and jet
black hair that was thick and curly. Some
day Teton would be strikingly beautiful.

But a skulking coyote interrupted his
musings. The hounds had followed him and
now they strung out after the coyote; Lance
forgot the girl in the thrill of the race.

But that night Pecos "hoorawed" him
about giving away the black gelding.

"Only last week you was sayin' how you'd

make a top town hoss outa Midnight. Now yuh go an' give away the best hoss in the Circle Seven iron. I'm gonna keep yuh away from the female sex er we won't have enough ponies left in the remuda tuh do our spring work."

"You go sit on an icicle," grinned Lance, flushing. He began pawing over the mail that one of the boys had brought from town.

"Here's a letter from Jack Parsons of the Quarter-Circle Z," Lance tossed the unopened letter across the table. Pecos had sent them the hide of the yearling and an explanatory letter. He opened the letter from Parsons eagerly.

As he read, Pecos scowled thoughtfully. "Damn Parsons!"

"What's the matter, Pecos?"

"Nothin' except that Jack Parsons is such a damn crook hisse'f that he thinks other cow-men is all crooks too. Him an' me has had a few run-ins from time tuh time. He as much as says here in black an' white that I meant tuh git off with that yearlin' only it was such a lousy job uh brand workin' that I got cold feet an' butchered it, then sends him the hide. That red-complected son of a cross between a dry water-hole and a hard winter never et a pound uh his own beef in his life. I'd like tuh work him over with a neck-yoke er the hot end of a brandin'-iron.

"Says he's takin' a drastic measure, whatever that is, next time anything uh the kind happens. An' I kin make a fair tuh middlin' guess who has bin runnin' off at the head to him. Buck an' Slim's in a line camp near the Z ranch an' Buck's a damn magpie after two drinks. I might as well tell yuh, son, that them two Bench-K waddies has some sort uh hen-yard idee that Tom Mansfield was kinda th'owed in with Tanner an' Jimson in some queer brandin'. Fact is, that yearlin' wa'n't a mistake brand a-tall. As a calf, he'd wore his Quarter-Circle Z. Then some jasper swings a long rope and changes the brand. It showed on the under side uh the hide, savvy?

"They musta had the yearlin' penned up somewheres weanin' him an' mebby so some more. When they find Tom's dead, they turn 'em loose an' mister yearlin', bein' only part weaned, hunts his mammy. Damn Buck, anyhow."

"You think father was a cow thief?" Lance's voice was husky with emotion.

"Tom Mansfield a cow thief?" Pecos laughed gruffly. "Kid, that dad uh yourn had his faults, God knows, but he was straight as a pine-tree. Don't let no man argue different. He never drawed a crooked breath in his life."

"Then why didn't you defend his memory that night when Buck sat in this room and called Dad a rustler?" Lance spoke before he thought. He sat in his chair, straight-backed, white-lipped, smiling Tom Mansfield's twisted smile. Pecos rose, gasping with astonishment.

"You heard us talkin' that night?"

"Yes." Lance's voice was barely audible. He did not look at Pecos. It was as if the boy dreaded what was to be seen in the old cow-puncher's face. But Pecos's big hands reached down and gripped the boy's shoulders.

"You kep' your mouth shut. You bin thinkin' all this time that I believed them two boneheads? That I wa'n't man enough tuh speak up fer a friend that was dead? Good God! Yuh bin goin' along all these weeks thinkin' that?"

"Yes." Lance looked up now into the hurt eyes of the big foreman. "I guess I'm a damn fool kid that needs a beating, Pecos. I know now I was wrong, somehow. I'm sorry, if that'll help."

"I kep' shut up, so's tuh learn what them two knowed, that's all. I don't blame yuh fer thinkin' like yuh did. It was my play tuh tip yuh off, but I figgered you was too much of a

61

kid tuh savvy the burro an' play yore cards clost to yore belly, sayin' nothin' ner startin' nothin' till the play was right. That's why yuh packed a gun when we moved the Figger Eight herd near Hell Crick?"

"I was going to get the truth out of those two roughnecks."

"I thought it was account uh the beatin' they give yuh that night. Hmmm. Kid, yo're close-mouthed. That's a good habit tuh learn in this country. But from now on, we splits our opinions an' augers things out. You got plenty sense — a heap more than lots uh men I know. We're gonna win out on this ranch, too, barrin' bad luck, oncet we're outa debt."

"Debt, Pecos?"

"Yeah. Seems Tom had some outstandin' notes that come in last week. Judge Truman paid 'em an' his bank'll carry our paper fer it till we ship next fall. You'll have that thirty-three thousand cash you saved outa the insurance money, if the worst comes to the worst. Truman kin take a mortgage on the ranch as security fer our notes."

"How much did Dad owe, Pecos?"

"Fifty thousand. This Parsons snake had twenty thousand of it. Man named Charlie Edwards, the balance."

"Charlie Edwards at Havre?" asked

Lance steadily. "The gambler?"

"Yeah. I reckon Parsons likewise won his at poker. I doubt, Lance, if yore dad knowed jest what he was doin', er if he had much recollection uh them notes he signed. He got right drunk at times. Reckon you'd orter know about things like that. Not that Tom Mansfield wa'n't a man, fer he was. But there was times he shore hit the licker, son."

"I've heard a few hints like that," admitted Lance.

Pecos nodded. "You was bound to. But he was a man, in spite uh all that — a white man, boy, an' never fergit it. Somethin' was eatin' at his mind. I've knowed him tuh set all night in front uh the fire, drinkin' one whisky after another, starin' into the firelight with a look in his eyes that was shore hell tuh see in the eyes of a friend. God knows what he was thinkin'. But he never whined, not oncet. An' when you was home, he hid it all behind his grin. Mebby, if he could uh talked 'er outa his system, he'd uh felt better. But he never talked. Jest sat there."

A silence fell over the two. Pecos put a fresh log on the fire. When he came back, he showed Lance the letter from Jack Parsons. It was coldly accusing in its phrasing. It hinted that this was not the first occurrence of brand working. And it finished with a cryptic warning:

"Don't let it happen again."

"Tanner an' Jimson'll bear watchin'," grunted Pecos. "The drift fence on Cottonwood was cut twicet lately. Our line riders is packin' Winchesters. They got it in fer Kirby's spread too since Bob whupped Lon Jimson at the Half Way House last month."

"Bob licked Lon Jimson?"

"So I heard. Reckon Bob an' Lon was both drinkin'. That licker at the Half Way House is shore rot-gut. More fights in one quart than there is in ten bulldogs."

"That was a month ago?"

"About then. Bob took Lon's gun, then licked him; somethin' about a poker hand. Don't say nothin' about it. Jim Kirby'd eat Bob's head off fer bein' there at the Half Way House instead uh at the line camps."

Lance was doing some thinking. . . . Bob Kirby thrashing Lon Jimson. . . . Evidence of Jimson being in the vicinity about the time of the blizzard. . . . Teton's accident and her screams.

"I'd hate tuh be the gent yo're thinkin' about," laughed Pecos. "Yuh shore kin look mean, fer a kid."

It was on the tip of Lance's tongue to

mention Teton's terror of some man who had laid hands on her. Then he recalled his promise to Jim Kirby. He smiled crookedly and said nothing. After all, it was Jim Kirby's affair; Kirby's and — yes, and Lance Mansfield's. And in due time Jim Kirby would hear of the affair at the Half Way stage station and, in his wisdom of men, make what he could out of its possible sequence. He knew that big Jim Kirby now carried a gun whenever he left his place.

But Lance lay awake a long time that night, thinking until his head ached with milling thoughts.

Chapter VII

But the winter passed without further developments. Jim Kirby still packed a gun. Teton was away at school. Storms kept every man too busy for trouble-hunting. Kirby had to buy hay to survive the winter, which was a hard one. Pecos rode with a worried scowl darkening his frost-seared face. Evenings he and Lance "made medicine" — figuring hay measurements, grub lists, cattle tallies, wages paid. Their running expenses were cut as low as possible, yet were appalling when totaled.

"Gonna be nip an' tuck, kid. We'll jest about make 'er without borrowin' more cash tuh run on. Gosh, them jaspers git away with a lot uh grub. Must put in half their time cookin', the rest uh the day eatin'. Hay's holdin' out, though. That Figger Eight stuff is winterin' in good shape. They tell me Rawlins is usin' snow-plows over on Seven Mile. Hay gone an' his pore stiff pilin' up in the coulées. He th'owed in some dogie stuff that can't savvy how tuh paw tuh feed. Seen one uh his boys in town an' he 'lowed the ol' man was shore up ag'in' 'er."

Lance, in town for the holidays at

Christmas, went to Helena to see Teton. He was breathless at the change in her in the few weeks she had spent here.

"Gee, Tonnie!"

"Like me in this frock, Lance?" A month ago she would have said, "How's this for a outfit?" And her greeting would have been clumsy.

"What'll you be by Easter?" he grinned.

"A lady or a corpse, pard. I'm getting the rough edges knocked off. It's a finishing school in more than one sense. But the girls are great and I'm learning the ropes; which fork to use, how to be happy though a wallflower, which I was at our dance last week."

"The guys must be blind!"

"Not blind — just considerate of their feet. I'm just learning to dance something besides hoe-down square dances. Now tell me about the ranch. I'm homesick but I won't act the cry-baby — honest."

Lance knew she was gamely hiding the bitter part of her experiences here — incidents like being a wallflower. She had her father's grit and his humor. She'd make good. But the ache of her homesick little heart showed in her eyes. She listened as he talked of the ranch and the horses and hounds and the work.

And with her quick woman's eyes she saw

the change in Lance Mansfield. He looked handsome in spite of his frost-blackened cheeks and nose, which were peeling a little. His forehead and the back of his jaws were white from the protection of his fur cap. His hands were hard and calloused, but well kept. And he sat his chair with the stiff-backed seat learned at military school.

"— so Pecos tailed up the cow while I took the calf up on my saddle. Then Drifter spooked and broke in two and I landed on the ice with the calf in my arms and the cow pilin' in at me, hookin' an' blowin' steam into my face. Pecos, darn him, had let go her tail an' stood back, bustin' with fool laughter. The calf kicked me in the eye. Gosh knows what I'd have done if she hadn't fallen down again and I got away. And those fool hounds yapping and running in at her. Lordy!"

"Gee, Lance, I bet it was grand!"

And so they both were changing, Teton Kirby acquiring her "slickin' down," as Jim called it, Lance getting broader of shoulder and dropping his letter "g" with cow-country negligence.

But he was too busy to see Teton at Easter-time. The winter had broken and Lance was in the saddle from dawn till past dark, combing the Bad Lands for cattle.

Easter Sunday he and Pecos worked all day in a chilling rain that ran down his back and into his sodden boots. Plodding in sticky black adobe mud in the wake of a hundred weak cows. Each carried a young calf on his saddle. They had not eaten since four that morning. Up the long, bare ridges and on to a flat that was a gray lake under a leaden sky.

Pecos grinned as he tilted up a leg to pour water from his boot. "Anyhow, kid, we won't have tuh worry about where we'll water these critters."

Lance had learned that only a tenderfoot ever mentions the heat or cold or snow or rain or hunger. Those things were to be borne in stoical silence or passed off with some jocular remark. They were part of the cowboy's existence, the same as the brief good times in town. The whisky and cards and dances at the school-house.

That night they unloaded their pack-horse and pitched a tepee on a high knoll. They cooked and ate in the rain, water dripping from their wide hats on to the ground.

"Give a month's pay fer a big jolt uh redeye," grinned Lance.

Pecos gave him a swift look, but Lance sipped his hot coffee without notice of that quick scrutiny. Pecos went on eating. But in the mind of the old cow-puncher was the germ of something akin to suspicion. He had heard one or two vague rumors. He came abruptly to the point.

"Didn't ever see yuh take a drink, kid."

"No, don't reckon you have, Pecos." Lance spoke with his mouth full of beans and meat.

"But you do take a drink now an' then?"

"When I want it, sure."

"Ain't you startin' sorter young?"

"When did you take your first drink, Pecos?"

"Hell, I musta bin all uh ten er twelve. But I didn't know no better."

"You think it hurts me?" There was a defiant note in the boy's question, and Pecos knew better than to openly preach.

"Well, I don't reckon it'll stunt yore growth none. Let's have that larrup. Every time I move I start a new rip in this damn slicker. I stole it off a sheep-herder an' never noticed it was about two sizes too quick fer me."

"You think I should let the stuff alone, eh?" Lance passed the syrup.

"I ain't no nurse. If yuh like a drink, take one. Take ten er fifty if you kin stand up under 'em. Only stick tuh singin' licker. Leave the wildcat stuff tuh them as likes tuh sober up in jail. Yuh'll never start nothin'

70

singin' pervidin' yuh ain't got a voice like ol' Foghorn Riley's. Now ol' Foghorn usta sing 'Sam Bass,' 'Annie Laurie,' and 'Nearer, My God,' all to the same tune, which same was the tune tuh 'The Star Spangled Banner.' An' nothin' less than a gun-barrel acrost his horns 'ud stop him when he set his mind on his warblin'. One good thing about rain. Saves dish-washin'."

And Lance let the subject drop. But he read the warning in the bantering words of Pecos, who was not one of the singing type when in his cups.

"We'll have tuh th'ow them cattle into yon pasture afore dark." Pecos chucked his empty plate and cup into the skillet, where nature would wash them. "I'll start 'em while you rustle some dry wood." And he rode away in the rain, humming tunelessly and dispassionately cursing the sheepherder who wore a No. 2 slicker.

"Hope the kid won't foller his dad's trail," he mused.

"Walk, doggies, walk along. Yo, ho, ho!" He shook his rope free and slapped his slicker skirts to make a noise that would move the leg-weary cattle.

"He'll need keerful handlin'."

Chapter VIII

The geese were flying north. Patches of green showed in the coulées. Summer crept across Montana and the calf work was in full swing.

"Bench-K on the left ribs. Big 'un fer yuh, Bob Kirby."

"We shore need them big 'uns," grinned Bob, going down the rope after a bawling calf. "Dang yuh, Pecos, can't yuh heel them big fellers?"

Lance and Bob Kirby were flanking calves together. Bob had been sent over from the Bench-K as rep for that outfit. Between Bob and Lance there had grown a sort of tentative friendship. They rode circle together, stood guard, and forgot their past quarrels in the fresh struggle that was uniting the cattlemen of that section. In many instances old feuds were laid aside as the cow country watched the invasion of sheep and nesters.

For the open range was fast shrinking. The freight platform in town was piled with barbed-wire. There was a new bank in town, financed by Eastern capital that was backing the new dry-land farming venture.

Each train brought in eager-eyed, horny-handed farmers. Sod-busters. Furrow-followers. Some brought families. Survey gangs were pacing across land that had been claimed by the cow outfits.

The sheep-men, made bold by the precedent of the farmers, now trailed bands of sheep across what had once been held as sacred ground — driving to summer range across the Canadian line, to return again in the fall, leaving in their wake range that was now ruined for cattle or horses. For a sheep eats close and leaves nothing.

"There'll be a hull slue uh loco weed here next year," prophesied Jim Kirby. "Don't ask me how sheep brings it, but they do. Damn 'em."

Judge Truman was backing his friends. He loaned no money to farmers. He would scowl at them from under his bushy white brows, grunt something that was none too complimentary, and point to the new brick bank across the street. There was a story that he had reached for the old .45 which hung on the elk antlers behind his desk, the day that a delegation of Eastern capitalists came for a conference.

But he went on making loans to such men as the Kirbys, Rawlins, and other cow outfits.

"We gotta take up more land to protect ourselves, Judge."

Land and more land. School sections leased. Cow-punchers filing on homesteads, grinning at the law that demands permanent residence for three months of each year. Now and then they slept in the cabin built by the cow outfit for which they worked.

"I got three hundred an' twenty slapdab in the center uh Jim's alfalfa. Part uh my place takes in his icehouse. Hell, them ol'-time surveyors musta ran lines with a rawhide rope an' a whisky bottle. Take off yore hats, gents, to a landowner."

Grinning at the law. . . . What were such damn fool laws to men who had come to the country in days when the Indians were hostile.

"Grind yore meal an' sift your bran,
You'll never make a livin' in the cowboy's lan'."

Truman bending banking laws on long loans. . . . Cow-men putting money into land. . . . Buying, leasing, grinning at homestead laws as they hired men to homestead with the understanding that they sell their land to the cow-man. . . . Stringing miles of barbed-wire. . . . Fence crews. . . . Land going into grain and alfalfa where there was water.

And across the street from Truman's bank, potbellied, white-vested men smoked fat cigars, smiled complacently, and waited. They roomed at the Parker House, greeted the incoming pilgrims, and pored over blueprints in the surveyor's office next door to the bank.

"The ol' town's boomin'," declared the residents. The saloon men were among the first to scent out the shallow foundation of that boom.

"There ain't the money circulatin' like there was last spring. These damn scissorbills buy one beer an' walk out. Dick Smiths, all of 'em. Wish the spring round-ups was over."

The tin-horn gamblers sat about idle. The "houses" on the south side of the track were dark at ten each night. The occasional tinny clang of a piano betrayed the presence of a wool-buyer in town. Wheezy phonographs mocked the quiet nights.

"Boom? Boom, hell. Burial, ya mean, don'tcha?"

The round-ups worked the Bad Lands. Cattle had wintered in fair shape on the Circle Seven range. One day in late June, Bob Kirby went over his calf tally, then strolled over to where Lance and Pecos sat on the cook's bed.

"Looks to me like you fellows have been wintering a hell of a lot of Bench-K stuff, Pecos. Looks like somebody done a rotten job uh throwin' our stuff back where they belonged. An' you've been pourin' Circle Seven hay into their bellies to pull 'em through the winter."

"We had a-plenty, Bob. An' Jim was kinda up ag'in' er fer feed. It wa'n't no more'n he'd do fer us in a tight. Fergit it."

"It — it was right white of you folks."

"How about a game of mumbley-peg, Robert?" Lance put in. "Quit tryin' to thank us for something that don't amount to a damn."

But Bob Kirby did not forget. He rode over to the Bench-K wagon a week later and found Dick.

"Look here, kid. Quit bein' so damned shirty with Lance Mansfield. We had him sized up wrong. They wintered a hundred head or more of our stuff last year."

"They probably stole enough calves to make up the feed bill," grunted Dick. He had never outgrown his childhood dislike for Lance.

"You listen to Buck an' Slim and you'll get to thinkin' everybody's crooked. You give the Circle Seven rep a square deal, too. You've made it so ornery fer the last two Circle Seven men that they cut their strings an' went home. Treat this third one right or I'll run this wagon like it orter be run."

"The hell you will! Robbie, the champion of the Johnnie Bull spread. A man can almost see your wings sproutin', you're that angelic. You give me a pain. I'm runnin' this wagon."

"Runnin' it into the ground," snapped Bob. "And since when has Paw allowed a whisky keg in the mess wagon?"

"I suppose the Circle Seven reps spread that glad news, eh? You don't see anybody drunk around here, do yuh, Mister Holier Than Thee?"

"You're half-shot now," growled Bob Kirby, and mounted his horse. He rode away without a backward glance.

"Smell whisky on him a mile off," mused Bob, heading for the Circle Seven wagon. "Poker game goin' in the bed tent. Jim'd raise particular hell if he knowed." Filled with foreboding, he rode slowly across the hills.

A week later a Bench-K man rode over to the Circle Seven wagon. He called Bob aside and the two talked for some time. Bob looked a little white about the mouth as he came up to Pecos. "This boy'll rep in my place a spell, Pecos. I'm goin' over to run the Bench-K spread a while."

"Anything wrong, Bob?"

"Dick got into it with some farmer — shot him up. There's a posse after the kid."

Chapter IX

Teton Kirby found the Circle Seven wagon camped on the banks of the Missouri at the mouth of Rock Creek. It had been three weeks since Dick shot the farmer, and rumor had it that the youngster had thrown in with the Dutch Henry gang in the Bad Lands.

"Now ain't you a sight fer near-sighted folks, young lady!" grinned Pecos, who had ridden into camp to tell the cook to have early supper. "Light an' set awhile. Gosh, yo're a lady! Growed up an' purtier'n ever. Excuse me if I don't dare git up off this wagon tongue. A cow ketched me with her horn an' jest nacherally plumb ruined these Levi pants. Have a cup uh coffee. Bet you smelt that son-of — that taller puddin', eh? How's Miz Kirby an' Jim?"

Teton swung to the ground. Midnight nibbled at her leather jumper as she sat down beside Pecos on the wagon tongue.

"The folks are all right, Pecos. Only Jim's mad as a hornet at Dick. Dick was drinking when he shot that farmer. Thank God, the man's going to live, but it will take a lot of money to square it. Have you seen Dick?"

"Nary sign, honey. But if yuh want him found, I reckon it kin be did."

"Could you, Pecos? Could you get word to him that there's no warrant out for him? Send him back home? Bob says he thinks Dick's trailing with some horse thieves."

"I'll hunt him up, Tonnie. Now pull yore hull off Midnight an' take a rest fer yorese'f. Yuh look tuckered out. Lance'll be in directly. Him an' the boys is brandin' down at the lower end uh the river bottom."

"If you don't mind, Pecos, I'll be going back."

"Back where? Home? Hell it's fifty miles, beggin' yore pardon."

"Midnight will take me back without turning a hair."

"An' will yuh tell a ignerant cow-hand what's so danged poisonous about the Circle Seven outfit?"

"Nothing. It's just that I have to be getting back."

"Then," said Pecos shrewdly, "I'll get Lance tuh ride back with yuh."

"No, no, no! I — He —"

"I — He —" mocked Pecos. "Sounds like a Injun song. Trot into that tent an' Tex'll give yuh some coffee with whiskers on it. Make a new man outa yuh. I'll take keer uh Midnight. An' while yuh may uh got finished off an' city broke an' high-toned at that she college, I'm still man enough tuh turn yuh over this wagon tongue an' take a hame strap to yuh. Git, now."

"But Pecos, I —"

"Nothin' uh the kind. Whatever you was about tuh say, I disagree on the subject. Hey, Tex, will yuh ride herd on this young lady while I'm gone? If she tries tuh quit the flats, hog-tie her." He turned Midnight loose, swung into the saddle, and rode away whistling tunelessly.

"Lance," he said carelessly when he reached the branding crew, "lope on back tuh camp an' change hosses. Ketch yore ridge-runner an' tie up Big Enough fer me. Wait at camp till I get there. Me'n you's goin' fer a ride this evenin'."

"What's up, Pecos?"

Pecos winked mysteriously and rode into the herd. Lance, puzzled, rode toward camp.

"Whatever's wrong between them two young 'uns," mused Pecos as he roped a calf and dragged it to the branding fire, "they'd orter git it patched up by the time we git in from brandin'."

The remuda was in the rope corral when Lance rode up. He pulled his saddle from his sweat-streaked horse and un-buckled his rope. He had not noticed Teton's saddle on the ground near the bed-wagon. The girl herself was inside the mess tent sipping coffee and listening to the garrulous Tex, who was bustling about in a clean flour-sack apron, beaming with all the genial bluster of a proud host. Lady visitors were scarce, and he was out to do himself and the outfit proud.

"Directly I build this here apricot pie, I'll show yuh how tuh mix up what I calls a Circle Seven Wowser; kinda like a cross between a fruit mulligan an' a horse-wrangler's delight. It marks the brand into the crust."

"I bet it melts in a person's mouth, Tex." Teton's seat on the cook's bedroll, which is the throne of honor in a cow camp, did not permit a view of the rider who had come up. She had heard horses' hoofs and the sounds of unsaddling — then the muffled thudding of the remuda milling in the corral. That meant that the rider was catching a fresh horse.

But Lance's loop had dropped with sudden limpness. He was looking at a sweaty black gelding that had been recently unsaddled and had acquired a coat of dust from a luxurious rolling. The presence of Midnight meant that Teton Kirby was at camp. Lance crawled back over the corral rope and strode toward the mess tent. He was dust-covered and frayed and altogether disreputable-looking, but his face beamed. He had not seen Teton since that visit he had made at Christmas-time.

"Gee, Tonnie!" he greeted her warmly, shoving out a hand that was none too clean. "Long time no see you!" His hat was off, and his uncut hair needed combing — combing and trimming and shampooing.

"Hello, Lance." She was on her feet — a slim, boyish figure flannel shirt, overalls, chaps and boots. Her face looked small under the big cream-colored Stetson. Her hand held no warmth in its greeting. Her voice was politely cold.

"I meant to write," he said, sensing the chill of her greeting and interpreting it as caused by his negligence in letter-writing, "but we've been on a high lope since the spring round-up began."

"Of course," she smiled coldly, and resumed her coffee. Old Tex pointedly kept his back to them and whistled to let them know he was not eavesdropping. Lance took the cup from her hand and lifted the tent wall behind them.

"Want to show you something," he said quietly, and almost shoved her under and outside the mess tent.

"Now," he said, smiling quickly, "what's the chip on your shoulder, pardner?"

"No chip on my shoulder," she said, meeting his eyes.

"I meant to write — honest, Tonnie."

"Oh, don't be foolish. I know you've been busy."

"Then what's the row, anyhow? Gosh, you'd think I'd done something!"

"Oh, let's not talk about it."

"But we're going to. What the Sam Hill have I done?"

"Is it necessary to swear?"

"Swear? Good Lord, I wasn't swearing!"

"There you go again."

"Look here, Teton Kirby, you ain't too old for spankin'. In about one short minute I'm goin' to give you what the small boy got for playin' hooky."

"Don't you think it's a little too serious to pass off with funny cracks, Lance? If you could see the way Mother cries at night, and how Dad worries!"

"What the deuce are you driving at?" he asked.

"At least be man enough to admit what you've done," she said scornfully, half turning away. He caught her none too gently by the arm.

"Look here, Tonnie. Come clean. What have I done?"

"You think I don't know what you've done? I've kept my mouth shut, Lance Mansfield, and Bob stuck up for you against his own brother. But that doesn't keep you from being guilty. It's you, not Dick, that should be in jail!"

Her eyes were blazing. Her cheeks were white save for two crimson spots. Lance looked at her with bewildered eyes.

"I didn't even hint it to Pecos. No use hurting him, if he don't know the truth. I can understand your silence as far as Pecos is concerned, but do you think it's fair to sit back and look innocent while Dick takes all the blame?"

"Blame for what?"

"For everything."

"You mean I'm to blame because Dick had a few drinks and picked a scrap with a farmer and plugged him?"

"Oh, Lance, be a man! At least be gritty enough to stand back of your so-called farmers!"

"I don't get you." Lance's voice was cold. There was no dodging the insinuation that he was mixed up in Dick Kirby's row.

"Then I'll tell you what everybody but the Circle Seven now knows. That you knew of the open-water rights on Wild Horse Creek. Land that Dad thought he owned, but which you, with your education and shrewdness, knew was open for homesteading. So you hired men to file on that land. Farmers? Do farmers pack six-shooters and sit around all day guzzling whisky? If that Zack Tanner is a farmer I'm the Queen of Sheba."

"You mean it was Zack Tanner that Dick shot?"

"As if you didn't know! The man admitted you were backing him. I guess if Dick wanted to tell what he knew, you would be filling a cell in the new jail. Not for land-grabbing, either." And she turned abruptly and went back into the mess tent.

For several minutes Lance stood there stunned. Then he picked up his rope and stepped back into the corral. A few minutes later he led out a rangy sorrel and threw his saddle on the animal. Teton, again sitting on the cook's bed and trying to smile as old Tex talked, heard him ride away.

Pecos and the group of tired cowpunchers rode in a little later. "Where's Lance?" he asked Teton. She shrugged and shook her head.

"Don't ask me. He caught a horse and rode off."

Pecos scowled uneasily, and as the boys filled their plates he slipped outside and pawed around in Lance's bed. His scowl deepened when he made certain that Lance had taken his gun.

Chapter X

Determined to learn the unvarnished truth of Dick Kirby's scrape, Lance rode along a dim trail that led into the heart of the Bad Lands.

Only the day before, a cow-puncher from up the river said that he had seen Dick Kirby in company with Dutch Henry and two other men at the Rocky Point saloon. He hinted that a bunch of stolen horses had been crossed there at the Point; another crime added to the list tabulated in black under the record of Dutch Henry, a rustler. And against Dick Kirby, if he were caught in such blackleg company.

Dutch Henry, wise in the ways of law and the men enforcing the law, was canny enough to do his stealing in other States and use Montana as a stopping station along his underground route to Canada. Barring a few "glory hunters" and deputies anxious to claim the generous reward on the outlaw, the law enforcers were content to attend to their own home affairs. So long as Dutch Henry confined his depredations to the Dakotas, Idaho, Wyoming, and Colorado, the Montana sheriffs would not lose many meals hunting him down.

Cow-men in that section had nothing to fear from Dutch Henry. He had even been known to reclaim stolen horses and bring them back to their Montana owners. Now and then he "borrowed" a fast mount, later to return it — with sometimes another horse or two for interest. So the outlaw, once he reached the breaks of the Missouri River, would rest up a week or ten days. In some remote hiding-place he and his men would eat, sleep, and drink in comparative safety. Horses would be shod and perhaps a few brands changed with a wet sack and a hot iron.

Lance had never come in direct contact with the outlaw fraternity. He had but a faint understanding of the sort of truce which existed between the stockmen and such fellows as Dutch Henry. But he knew the approximate location of the hidden corrals and cabins back in the scrub pines, and he knew that he would find Dick Kirby there.

Teton's scorn had cut him to the quick. He felt like a man condemned without a hearing. He had no way of knowing that the hurt in the girl's heart was more poignant than his own bitterness. For Teton had lost more than friendship. Dick was her favorite,

89

her chum. Bob, being older, had never been as close to her as Dick. Bob had taken Lance's part. There had been quite a scene that night when Bob brought Dick to the Kirby ranch to talk it out with old Jim. Jim had sat like a big grizzly by the fire, smoking, silent, grief loading him with pathetic gravity. Mrs. Kirby fluttered about packing Dick's war-sack with clean clothes. For it was Jim's advice that Dick hide out until Zack Tanner's condition was ascertained.

Hot-headed Dick, with his quick accusations, his hair-trigger condemnation of Lance Mansfield; Bob gruffly defending Lance; Big Jim wrapped in brooding, grim-lipped silence: Teton had taken Dick's part, but somehow she could not believe all the things Dick was saying of Tom and Lance Mansfield.

"A whelp of the Mansfield breed," snarled Dick. "He don't belong here. Needs a coat of tar and feathers, then a ride on a rail. The damn dude nester-lover. The sneakin' calf thief. Jack Parsons aims tuh hang his purty hide on the fence. By gosh, I'll lend Jack a hand!"

"You'll mind your own game, Dick," growled Bob. "I tell you, you're all wrong. Somebody else is framing this. There's a big bug behind it, and I'm goin' to locate him."

"Because Mansfield's slick enough to kid you along, you think he's a real guy," scoffed Dick. "He's damn cute, wintering a handful uh our stuff. You hang a halo around his curly head. Why the hell don't you herd with him?"

"You're sore, Dick. Quit cussin' in front of Tonnie. I'll stick by you, and you know it. So shut up and listen to Jimmer. You don't hear him blackguardin' Lance, do yuh?"

"I ain't forgettin' the night he brung Tonnie home," said old Jim Kirby softly. "Nobody but a yaller dog 'ud do what Dick's accusin' Lance Mansfield uh doin'. I ain't sayin' nothin' till I've done some lookin' around."

"Didn't I make that Zack Tanner snake cough up the whole yarn? Didn't he admit it was Mansfield money backin' him?" Dick's eyes blazed with indignation. "I never had any use for Lance Mansfield. I never expect to do anything but hate him. He's hated me'n Bob since we was kids. He put up with Tonnie because she was a girl and a kid and trailed him like a sheep-dog, waitin' on him. You don't see her hangin' any crown on his dome now. She's got sense enough to see through him."

"Leave Tonnie out of this mess," snapped

Bob. But Teton put her arm around Dick's shoulder and stood there, very slim and straight and with her lower lip caught between her teeth. She had seen the heavily armed men who had come to the ranch hunting Dick, and her heart was with the hunted boy. No matter what he had done, he was the under dog now. Men were hunting him down like a wild beast — like the hounds after a coyote. And Dick's chances were those of the running, dodging coyote. She found herself almost hating Lance. For hate is, after all, but second cousin to love.

Dick rode away later, filled with a sort of bitterness. Jim had given him a few brief words of advice.

"Yo're not tuh go makin' any fool gun plays, savvy? Take yore pack-horse and slip into the breaks fer a few weeks. Me'n Judge Truman'll handle yore case. When I send fer yuh, you come. An' no more booze — understand that? You ain't learnt tuh handle the stuff. I'll git word to the sheriff that you'll be on hand when the right time comes. So long, son. God look after yuh, fer yuh need His help."

"So long, kid," Dick kissed Tonnie, who was trying to keep back her tears. "You're a brick."

"Dick! Dick! Don't let them kill you!"

Mrs. Kirby kissed her son, who, in her mother's heart, was her baby — even more than Teton. Dick, the hot-headed, impulsive, sometimes wonderfully kind and gentle Dick, going into the night to skulk like a coyote while men shot at him! She buttoned his shirt-collar and reminded him of the liniment and pills in his war sack.

It was Bob, growling, scowling, loyalhearted, who waited with the horses out in the brush till Dick slipped from the dark house, crawling along the piles of cordwood to the willow thicket. It was Bob who rode with Dick to the edge of the brakes.

"Reckon you can cut 'er a line now, kid. I'll keep yuh posted. Check in at the burnt cabin on Rock Crick every few days. I'll leave a note under a rock at the base uh the big pine there. Keep clear uh the Rocky Point saloon an' the gang that hangs aroun' there. Trailin' with that gang won't do you any good."

"To hell with your sermons!"

"Let's don't quarrel, Dick — not tonight. But just don't be the damn fool, that's all. You know I'll go through hell an' high water for yuh, Dick."

"I'm not worth it, Bob." Dick was suddenly contrite. "I know I'm a damn fool —

lettin' you all in for trouble this way. I'm a bum, that's all. Not worth botherin' with."

"Quit it, kid. That Tanner had it coming. If he croaks, it's self-defense, anyhow. It's the scissor-bill bunch that's hollerin' for your head. The sheriff ain't bustin' no blood-vessels lookin' for yuh. An' them sodbusters in his posse can't hit a barn door. Nothin' to worry about. But Kirby blood don't mix with licker. I know it. That jamboree at the Half Way House kinda learnt me a lesson. Only by luck I didn't kill Lon Jimson. So handle yore licker easy, Dick, old-timer. Good luck an' gosh darn yuh. They gotta whup the whole Kirby tribe tuh get yuh, kid."

"I'm sorry I talked so damn—"

"Shut up or I'll take yuh down an' sit on yuh."

"You ain't man enough!" grinned Dick.

"That's the old spirit, kid. Now drift, outlaw. Remember the big pine at the burnt cabin. Gosh, wish I was you. No calf-wrasslin' or night guards. Just roundsidin', like a dang bear. So long."

"So long, Bob." Dick rode into the Bad Lands leading his laden pack-horse. For a week he had minded Bob's advice. Then he ran across a bearded man with an easy grin and a bottle of whisky. That night Dick

Kirby moved his bed to Dutch Henry's camp. Bob's notes lay untouched under the rock at the big pine.

"Hired fer a tough hand, Henry," announced Dick thickly as they played stud-poker with a saddle blanket for a table. "I'm playin' my string out."

His boy's vanity was tickled by the easy conviviality of these men who rode their hidden trails with a price on their heads. To the youth of the cow country Dutch Henry was a sort of hero. Dick listened to tales of the outlaw trails, drank when the jug came his way, and lost steadily at poker. When he became a little unsteady of tongue and feet, he bragged a little of his shooting scrape and hinted what lay in store for Lance Mansfield when he cut the sign of the damn dude nester-herder.

Lance rode unchallenged into the deep cañon that led to the hidden corrals. It was growing dark when a coldly sinister voice halted him.

"That'll be about far enough, cowboy! Set with yore hands kinda uplike while we reads yore brand."

Chapter XI

"Got a young feller here," announced a bearded, swaggering man to the group at the camp-fire, "that 'lows he's honin' fer speech with Dick Kirby."

"Is it my brother Bob?" asked Dick nervously.

"Says he's Lance Mansfield."

"Bring the coyote up." Dick was on his feet. He now wore his gun in a scabbard and, aping the outlaw leader, he had the scabbard tied low on his thigh after the mode of the old-time gunman.

Lance, a little white but smiling twistedly, was ushered into the circle of men. He stood there, erect, inwardly afraid, but steady-eyed. Dick broke the silence.

"Well, Lord Fauntleroy?"

"I rode here to talk to you, Dick — alone." Lance's face was hot under the curious, half-amused, half-hostile scrutiny of these men.

"What I got to say," said Dick, "I ain't ashamed to say before witnesses. This suits me right here. We got a bone tuh pick, Mansfield, an' this is a damn good place tuh do the pickin'."

"I came to find out about your mix-up with Tanner."

"Then why don't you ask Tanner? You're payin' him an' entitled to a run for your money."

"You lie when you say I hired Tanner."

"I'm a liar, eh? In my language that means fight!" Dick, overanxious to prove his gameness before these men, and fired with bad whisky, dropped his hand on his gun.

"Fill your hand, Mansfield!" He barked the gunman's challenge.

But Lance made no hostile move. Instead, he grinned.

"You must be readin' 'Diamond Dick' or something," he said, actually rather amused by Dick's swashbuckling sincerity. "I haven't a gun. If I did have one, I wouldn't go for it. Looks to me like you'd done enough shootin'."

"Here's yore hawg-laig, bub," grinned the man who had brought Lance into the outlaw camp. "Looks like yuh might need it."

"If he ain't too damn yellow," sneered Dick. "What's the idea in packin' a gun if you won't use it?"

"It's a damn poor way to straighten out the mess; that's one reason." Lance was not afraid, but his voice shook a little. Inwardly he was hot with anger. He wanted to smash the jeering grin from Dick Kirby's mouth. He voiced that wish now.

"I may be yellow, but I don't reckon I am," he said, shoving his gun in the waistband of his overalls. "I might be able to use a gun if I had to. For one thing, you're filled with the Injun's brave-maker. I'll call your drunken bet on one condition."

"Name it, Launcelot."

"Lick me with your fists. I'm giving you twenty pounds weight and you're among your friends. But lick me and I'll try you with a gun. Have you the guts to fight?"

"Now," said Dutch Henry, who was not at all anxious to see any gun play until he had delivered his stolen herd across the Canadian line, "you're talkin' sense. Have at 'im, Kirby. I'll take charge uh both yore guns."

Dick nodded, inwardly certain that he could thrash Lance. He had done it before, many times before. He'd do it again here and show his new comrades the toughness of his fiber. He winked at Dutch Henry as he passed over his gun. Lance parted from his weapon without a word. His eyes were blue slits of smoldering wrath and his mouth smiled. The outlaw leader, who knew men, especially fighting men, could not but admire the courage of the much maligned son of Tom Mansfield, whom he had always held in good-natured contempt.

"I'm going to muss up that grin of yours," warned Dick, squaring off.

"Yeah? Step to it, then, instead of chinning about it." And Lance met Dick's rush with an uppercut that should have been a warning that this was not the Lance Mansfield of a year ago.

The fight was an example of science against fury. Time after time Dick came in, head lowered, body crouched, his thick, muscled arms like twin pistons. And Lance met each rush with cool precision, hooking, jabbing, side-stepping. Dick's blows missed by the fraction of an inch or glanced off Lance's head or shoulder, who caught some with his forearms and countered with short jabs that made Dick grunt.

"From where I'm settin'," grunted the grinning Dutch Henry, "I'm damned if I kin see no yaller in the Mansfield kid. He fights right purty. Ugh!" For Lance dropped Dick with a terrific jolt that had not traveled a foot. Dick was up again, sobbing curses, badly winded and bleeding from a smashed nose. He rushed again and Lance swung. This time Dick did not get up. To the surprise of the outlaws, Lance did not kick the fallen man. He did not even fall on him and beat at the other's battered face until Dick called "enough." Instead, he stepped back and waited for Dick to get up.

But Dick Kirby was out for a long count. The blow had caught him on the point of his jaw.

"Gawd, he's dead!" said someone.

"Stand away from him," snapped Lance. "He ain't dead. This is my scrap. Unless you want to take it up where he left off?"

"Not me, kid," grinned the man. "I've known men tuh git kicked by mules an' be in better shape than young Kirby. I ain't no hand-fighter."

Presently Dick moved and sat up. He looked about a little dazed; then his eyes found Lance.

"Want any more, Dick?"

Dick Kirby got on his hands and knees, to stand for a moment, swaying dizzily.

"More? Me want more? Yes, damn you!" And he rushed weakly. But Lance did not hit him. He countered Dick's feeble swing — held him with a hammerlock. Then he flung Dick down on the stump where he had been sitting when Lance came.

"Get up again and I'll knock the can clean off your shoulders, Kirby. I've showed you I could do it. Just because I'm not killing you,

100

don't get the mistaken idea I'm yellow." He faced Dutch Henry. "That goes as she lays and takes in Kirby's friends."

There was nothing of the braggart about Lance Mansfield. He was too much Tom's son for that. His voice was flat, deadly calm, and he faced the men without flinching.

"Now," he asked, "where do I stand here?" He expected some one to take up Dick's quarrel. They were a hard-looking crowd.

"From where I'm settin'," grinned Dutch Henry, "it looks like yo're standin' on yore two feet. It's none uh our scrap, kid. Have a drink."

Lance took the proffered jug and looked at Dick, who sat with lowered head, blood dripping from his nose to the ground.

"Here's how," he said, and tipped up the jug.

"Looks like I come about in time," drawled a voice from the brush, and Pecos stepped into the firelight.

"Howdy, Pecos," Dutch Henry greeted him. "How's the weather up yore way." He looked up at the giant Texan's head. Pecos took the jug from Lance and, without further preamble, drank. Then he grinned at the battered Dick Kirby.

"I brung word fer you tuh go to the

Bench-K ranch, Dick. Tanner's gonna live, worse luck. Next time shoot straight." Pecos turned to Lance.

"You done enough hell-raisin' fer one evenin'. Drag it fer camp. Me'n Dick will be along directly."

"Kin I borrow the loan uh yore wildcat some day?" said Dutch Henry. "I'd like fer tuh sic him on a big 'breed that kicked a tooth outa me oncet."

Dick looked sullenly at Pecos. The boy was sober enough now. He felt that in defeat he had lost caste among these riders of moonlit trails. Bitterly he blamed Lance Mansfield for it all. Lance took his gun from Dutch Henry but made no move to leave.

"Vamoose fer camp, kid," growled Pecos.

"Not till I get this Zack Tanner business straightened out. You knew it was Tanner that Dick shot?"

"Not till this evenin'. You can't learn nothin' here. We'll have a pow-wow at camp. Now git."

Lance obeyed in silence, Dick Kirby's sullen eyes following him. He was a little relieved to find Teton gone when he reached camp. An hour later Pecos rode in, looking tired and worried.

"We'll talk 'er over to-morrow," he said wearily. "I gotta do some thinkin'."

Chapter XII

Zack Tanner, under the protection of two special deputies, was back on his homestead. At midnight the following night a group of masked men wearing slickers rode up to his cabin. The two deputies were escorted to the edge of the homestead and the group leader returned their guns. The guns had been unloaded.

"Now, you plow-herders," said the masked leader gruffly, "there's the road tuh Chinook. Git on it!"

"We're law officers," protested one of the farmer-deputies. "You can't do this."

"Mebbe not, son," came the soft reply, "but it sorter looks like we are doin' it, jest the same. There's enough tar an' feathers tuh split three ways, if you gents are rarin' tuh linger." They left without further argument.

An hour later Zack Tanner, his naked body smeared with tar, dirt, and chicken feathers, managed to catch his horse. He headed for his place on Hell Creek, across the Missouri and a hundred miles away. As he topped a ridge, he glanced back over his shoulder, coyote-like. His cabin was in flames.

The riders separated, scattered in different directions. The following morning Pecos rode over to the Bench-K.

"Mornin', Miss Teton. Where's Jim? At the corrals? *Bueno.* Yo're lookin' right peakèd. Hope you ain't reducin' er somethin'." Pecos rode off to find Jim Kirby on the top log of the corral watching a bronc fighter saddling a colt. "Still on the prod," he grinned when she gave no reply.

"Mornin', Pecos."

"Howdy, Jim. Kinda warmish, eh?" Pecos climbed the corral and bit off a corner of plug tobacco. They sat for some minutes in silence.

"I bin readin' up on laws, Jim — land laws. Seems like if one uh these homestead jaspers kinda stays off his place fer a spell, he loses his rights; somethin' uh that sort. I reckon that law sharp uh yourn kin tell yuh about it."

"Reckon so, Pecos."

"Dick ain't used up his homestead rights, has he?"

"Nope."

"It might be a kinda good idee fer him tuh show up at the land office in Chinook when the sign is right, an' take up that hunk uh land Tanner's taken. I hear Tanner ain't gonna file no second papers."

"How's that?" Jim looked at the old cow-puncher curiously. Dick had brought home his own version of the clash with Lance. Galled by defeat, the younger Kirby had not been too scrupulous as to the veracity of the tale. But if Teton believed Dick's every word, Jim took his dosage of the tale with the proverbial grain of salt.

"Seems like Tanner had some bad luck last evenin'. Cabin burned."

"Hmmmmmm. Yeah?"

"Uh-huh. Shore too bad. Nothin' tuh show he ever built a cabin. I come by there this mornin'. Nothin' left but ashes." Pecos spat into the dust. "That's a good-lookin' bronc, Jim." And again a silence fell over them. Presently Pecos chuckled softly. Jim sent him a sidelong glance of inquiry.

"I like tuh got th'owed this mornin'. This fool hoss ain't pitched fer years neither. But he shore boogered at what we meets along the trail. First off, it kinda had me thinkin' I was took bad with a set uh D.T.'s. Yep, I shore thought I had 'em. Fer a-comin' along the trail was a big he-chicken settin' on Zack Tanner's hoss. But when me'n my fool hoss gits closter, it's a man wearin' feathers. In his hair an' all over his carcass — white feathers an' gray feathers an' prairie-chicken feathers an' sage-hen feathers. I

105

reins up some for tuh git a good look. I sees them feathers is stuck on with pitch tar. When I taken a good look, danged if it ain't Zack Tanner."

"What the hell you tryin' to git at, Pecos?"

"Me? Nothin', Jim; only what I seen. He was headin' fer Hell Crick, near as I could make out. Looks like a hoss as old as that fool Pilot had orter quit tryin' tuh pitch. Well, reckon I better be movin' along."

Pecos bent over to pick something from his overalls. The object was a feather. There were spots of fresh tar on his boots, another feather or two. He picked them off and swung a leg back over the corral. Then he climbed off the corral and on to his waiting horse. "Shore a-gittin' warmish for this early in the day," he announced. "Mind about that law, Jim. The Tanner place orter make Dick a right good homestead." And he rode away.

When Dick got in that evening from horsehunting, Jim Kirby met him at the barn.

"I never thought I'd live tuh see a Kirby that was a damned liar," said old Jim, his voice as hard as the glint in his eyes. "Now, by God, I want the truth outa you about Pecos an' Lance Mansfield. I'll git it if I have tuh jerk it outa yore hide with a blacksnake." Dick went white. For in Jim Kirby's hand was a coiled bull whip.

"God, Jimmer!" Dick looked sick, there in the afterglow of the sunset. Jim Kirby had been more like a chum than a father. "You wouldn't!"

"I'm askin' fer the truth uh what happened at Dutch Henry's camp. Out with it." Jim's voice was terribly quiet.

"I told you the truth once." Dick, white-lipped, tried to meet his father's eyes.

"You lied like a yellow coward. Pecos never laid a hand on you. Lance licked you and yo're ashamed to admit it."

"That's a lie! They both jumped me!" Dick was determined to stick to his varnished version of the affair.

"Furthermore," he said in sullen defiance, "you lay that whip on me an' I'll fight back! I'm no damned dog!"

"Fight back, eh?" Big Jim Kirby's face went white. "I'm yore father. I reckon yo're forgettin' that?"

"A hell of a father you are!" exploded Dick. "Takin' sides with them damned nesters an' rustlers against your own son. To hell with you!"

Because Jim had always treated his boys more as a brother than a father, and had never in his life laid a hand on either of them, Dick's words were like a slap across his face. He was a big man, a man who had fought his way in the world with his two hands. Few men cared to cross him. In his younger days he was said to have had a terrible temper. Years had sobered him, suppressed that hot temper. But it flared now.

The long black lash slithered out like a striking snake. Once, twice, it ripped across Dick Kirby's back. Dick, white, his eyes slitted with a terrible white hate, jerked his gun and shot. The lash dropped from big Jim Kirby's hand. His whip arm hung useless, broken below the shoulder by Dick's bullet.

With a choking sob, the boy flung himself into the saddle and spurred into the night, just as Teton Kirby, alarmed at the sound of the shot, opened the kitchen door.

Lips pressed to a thin, grim line, Jim Kirby walked slowly to the house. Teton ran to meet him, fear in her dark eyes.

"Gun went off accidental," he said in a husky voice. "Dick's gone fer a doctor. It don't amount to nothin'." He tried to grin.

"Land uh mercy," wailed Mrs. Kirby as she bathed and dressed the wound. "Never rains but it pours. Goodness, if we ain't havin' the wust luck. Teton, fetch the hot water."

"Then build me a cigarette, Honey. Liz, quit frettin'. It ain't but a scratch. That bottle uh Old Crow had orter kill the poison," he suggested. He was wondering if Dick would ride for Doc King. Or would the boy ride for the Bad Lands and the rustler gang? He forgot physical pain in his agony of mental torture. He regretted his haste. He had gone at Dick altogether wrong. Dick was like a blooded, high-strung colt. By tact and understanding, not by the whip, could the boy be handled.

But Dick had gone to town. He had sent Doc King. Then the boy had ridden away. No, Doc didn't know which direction. Seemed kind of flighty. Said to get word to Jim that he was sorry. That he wouldn't be troubling Jim no more. Something like that. He reckoned the boy was upset.

It was Teton who found the black-snake on the barn floor. She was in the room when Doc King delivered his message from Dick, even as he splinted the arm and grinned admiringly at old Jim's gameness.

The girl slipped out of the room and out to the barn. There she crept into the darkness and sobbed brokenly.

"I hate him! I hate him! I hate him!" she sobbed over and over. For she was blaming Lance for these days and nights of trouble.

★ ★ ★

At about that same hour at the Circle Seven ranch Pecos and Lance quit their tiresome game of seven-up and made ready for bed.

"Reckon you'll be takin' a ride about Sunday, eh, boy? If I know female wimmen, Teton'll be shore glad tuh smoke the peace-pipe. Gosh, I never thought I'd git sick uh chicken. Fried, roast, an' chicken hash — an' more on ice. I've heard how the buffalo-hunters usta kill buffaloes fer their tongues, but I never slaughtered no chickens fer their feathers before."

"But we're not through with the job till we find out who hired Tanner."

"You leave that to yore Uncle Pecos. I'm plumb bird dog when it comes tuh trailin' human skunks. Yore job is tuh patch it up with Teton." From the sofa came sounds of gentle snoring. Pecos heaved a book at the sleeper.

"Come alive, Bob Kirby, an' pay fer yore bed. How about a cold snack uh chicken sandwich?"

Bob Kirby groaned feebly. "I was dreamin' uh green roosters bigger'n a native four-year-old. Stampedin' — an' a-crowin' — me a-tryin' tuh outrun 'em. Gosh, don't talk chicken to me. An' I never will get the

110

tar off these new boots. I'd better light out, come mornin'. Jim'll think I'm roundsidin'. I'm supposed to be huntin' horses."

As Bob and Lance undressed for bed, Lance handed him a thick envelope.

"Wish you'd give this to Tonnie, Bob."

"Sure." Bob grinned and ducked Lance's swing. "Yuh don't mind if I read it, uh course? Say, yuh seen the papers?"

"Pecos roped me into the card game. What's new?"

"Price uh candy's gone up."

Chapter XIII

But there had been other news in the papers. For this was the summer of 1916. The distant war meant little to the cow country. Now and then when a French or English officer came out to buy horses, the punchers stood about and snickered at the funny clothes of those men who, in spite of their queer garb, were keen judges of horseflesh.

"A year ago they was more fussy. Now they're takin' hosses they turned down cold last year this time."

"We'll be drawed into the whole thing yet."

"Aw, what's eatin' ya? It ain't our war."

"Man, I'd be proud tuh be settin' by when one uh them Frenchies steps into the middle uh that cyclone hoss!"

"Er ol' Bogus. He'll get hisse'f a sojer."

"Did yuh hear that army feller say Treasure Box 'ud make a good officer's mount? Yeah. If the officer kin mount 'im."

"Jest the same, Woodrow Wilson's sent a shore hot note."

"Ain't no killin' power in a note, cowboy. He'd orter slip in a bomb with it. Them

Dutchmen is shore mistreatin' the Belgian folks. I'd like tuh git a runnin' shot at that Kaiser Bill myse'f."

"Runnin' is right, feller. But you'd be runnin' so fast, yuh couldn't hit nothin'. Speakin' uh shootin', how's Jim Kirby's arm, Pecos?"

"Not so good. Doc tells Lance them sawbones fellers at Great Falls is talkin' about takin' it off below the shoulder."

"That'll be kinda hell on Jim. I come past the Bench-K yesterday. Bob's batchin' since the folks moved tuh town. He swole up when I ast about Dick. There's somethin' shore queer about that shootin'."

"If you was as good at fixin' fence as yuh are at pokin' into folks' affairs," said Pecos, "I could fire the rest uh the fence crew. What the hell was you doin' over there, anyhow?"

"Run outa staples," explained the cowboy.

"Hmmm. Now ain't that odd? With a sackful tied on yore saddle. You cowdodgers shore make fine fence hands. Yuh work fine as long as you kin tack in a staple without gittin' off yore hoss. Too proud tuh pack a hammer. I picked up seven hammers along that fence line this evenin'. Yuh must think that a hammer's plumb spoilt after

113

yuh pound a staple with it. So yuh drop it there. An' if the wire's broke yuh set up a holler fer a fence crew." Pecos bit off a fresh chew.

"Fer the good uh all concerned, I'm tellin' yuh that Teton Kirby won't be back fer a month. Yuh jest as well save yore hosses. Anyhow, Jim ain't a-marryin' his gal off to no forty a month cow-hand."

With which parting shot, Pecos stalked off to the house to find Lance in the living-room sitting with a half-empty whisky bottle on the table staring at nothing in brooding silence. On the table was the mail that had come out that day, lying in an unopened litter.

Pecos scowled at the half-empty bottle, but grinned as Lance looked up.

"That you I heard singin', kid?" He reached for the bottle, took Lance's glass, and poured himself a drink.

"Here's to the achin' hearts that bleed. May she be a wet summer an' lots of feed. Here's mud in yore eye, young 'un. Didn't she write again?"

"What do you mean, again?"

"I was taken down oncet, the same way," said Pecos, sliding into a chair and again reaching for the bottle. "Down at some place acrost from New Mexico. I reckon it was Chihuahua. Her name was Maria somethin', but she looked more nigger than she did Mex. Kinda brunette fer markins. Her ol' man made the best tequila I ever th'owed a lip over. I think they hung him later.

"I was roddin' a spread down near their place an' come over there tuh pinch the ol' man fer butcherin' beef. But I fergits the beef when I looks up into Maria's eyes. Yeah — *up*. She was nigh seven foot an' wore about a 'leven shoe — if she'd uh wore shoes; which she didn't, her bein' one uh the barefooted kind. I've struck many a match on the sole uh her foot.

"She greets me with a bottle an' a smile that won't wear off. Her bein' a mite cock-eyed, I can't tell whether she's lookin' at me er past me.

" *'Amigo,'* she says.

" *'Amigo,'* I says. I don't savvy more Mex than the law calls fer. I knows that *amigo* means friend. So I takes the bottle. After the third drink I'm willin' tuh give her the herd. Half a hour later I'm warblin' a sour tequila tenor to a song that 'ud git a man ten years hard labor in this country. I leaves soon, wearin' the ol' man's hat an' packin' two-three bottles uh this paisano fire-water. I'm full uh tortillas, beanses, Chihuahua hooch an' love. As I'm goin' along the trail I runs into some greaser fellers in 'dobe soljer clothes. The leader is a big black-complected gent with rollin' white eyes an' nigger lips — ugly an' ornery. An' he gives me a shore mean look as I passes. Then he pulls a crack in his language which I savvies. I'd picked up spic durin' the Spanish War, an' while I can't hold no conversation at a church gatherin', I can make myse'f understood when I cuss.

"What this black feller says ain't easy tuh take, drunk er sober. But I'm in Mexico an' in no shape tuh fight no twenty er fifty men single-handed. But I knows this jasper fer a rebel general er somethin', an' I'd sighted him over on our side uh the line. Thinks I, he'll show up some fine mornin' on my side uh the border an' he's gonna shore turn up missin' aroun' home. I takes me a drink an' goes home.

"When I git time, I rides down to Maria's place an' we gits right chummy. Barrin' a herd uh bugs I gits from wearin' the ol' man's hat, I can't say nothin' ag'in' the ol' man er his gal. She's kinda high-withered an' long-backed an' her eyes ain't mates an' she steps in behind a mule an' loses some teeth, but she makes grand chicken mulligan an' the ol' man's tequila is plenty good.

116

" *'Muy amigos,'* says Maria.

"*'Muy amigos,'* I says. We'd got that far. Take her of a moonlight evenin', er about dusk, an' she ain't too hard on the eyes. Er mebby so it's the ol' man's licker. Anyhow, I'm gittin' handy with a guitar.

"Then one evenin' as I rides fer home, this buck general blocks the trail.

" *'Aviso, gringo!'* growls Mister General — meanin' beware. An' he shoots. He misses me a foot an' I fans my cannon his direction. But he don't git hit. Why? Because somebody done taken the shells outa my gun. I recollects takin' a nap at Maria's place. Her er the ol' man has fixed my gun. An' I knows by the way this buck general grins that he knows my gun is *no bueno* before he opens the jack-pot.

"But a ol' single-action gun is a right handy weapon, even empty. But this greaser hits me with two-three bullets before I warps my gun-barrel acrost his eyebrows. When I make sure that he's a sure enough corpse, I reloads my gun an' ties up the bullet holes in my hide. Then I takes a drink an', snaggin' my rope on Mister Bushwhacker, I drags him back to where I bin spendin' my evenin's. Maria is standin' under a tree, dressed up like she's goin' somewhere. The ol' man has a fresh bottle set out on a bench by the well. I don't need specs tuh see that they're waitin' fer the rebel feller.

" 'Here he is," says I, draggin' up the greaser's carcass an' handin' her the rope. Her knife grazes my cheek. I glaums the bottle on the bench, kicks the ol' man in the paunch, then rides home filled with sorrow an' thinkin' heavy on the ways uh female wimmen. It taken me all uh three weeks tuh git shet uh that bogged-down feelin' in my heart." Pecos sighed and set down the bottle. It was almost empty.

"Sad, eh, kid?"

"What's sad?"

"About me'n her."

"You and who?"

"Me'n Maria, dang it."

"Who is Maria?"

"You mean you ain't bin listenin'?"

"I was thinking."

"What yuh usin' fer brains? Yuh mean yuh never heard about what I was tellin'? Then I'll begin over." Pecos sighed and reached for the bottle.

"It happened down acrost the Mexican —"

"Don't. You'll have me bitin' my fingernails in grief. Has Bob located Dick?"

"Nary sign. Hell, don't let 'im whup yuh, Lance. You ain't to blame."

"Teton thinks so. So do a lot of other fools. They say Jack Parsons has made some nasty talk about us stealing beef. Buck and Slim passed me up in town like I was a drunk sheep-herder. It's hard to laugh off that sort of stuff. Poor old Bob's trying to be loyal to both sides. If anything happens to Dick Kirby, I won't have a friend left in the country. They're already down on me." Lance poured himself a stiff drink.

"Hmmm. Got a check-book handy?"

"Right here on the table. Why?"

"Yuh jest as well figger up my time."

"You mean you're —"

"I'm quittin'. So long as you fight like a man, I'll stick by yuh. I'll hang an' rattle plenty fer a game man. But I ain't workin' fer no man that lays 'em down because a fool gal sticks up her nose an' a damn cow thief like Jack Parsons makes a flash play. Instead uh provin' 'em liars, you bog down with a bottle an' feel sorry fer Lance Mansfield. Any fool kin laugh when he's winnin', but it takes a man with guts tuh grin when he's gittin' tromped on. I'll git my check directly I git my stuff packed." And he walked out.

When Pecos came back into the house an hour later, sounds of a song mingled with running shower water. When Pecos shoved his head inside the bathroom a wet sponge caught the old cow-puncher in the face. Pecos grinned, called the boy a few pet names, and went out of the house whistling. It was significant that the old foreman had not packed so much as a sock.

Chapter XIV

They amputated big Jim Kirby's arm below the shoulder. But they could not mar the courage of the old cattleman.

"I was lookin' around fer a excuse tuh set back an' let Bob do it. Man don't need a gun arm these days, an' I don't have tuh rope ol' Ji to ketch him of a mornin'."

"I hear Dick joined up with the Canadian army, Jim."

Jim Kirby's smile became a little forced, but his voice was hearty enough. "He writes that he's ridin' out them skates that us folks unloads on the English hoss buyers. Says they couldn't hand-pick the world an' git meaner hosses. He's at Calgary. Sarcee Camp, they calls it; kinda remount camp. He aims tuh git transferred when our country steps into the scrap."

He did not add that Dick's letters all came to Mrs. Kirby and Teton — that Dick still nursed his grudge against his father and Lance Mansfield. Nor did Bob hint of it to Lance or Pecos.

Winter whitened the hills. Cowboys wrapped in chaps and mackinaw coats rode the ridges. The check for the last shipment of Circle Seven cattle came from Chicago, and Lance saddled up and rode to town with it. Judge Truman greeted him warmly. The old banker seemed to be aging.

"Damned rheumatism, son. Have a seat."

Lance took off his fur coat and laid a small ledger on the table. Then he laid a checkbook beside it. He smiled twistedly, and the Judge was reminded of Tom Mansfield.

"I think you'll find my account accurate, sir. With this last check for the steers, we just about break even. I'm transferring my thirty-three thousand over to the ranch account."

"Throwing away your nest-egg, eh?"

"I'm not going to borrow from the bank to run on, sir. It wouldn't be fair to you."

Judge Truman nodded thoughtfully. He seemed about to say something, then changed his mind and remained silent. Lance transferred the money from his private account at Helena to his ranch account at the town bank. The money for the steers paid off Lance's notes to the bank. There was no denying it, Judge Truman looked older, older and almost ill. Lance noticed a stranger in the cashier's cage. The cashier's face was set and unsmiling as he and the stranger bent over a huge ledger.

Lance stabled his horse and walked down

the street toward the hotel. Teton Kirby was coming toward him. She looked up through the falling snow, glanced about swiftly as if seeking an avenue of escape, then came on with her head held high. But Lance blocked her way, smiling a little, his fur cap in his hand.

"Hello, Tonnie. Going to pass up an old friend?"

"Friend?" Her voice was a hard little whisper. "Friend? No, I always greet my friends." And she brushed past him. He looked after her, the hurt of her words reflected in his eyes. Then he jammed on his cap and went on down the street.

"What was Teton doing in town anyhow?" he mused bitterly. "Why wasn't she at school?" Then he suddenly remembered that it was almost Christmas and she must be home for the holidays. Christmas! He laughed a little bitterly and swung into the barroom of the hotel.

Big Jim Kirby was at the bar, talking to a tall man in a bearskin coat. The tall man eyed Lance without curiosity. Jim Kirby nodded curtly. Lance took the old cowman's brief nod for unfriendliness. Coming on top of Teton's snubbing, it rankled, for Jim had been friendly always. Lance, determined to probe this antagonism to the bottom, stepped up to the bar. "Have a drink, Jim?" His glance included the tall stranger. It was more than an invitation. It was a challenge, a test of friendship. For only friends drink from the same bottle in the cow country.

"Why — why, sure, son. Don't reckon you two gents ever met. Lance, shake hands with Jack Parsons. This is young Mansfield, Parsons."

So that was the reason for old Jim Kirby's brief nod? He had hoped Lance would pass on through the saloon into the adjoining hotel lobby.

Parsons's black eyes narrowed a little as he studied the younger man. Neither had offered to shake hands. Jim Kirby stirred uneasily. That moment's silence seemed never-ending as those two men eyed each other.

This was Jack Parsons of the Quarter-Circle Z — the man who had called the Circle Seven outfit cow thieves. Parsons twisted an end of a neat black mustache, smiling thinly at the hot-eyed stripling who was not yet out of his teens. It was the tolerant contempt of seasoned manhood for mere youth.

Perhaps it was Teton's snubbing rather than Parsons's smile that roused the boy's hot wrath. His voice shook with emotion when he broke the pregnant silence.

"I've been looking forward to meeting you, Parsons. You've called me a cow thief, without proof. You've fouled the name of my dead father. Shed your coat, you damned skunk!" Lance threw his own coat into a corner.

"Easy, kid," cautioned Jim Kirby.

"My scrap, Jim. Keep out. I'm waiting, Parsons."

"I don't fight kids," sneered Parsons.

"There's logic in that," said Lance bitingly. "The present heavyweight champ of the world is a kid. There's a lot of nice fighting names in my vocabulary. Want 'em? Or how about this for a teaser?" Lance stepped forward and his open hand caught Parsons across the mouth.

"You damned young whelp!" Parsons flung off his coat. He was a well-built man, slim-waisted, heavy-shouldered; and he stood on his feet like a boxer. Lance's quick glance took in these little details, even as he met Parsons's attack.

It was no bullheaded rush, that attack. Rather, it was the light-footed spring of a panther. Lance caught the blow on his shoulder and countered with a jab that split Parsons's lips.

The bartender stood back admiringly behind his polished barrier. In two minutes a crowd was gathering — a silent, eager-eyed crowd of townsmen, cow-punchers, and traveling salesmen waiting for Number three.

The shuffle of feet, the thud of blows, the audible murmur of the onlookers. Smashing, ducking, jabbing, sidestepping, the two men fought. Each man battled with cold fury in his blows. They were evenly matched in skill and weight. The crowd formed a human ring.

Minute after minute they battled. Both fighters were bleeding. Parsons wore a heavy ring that drew blood every blow. He was using that ring with cruel skill, cutting, ripping. And Lance fought without notice of the gashes in his face and arms and shoulders. He was smiling crookedly; forcing the fight now; advancing on flat feet; smashing at the handsome face of the man who had branded his father a thief. Parsons ripped in terrific body blows but Lance kept on coming; his feet never off the floor, shifting always forward; meeting the older man's blows with hooks and jabs and uppercuts that rocked Parsons's head. Chinook had never seen such a fight, inside the prize-ring or out of it. These men were fighters who used no padded gloves and fought on without pause, minute after minute.

In the adjoining lobby, men bustled wives and daughters and mothers upstairs; then joined the crowd in the barroom. The lobby was empty when Teton Kirby entered, crossed the deserted place, and was about to go up to her room when a voice from the bar halted her.

"My money's on Mansfield. Go to it, kid. A hundred on the kid!" Teton paused, frozen in her tracks. Then she mounted a few steps and looked through the open doorway, across the crowded heads, into the cleared circle where two men, their shirts ripped in bloody shreds, fought like two beasts. There was no mistaking that close cropped blond head of Lance Mansfield, nor the dark featured Jack Parsons, who was known as quite a dandy in dress and manner. Teton sank weakly on the steps, her fascinated gaze on the two fighters. Dimly, as through a haze, she saw her father keeping back the crowd, his big voice raised in gruff command.

"Back, gents. Give 'em room. More room, boys."

Winded, their breath coming in terrible sobbing gasps, the men fought on. Lance shuffling forward, crouched, smiling terribly through a smear of oozing blood; Parsons, weaker each minute, beating at the boy with ripping, slashing blows. A low murmur of disgust followed Parsons.

"The kid's fightin' fair. That damn ring is worse'n a knife. Always said there was greaser in Jack Parsons. Git him, Lance."

Lance paid these comments no heed. He had fought in the ring enough to disregard comments. But Parsons snarled something at the man who had spoken. Lance stepped inside, blocked a hook, swung upward at the snarling face that was jolted backward. Parsons reeled, staggered back, and almost went down. Lance stood crouching as the other man came for him.

Parsons swung an uppercut that would have landed low had it connected, but Lance's forearm had warded the blow and they were locked in a clinch.

"Your fighting's as dirty as your tongue, Parsons." Lance broke away and smashed a short one into the other's face. It was not the first low shot that Parsons had tried. And he had roughed it in the clinches.

They met again in a clinch. This time Lance, grinning widely, shoved Parsons's head back with the heel of his hand. Then he slid from the clinch and slapped with his open palm. The blow cracked like a pistol.

It was deliberately done and those who saw it grinned or laughed outright.

"Slap him on the other cheek, kid." And a roar of ribald applause went up as Lance, catching an opening, swung an open-handed blow against the other cheek. Parsons, crazy with rage, rushed in, dropping his guard to swing. Lance shifted a bit, stiffened, swung. Parsons went down in a sodden heap. He got up slowly. A ready chorus was counting.

"Five — six — seven!" Parsons came up from the floor in a crouch. He put all his vanishing strength into a blow that caught Lance low in the groin. But even as the blow landed, Lance's swing spun Parsons about and sent him sprawling, face downward on the tobacco-stained floor. Lance sank weakly, a gray pallor spreading over his ripped face. Twenty men had seen the foul blow that had dropped the boy.

"Carry the kid upstairs," said someone. "Where's his room?"

"He ain't registered."

"Take him to my room," said Jim Kirby.

"Oh, hell, Jim, I'm — I'm —"

"Number five," instructed Kirby. "Somebody fetch Doc King."

"What'll we do with Parsons?" called a voice.

"If it was left tuh me," said a big cow-puncher, "I'd say hang 'im. That kid was scrappin' clean all through. I kin lick the liar that calls Mansfield a cow thief."

It was none other than Buck who spoke. Slim nodded his approval.

"I'm beginnin' tuh kinda like that kid," announced Slim. "An' the more I see uh Parsons, the more I want tuh stay clear uh the Quarter-Circle Z. We'll kinda ride close herd on Jack Parsons when he wakes up, eh?"

"Shore thing. Mebby learn some new swear words."

Big Jim Kirby, guiding the men who carried the agonized Lance upstairs, smiled queerly as he saw Teton vanishing at the top of the stairway. But she did not come near her father's room. It was noticeable, however, had big Jim taken the trouble to observe such a trifle, that Teton managed to waylay her father at the first opportunity.

"Wasn't that Lance Mansfield that was fighting, Jim?"

"Yeah." Jim nodded indifferently. Doc King had just left the room where Lance lay in Jim Kirby's bed.

"Was he hurt badly?"

"Uh? Who? Oh, Lance, yuh mean. Nope. His looks is kinda spoilt fer parlor work, though. Purty bad cut up aroun' the face."

"What were they fighting about, Jim?"

"Mmmmmm. Lemme see now, what was it? Somebody called t'other a skunk er somethin'."

"And Jack Parsons licked Lance?"

"Parsons lick Lance Mansfield? I reckon, hardly. That boy is about the one fightin'est human I ever seen. He's a bearcat, that boy. I bet Parsons is still sleepin'. Wasn't Jack Parsons gonna take you to the picture show to-night, Tonnie?"

"He still is, if he don't back out. Now quit scowling."

"Ain't he kinda oldish fer you, kid?"

"Oh, I don't know. These boys give me a pain. All they know is kid stuff. Jack Parsons knows something about the world. Besides, he's the best-looking man in town and the girls are all crazy about him."

The old cow-man snorted. He was about to make some explosive statement, when he caught a twinkle in his daughter's eyes. Teton was not the sort of girl to lose her head over a man like Parsons and Jim knew it. Jim went downstairs humming softly under his breath.

Chapter XV

There was a dance after the picture show. Jack Parsons, in spite of the marks of battle, was easily the most handsome and romantic man on the floor. His clothes were well tailored, his white-toothed smile flashed with proper frequency, and his dancing was superb. He had brought Teton Kirby, who rather outshone the town girls. Her clothes were those of the city, and her poise and talk rather cheapened the town girls by comparison.

"Parsons is shore buildin' to Jim Kirby's gal."

"She's flirtin' with him somethin' scan'lous. Too bad her maw ain't here tuh put a stop to such brazen carryin' on. I don't see what Jim Kirby's thinkin' of, lettin' that young one go gallivantin' aroun' with a man old enough tuh be her father."

"Parsons has got a gall," said the husband of the last speaker, "showin' up after that scrap he had. The Mansfield boy shore trimmed him. Never seen such a scrap."

"Hmm. And you told me you was over at the depot askin' about them packages I had comin' from the mail-order house. Like as not you never went near the depot, an' here I set in my last winter's dress, while you —"

"Now, maw!" The husband squirmed, reddening with guilt.

"Pardners fer a quadrille!" shouted the caller. The fiddle scraped and the floor filled.

"Jumpin' centipedes, Slim, he's dancin' this set with Teton. I'll tell a man that purty Jack has a sight uh nerve."

"Yeah. Well, he'll be cuttin' his capers fer a few minutes. How about slippin' over to the Dew Drop an' h'istin' a light 'un, Buck?"

"Cowboy, you shore think in sweet terms. Let's go."

"He ain't likely tuh give us the slip, do yuh think?"

"Naw. Not so long as he kin be the he-belle uh the ball."

The two Bench-K cow-punchers seemed to have taken an unusual interest in the activities of Jack Parsons. Since that battered gentleman had gone to his room and come forth an hour later looking very little the worse for wear, they had cautiously shadowed him. At supper time they had turned in a listed report of Parsons's activities to Jim Kirby.

"Good work, boys. Keep sober an' don't

let him git on to you. Don't let him give yuh the slip now."

"He's slippery but he ain't smooth enough tuh fool us boys." And they had obeyed orders. Now they stepped into the Dew Drop to take the chill from their bones.

The saloon was well filled. Among those who lined the bar were Lon Jimson and Zack Tanner. Both these men were spending freely and were, as Buck put it, "well oiled." They were listening to a cow-puncher's drunken version of the fight between Parsons and Lance Mansfield. Buck and Slim unobtrusively took a stand at the bar and were served with two glasses and the bar bottle.

"What yuh say started the ruckus, feller?" inquired the one-eyed Lon.

"Somethin' about Mansfield bein' a cow thief. Shucks now, it ain't healthy tuh call that kid no names."

The two rustlers exchanged knowing glances. "Don't look's though a man like Jack Parsons 'ud be lettin' a bald-faced kid whup him. He musta bin shore drunk. Eh, Zack? Me'n Zack's seen that Parsons feller fight."

Zack spotted Buck and Slim and nudged his tall partner. Lon stooped as Zack whispered something, and when the tall fellow straightened there was an ugly grin on his wide mouth. But Zack growled something in the nature of a warning, and a cunning look crept into Lon's one eye. He looked down the bar and met Buck's glance.

"H'are ya, Buck? Howdy, Slim. Licker?"

"Got one in front of us an' one comin' up. Thanks jest the same, Jimson ol'-timer. How's the winter on Hell Crick?"

"Tol'able."

"Fetch Zack with yuh?"

Zack shoved his head past his tall partner. "I come without bein' fetched," he said acidly.

"Gosh, now," grinned Buck, "I didn't see yuh, Tanner. Lon takes up so much light u man can't sight what's hidin' behind him."

"Hidin'?"

"Well, standin', then. The mistake is all mine, as the feller says."

"Fer Gawd's sake, Buck," breathed Slim, "don't start nothin'. That snake's got a gun. Mind Jim's orders. We gotta trail Parsons."

Buck needed no warning to tell him that Zack Tanner, screened by Lon, had a hand on his gun. The temptation to hooraw Zack about his sudden quitting of his homestead was almost overpowering. While Buck was no gunman, still he was a fearless sort of fellow. He grinned at his reflection in a flyspecked bar mirror.

"Slim," he said solemnly, "I'm gittin' purtier every day. I paid a dollar fer a shave an' haircut an' pink hair tonic that's shore soothin' to the nose. Likewise I'm wearin' my store clothes an' a tie that set me back six bits. Shame tuh waste such manly beauty in a low-down barroom. I'm goin' back to the dance an' swing some purty gal aroun'. Come on, yuh bony thing, an' set off my manly charms. Foller me, cow-servant, an' git some pointers on ball-room manners." And winking at the crowd, Buck swaggered out with Slim following.

"Whew!" gasped Slim. "That was a close 'un. Them two wart-hogs was itchin' fer trouble. An' my gun's at the Last Chance."

"Gosh, I was dyin' tuh ask Zack how he got the tar off his hide."

"You'd uh no doubt died, all right. He knows we wasn't in on that feather an' tar part, but jest the same it was Bench-K land that he taken up an' was run off of."

They reached the dance hall just as the strains of "Home, Sweet Home" droned to silence.

"Gosh! Jest in time." And they stationed themselves to one side of the doorway, well in the shadow. They watched each group that came out, one couple after another. But when the last group had left the lighted hall, they faced one another in blank dismay. Jack Parsons and Teton Kirby had not passed them.

"They musta left before the last dance, Slim."

"While we was jawin' over at the Dew Drop. Dang it, we've lost him."

"He'd take the kid right back to the hotel."

"Shore thing." Buck led the way to the hotel. Jim Kirby sat in the lobby reading the "Drover's Journal."

"Well, what you boys find out?" he asked in a low tone.

"Tanner an' Jimson is in town."

"Yeah? Ain't the dance over?"

"Shore. Jest let out."

"Where'd Parsons an' Tonnie go?"

"Yuh mean they ain't back here to the hotel?"

But at that moment Teton entered the lobby, followed by Lance. The girl's face was white and her chin held high. She swept past Jim and his two punchers and up the stairs. Lance followed her with his eyes, a twisted, wistful sort of smile on his bruised lips. His left hand was badly swollen and bleeding.

Buck caught the message in Jim Kirby's

sharp glance and stalked out with Slim at his side.

"Where's Parsons, Lance?" Jim asked abruptly.

"Last I saw of the gentleman," said Lance grimly, "he was bedded down with his head under him. What the devil got into you, Jim, to let her go with that damn snake?"

"Shucks, son, Teton's no baby. No harm in her goin' to a dance with Parsons. He's old enough tuh be her daddy — er almost."

"He's about thirty, I'd say. Teton's sixteen an' looks twenty. The low-down polecat was tryin' to kiss her when I came along."

"The hell! What happened?" Kirby stiffened a little.

"I hit 'im, that's all."

Jim Kirby suppressed a smile. "What did Tonnie say?"

"Bawled me out for being a rowdy. Can you tie that? Said I'd spoiled a perfectly good evening."

"That hand uh yourn looks like it's busted. Doc's in the back room playin' solo. Better have him take a look at it, son. An' I'm obliged, Lance. So's Teton, only she's too mad tuh say so. Gosh knows why she went with Parsons. She's a close-mouthed kid. But ever since she found out that Dick had stayed at his place after he quit home, she's bin rarin' tuh meet him. Teton thinks a heap uh Dick; overlooks all his faults, kinda motherin' him. Will yuh do me a favor, Lance?"

"Why, sure, Jim. Name it."

"Soon as Doc fixes that hand, you git yore hoss an' go home. Jack Parsons is ornery. He ain't lettin' you git away with anything. I'm older'n you; I wouldn't ask yuh tuh do anything that ain't fer the best."

"If you mean Parsons will go gunning for me, Jim, two can play that game."

"What'll it git yuh? Lose, an' yuh git a pine board overcoat. Win, an' they'll mebby no give yuh life at Deer Lodge. The best you get is the worst of it."

"They'll say I'm yellow if I leave town, Jim. God knows they're calling me enough names as it is. I'm not a cow thief and I'm not cowardly enough to run from Jack Parsons." Lance's jaw bulged stubbornly.

"Then yuh won't go home, son?"

"Not till I'm ready to go, Jim."

"Are yuh packin' a gun?"

"It's upstairs."

"Parsons always packs one. Long as yo're stayin' in town where he is, you better go heeled."

"I will, Jim."

"An' don't crowd the play. Keep yore mouth shut an' yore eyes open. Keep away from the places he hangs out. . . . An' when yuh can't do nuthin' but fight, shoot fer his belly."

Chapter XVI

"Some day," said Jack Parsons, cold anger shaking his voice, "I'll get young Mansfield — and I'll get him for keeps."

The three other men who sat in the log cabin scowled at Parsons and nodded. Heavy green blinds were lowered across the cabin windows, and above the door hung the legend: "Ben Fisk, Land Locater." The place was thick with tobacco smoke and a bottle of whisky sat on the table.

Ben Fisk, a man of fifty, with hawklike features and sharp black eyes, drummed nervously on a drawing-board with a pencil.

"It's rather unwise, Jack, to attract attention just at this time. The whole town and its kids know you and young Mansfield had a scrap. It puts you in the public eye. Get him? Hell, we're getting him now, ain't we? What more can you ask for? Frankly, I'm skating on damn thin ice. These farmers think I'm locating men like Zack and Lon here on the best land. The cow-men give me a damn fishy eye. I'm not exactly popular.

"To-night, because you pinned a low one on Mansfield, you're none too popular yourself, and young Mansfield has gained a score of friends. Unless you agree absolutely to drop that fight and keep your mitts and your guns in your pockets, I'm quitting. That goes as it lays. I've too much at stake."

Zack Tanner and Lon Jimson exchanged sly grins. Parsons flushed darkly. . . . The two had come along as he awakened from Lance's blow. Lance and Teton were nowhere to be seen. The street, save for the approaching Lon and Zack, had been deserted.

"I slipped and twisted my ankle," Parsons had lied. They had grinned a little derisively.

"Shore thing," chuckled Lon, "I bin drinkin' the same brand uh tanglefoot. Bin huntin' yuh, Jack. Ben's sittin' in his shack fightin' his head. Bin waitin' a hour fer yuh."

Parsons had gone with the two rustlers. His head was aching and his jaw was swollen and stiff. Lance's one blow had been like the kick of a mule. Inwardly fuming, covering his chagrin and anger as well as he could, he entered the cabin of Ben Fisk. Lou had produced a bottle and Fisk set out glasses.

"Should anyone see us in here, our game is a flop," said Fisk uneasily. "It's risky. Let's get it over." He turned the lamp lower.

142

"Going back on your homestead, Zack?"

"Not while I've still got my right mind," came the emphatic reply. "It'll be a rope instead uh tar, next time."

"How about Lon, here?"

"Jest figger me out, Ben. It's taken me a week tuh git Zack shed off. He's still got spots showin' where the hide come off with the tar."

"I'll get some one on that land," said Parsons grimly, "if I have to take it up myself."

"Better leave that to me," suggested Fisk. "I have a man that will fill the bill. Did you feel out the Kirby girl about how Jim Kirby and the Circle Seven stood?"

"I did," snapped Parsons. "Jim and Bob Kirby are saying nothing and damn little of that. Dick and the girl hate the Mansfield outfit. I filled Dick to the eyes with whisky and ideas when he stayed at my place after he shot his old man. But I'm afraid the young idiot spilled too much to his sister about who ribbed him against Mansfield. There were times this evening when it looked like she was trying to pump me. Wish they were all as easy loaded as Dick." He did not mention his sudden meeting with Lance.

"Did you vamp the girl like you said you would?"

"Well, I think I had her going. Can't work too fast, you know. You leave that to little Jack. She'll fall." For Jack Parsons flattered himself that he had a way with women, young or old.

"I can't say I'm keen on this cradle-robbing, though. She's younger than she looks — full of kid ideas. But she sure hates Lance Mansfield."

"She's as purty as a spotted colt," leered Lon Jimson. "Built like a quarter hoss."

"Shut up," growled Zack. "Yo're drunk." He gave his partner an ugly look that was heavy with meaning. . . . Lon knew that Zack was thinking of that snowy night a year ago when Lon, drunk and half-froze, had stumbled into a cabin where the two were living for a few weeks. Lon had talked later on, when he had lowered the liquor in their jug. Lon's confession had sent the two rustlers into the storm, and they had not stopped till they reached Hell Creek. For by his admission, Lon had left the Kirby girl to freeze in the blizzard, pinned beneath a crippled horse.

"But I tell yuh she never seen my face, Zack. I had it covered," Lon had insisted drunkenly.

"I ain't chancin' nothin'," Zack had maintained. "We gotta git." They had almost shot it out with each other that night. Theirs had never been a comradeship of love. Rather, it was a partnership in crime that had more than once threatened to end in powder smoke. . . .

"You saw Truman to-day, Jack?" asked Fisk.

"I did," Jack Parsons smiled thinly. "I drew out every dollar I had and banked it across the street at the Farmer's Bank. Gad, old Truman looked positively green. There was a bank examiner there, going over the books."

Fisk nodded. "And I'm thinking that old Truman's about at the end of his rope. As I told you, he's loaned money with both hands. He's loaded to the guards with cowmen's paper — Kirby's and Mansfield's and others. He'll wish to God he'd pooled with us now. But he wouldn't listen to reason. He stuck by his cow-men. Now let's see how much good they can do him. They're all land-poor. They can't borrow a dime to pay Truman. He's holding the sack. No wonder he looked sick when you drew out your money. Parsons, I'll bet a hat that Truman's bank closes its door this week."

"That'll be sure hell," smiled Parsons. "Truman and Kirby and Tom Mansfield were always of the opinion that I was not good enough for them. It's my turn now. Kirby's in debt over his head. Truman is going to the wall. And I've got a little scheme that is going to put that cub of Tom Mansfield's in the pen for a long stretch. Then, when things are right, I'll buy the Circle Seven and the Bench-K outfits at Jack Parsons's own price."

"You mean shoving farmers in on their land?" asked Pawn Ben.

"That's just preliminary. Ben, stick in my game and you'll wear diamonds. All this is just marking time. Setting Kirby against Mansfield and so on. Man, when I spring my trap, Lance Mansfield is going to be making pebbles out of boulders with a nice striped suit on and a guard over him." Parsons, intoxicated by bitter hate, was talking more than he intended.

"I damn near had Tom Mansfield in that trap. But he was too cute for me. He took a gat and blew his brains out. Huh? Accident? Hardly, Ben, my boy. He was staring Old Man Law in the eye and he knew it."

"Then Tom Mansfield was a crook?"

"That John Bull a crook! Don't make me laugh. He didn't have the brains to be a crook. It ain't always the guilty that look out through the bars. I gave him his chance to make some easy dough and he got shirty and

146

ordered me out of his house, like I was a buck nigger with leprosy. No way to treat a gentleman, Ben. So when I got back home, I had a little medicine-talk with Zack and Lon.

"Tom Mansfield was paying five dollars a head for all his stray stuff brought back from across the river. For after Pecos quit him, his stuff drifted south beyond the Missouri. I've been accused of eating his beef. Can you imagine that?"

Parsons chuckled and went on glibly.

"So Zack and Lon delivered some of his stray stuff. They were paid by check. But it seems like there's somethin' odd about those cattle. Their brands are rather queer. Tom Mansfield ain't cow-man enough to see it, but the Circle Seven on their hides is really a Quarter-Circle Z. And Lon and Zack are clumsy enough to get caught by two Bench-K cow-punchers as they're working one of these brands. Fact is, Lon and Zack purposely get themselves watched."

"Sounds to me like they were putting their heads in a noose," said Fisk.

"In a way, they are. But after they had been jailed, Ben, and after their confession implicated Tom Mansfield, they would escape. Get the idea? They're gone. Not so

147

hard to get away if you have outside friends with a little money. That leaves Tom Mansfield facing a charge of buying stolen cattle. Lon and Zack leave signed confessions. Buck and Slim, the two Bench-K riders, are witnesses. Their innocence makes their testimony bullet-proof. That's what Mansfield was up against that evening when he killed himself. I'd gotten word to him a few days before that I was going after his scalp. Hell, I thought he'd see things right and throw in with me. But when I sent Lon and Zack to feel him out and further explain how we had him sewed up, they found the damn fool dead with a flag on his carcass. He'd beaten me, see, but he had to commit suicide to do it."

Jack Parsons laughed, but somehow his mirth fell flat. He muttered something and tossed off a stiff drink.

"Victory in death," said Ben Fisk softly, and drank. Then his eyes narrowed shrewdly.

"Have you any proof of the suicide theory, Jack?" he asked.

"Proof? No. Why?"

"Nothing. What's this new scheme of yours?"

Parsons winked knowingly. "I'm not telling, Ben. Too many crooks spoil the pie.

It's good. It'll work. And you'll come in for your cut. Time we adjourned, ain't it?"

"Me'n Zack kin use six-bits," leered Lon.

"Hell, you must think I'm a bank," growled Parsons, pulling out a check-book. "How much?"

"A hundred apiece'll do," suggested Zack.

"A hundred between you is what you get," snapped Parsons.

Lon leaned across the table and Jack Parsons saw a bit of lavender cloth on his knee — Teton's handkerchief. Something in Lon's leering grin told Jack Parsons that the two rustlers had seen his interrupted attempt to kiss Jim Kirby's daughter. He flushed hotly and wrote out a check for two hundred dollars. "Cash this at the Farmer's Bank — no place else."

"Told yuh we'd git a reward fer pickin' that purty nose-rag outa the snow, Zack," said Lon later.

Neither Jack Parsons nor his two hirelings saw the two shadowy figures that crouched under a window outside Ben Fisk's cabin. Parsons left first, walking swiftly toward the hotel.

Lon and Zack quit the now darkened cabin and strolled leisurely toward the Dew Drop. The two men under the window quit their chilly post.

"If I was a corpse, Buck, I couldn't be no colder."

"But, man, it was worth it. Gosh, it must be dang nigh daylight. Let's git a shot uh redeye, then wake up ol' Jim."

"We'll wake Jim first," said Buck firmly, his teeth chattering. "Then it'll be time fer the licker. Jim'll have a bottle in his room, mebby. We lost one bet by playin' bar-fly tonight. Anyhow, I'm rarin' tuh give the ol' man a earful uh what we nigh froze tuh death hearin'. Rattle yore hocks, cowboy, we got news tuh tell."

They passed Judge Truman's house. A thread of light showed through a torn window-shade.

"Judge's keepin' late hours," said Slim. "Else he's dropped off tuh sleep with his light on."

Chapter XVII

"Greater love hath no man than this, that he lay down his life for his friend."

Judge Truman was dead. Beside his bed lay the old Colt's that had seen the frontiersman through many a dangerous day when Montana was a wilderness and Sitting Bull and his Sioux were chanting their war-song.

He had known, even when he made loans to his old friends, that there would come a day of reckoning. He had known that the laws of friendship are not bunking laws. Vaguely, in his bluff, cow-man's way, Judge Truman had known. Yet he had kept faith with men like Jim Kirby. And they had never guessed the price that this old gentleman from Virginia must pay in the name of loyalty.

He left no message. His friends would understand. He had preferred death to prison. Men like Kirby, who loved the open sky, would understand and know that he had not died a coward. He had never married. There was no widow to bow beneath the burden of disgrace, if such a simple gesture of heroism might be so distorted and labeled.

In Lance Mansfield's mail was an envelope. Inside were some bits of torn paper. It was the check he had given Judge Truman — his check on the Helena bank for thirty-three thousand dollars. Lance Mansfield knew that in the passing of the soft-spoken old southerner he had lost a friend. Tears blurred his vision as he gently put the envelope and its contents into the stove. Its mute message was probably the last, the final act of loyalty and friendship in the life of the man who had been his father's friend.

Jim Kirby rapped on Lance's door, then entered. He sank into a chair and sat there in silence. Lance, for all his youth, knew better than to break that silence. Later he learned that big Jim had knocked down some man in the lobby who hinted that Judge Truman had defaulted and lost the money in speculation.

"I sent Buck to the ranch after Bob," Jim spoke finally. "Bob'll fetch yore school uniform. It'd be what Judge'd have yuh wear at the funeral. He went tuh one uh them soldier schools hisse'f — West Point. I dug up a flag." He did not explain that it was the new flag that belonged to the school. "Him havin' fought in the Civil War, I reckoned he had it comin' like Tom had."

Lance nodded. Jim was on his feet, pacing

to and fro, deep in thought.

"There'll be them, son, that'll be talkin' nasty. Best not tuh let on yuh hear. Judge his friends by them as stands by his grave. You'll be one uh the pall-bearers. Teton wired fer flowers an' Brother Van. Judge an' Brother Van is ol'-time friends. He'll give him the right kind uh send-off. Pete Rawlins an' Doc King an' some more'll be there. Bob'll fetch Maw. She's right good at funerals an' weddin's."

Teton entered without knocking. She was dressed in black and her eyes were a little swollen. She looked more of a woman than Lance thought possible. Her eyes were misty with unshed tears when Lance seated her in a chair. She found his hand and clutched it tightly, as she had held it that evening when Tom Mansfield lay draped in his country's flag.

Haltingly, a husky catch in his voice, Lance told them of the check Judge Truman had destroyed.

"He always thought a heap uh you, Lance," said big Jim. "He knowed what it meant, too, when he went on my note six months ago fer them Idaho two-year-olds I bought."

"Who will suffer, Jim?" asked Teton.

"Nobody, Honey. Mighty few town folks

153

banked with him. It was us cow-men that made his bank possible. It was us that ruined him. The odds stand in our favor. God has balanced Judge Truman's books."

It snowed heavily the day of the funeral. Teton had ripped and sewed at Lance's blue-gray uniform until it fitted him. He had grown heavier since he left school. They stood beside the flag-draped coffin, those white-haired men who followed the horse-drawn hearse to the cow town's cemetery. Snow fell in thick, soft flakes, as if God were blanketing the coffin with the eternal whiteness of peace. Lance, standing at attention, looked very young and clean and courageous. Teton again saw him through the eyes of girlish adoration.

Brother Van, himself a pioneer, spoke gently, understandingly of the dead man who had been his friend. And finally the casket was lowered into its white resting-place. Lance, through a mist of tears, caught the colors of the flowers.

"I am the Resurrection and the Life —"

Teton held Lance's hand all the way back to town. No mention was made of Parsons. The man had not been seen. He had probably gone home. Zack Tanner and Lon Jimson had also gone. But in Jim Kirby's wallet was a check made out to Zack Tanner and signed by Jack Parsons. It bore Tanner's endorsement. They had cashed it, as Buck thought they would, at the Dew Drop, and Buck had bought if from the bartender.

But Lance knew nothing of the sinister meeting at Ben Fisk's cabin; nor did Teton.

"Reckon I'll be drifting on home after dinner," said Lance at the hotel. "Can't let Pecos do it all."

"You'll come over for Christmas Day, Lance? We want you."

"You bet I will, Tonnie. Gee!"

Torn between grief and happiness, Lance rode home in the snow.

That was the day that Dick Kirby, in a Canadian uniform, was loaded on to a British transport and sent to France. . . .

"It's a long way to Tipperary. . . ."

Gray faces filing silently up the gangplank — the faces of boys fated to do a man's job. Some would come back; others would die. And still others were to return horribly maimed.

Mud and cognac and blood, and the stench of dead flesh . . . barbed-wire and billets . . . songs and curses, and the laughter of men fresh from a glimpse of hell.

They had canned willie for Christmas dinner. No lights were allowed for fear of submarines. Dick won fifty dollars shooting craps. There was liquor on board. Dick laughed and joked with the others, but there was no laughter in his heart.

"Wonder what Dutch Henry 'ud say if he saw me takin' orders from that sissy-lookin' loot?"

"Who's Dutch Henry? Sounds like a bloomin' Boche."

Dick chuckled musingly. "That major with the decorations looks like Tom Mansfield. Gimme that bottle, kiddo. I gotta take the taste uh that name outa my mouth."

While back at the Bench-K ranch, Lance carved the turkey and did his best to bring cheer to the Kirby home. He knew that Dick had been ordered overseas. Also he knew that big Jim would be hard pressed to pull through the winter. But Bob had agreed to let Lance winter some of the poor stuff.

"Send over Buck or Slim. I'll furnish the hay. I've got plenty — more than enough to go around."

Big Jim did not tell Lance what he had learned about Jack Parsons. He feared the boy might do something rash.

"Put Pecos wise, Bob. Then let Parsons play his cards. And don't let on to nobody that Tom Mansfield committed suicide.

The insurance folks 'ud just nacherally take the whole outfit, lock, stock and barrel. An' Lance 'ud go to the pen for about twenty-five years. I always suspicioned that Tom killed hisself a-purpose. Judge Truman, I think, had the same hunch, but he never said nothin'."

"Do yuh reckon that's what Parsons hopes tuh prove, Jim?"

"Don't think so. Still, Parsons is foxy."

So Lance, blissfully unaware of the danger that clouded his future, laughed and sang while Teton played popular airs on a wheezy little organ. Out of respect for the memory of Judge Truman, they did not go to the Christmas dance at Chinook

He was glad, afterward, that they had been together that day. For this was the winter of 1916–17. Even in the remote sections of the cow country men were feeling the fever of unrest. Bob Kirby voiced the fear that was to see fulfillment before another winter came.

"It's a long, long way to Tipperary, but I'm going there."

"Bob's got a good voice," grinned Jim; "but he kinda warped it a-warblin' to beef herds." He turned to Lance. "Where is this

157

Tipperary range, anyhow?"

"A long ways from here, Jim." Lance smiled a little wistfully. "I wish I was with Dick. If Dad were living, I'd be going. His old regiment lost heavily. And the Princess Pats were wiped out, almost to a man. I reckon Dad would want me to go."

"But you're not British, son. You're an American."

Lance nodded, his eyes filled with memories of the man who had been his father — Tom Mansfield who would inherit a title if some older brothers died. . . . He wondered about his mother.

Chapter XVIII

One sunny morning in early April three men rode through the gateway of the Circle Seven ranch. One of these men was a deputy sheriff, another was a cattle inspector, and the third was a hatchet-faced man who wore a stock detective's badge. The third man led the other two men to a haystack. With a hayfork they dug into the stack. Presently they dragged out a green cowhide.

"That's one of the hides, boys. There's more."

"This one's a Bench-K hide," said the stock inspector.

The detective located another hide buried under a cutbank. It was dry and wrinkled, but they made out part of the Quarter-Circle Z iron on the warped hide.

Jack Parsons had struck. Pecos was off on the horse round-up. The three men were waiting when Lance came in that evening from town.

"Anything you say in our presence," said the deputy sheriff, "may be used against you at the trial."

The stock detective laughed shortly.

"You're a smooth article, kid. But you should have cut the brands outa those hides an' fed 'em to the dogs. If I was you, I'd plead guilty."

"I thought there was something snaky about you when you hired out to me in town," said Lance. "Bronc rider, eh? I need just one guess to name the man that planted you here and who paid you for caching those hides on my place. Sheriff, if you'll let me have just one healthy swing at this polecat's jaw, I'll trot along peacefully to your little jail. I'll only need one swing."

"Sorry, kid," the deputy smiled at Lance's earnest plea, "but I can't allow it. Will you come without the bracelets?"

"Bracelets? Oh, I see. I'm not going to try to escape, if that's what you mean. I've done nothing against the law. I'd like to get word to my foreman, though."

"I'll see to that," said the deputy. "Don't worry."

Lance slept in the county jail that night. Jim Kirby and an attorney visited Lance after breakfast the next morning.

"This is Jack Parsons's doin's, Lance. Damn him, he outfoxed me." The old cowman told briefly of the plot Parsons and his confederates had talked of that night in Ben Fisk's cabin.

"I figured he'd try the same trick again that he tried on Tom. Had Buck an' Slim watchin'. Then they had tuh go with Bob on the horse round-up. Parsons plants them hides and this gimlet-eyed detective. He shore outfoxed us. But we'll whup him, son."

Big Jim rubbed the stump of his maimed arm and tried to grin.

The attorney took a less optimistic viewpoint. "Plant or no plant, it's evidence — damning evidence, Mansfield. The testimony of Kirby's men won't win your case. You'll need positive proof that those hides were planted. The stock association is out to punish such cases. It's a tough proposition. What we need is eye-witnesses to prove that this detective, Harry Winn, has planted the hides — direct testimony. I'm afraid the testimony of Kirby's men will be thrown out. Or if it is admitted, it won't weigh heavily with a jury of grangers. For eleven out of twelve jurymen will be farmers. I'll demand a hearing and get you out on bail. That's the best we can do right now. By postponing trial, we'll have time to build up some sort of defense."

"Cheerful cuss," growled Kirby, when the attorney had taken his leave. "Reminds me of a undertaker lookin' over a new corpse. Damn law sharps, anyhow. But we ain't licked yet."

Pecos came to town a few days later. He brought Lance's mail and a caddy of tobacco.

"I was in the can once fer ten days an' run outa smokin'. Like tuh went loco." He looked over the cell with critical eye. "Hell, a man kin git outa here with a good jackknife. The bartender at the Last Chance is gonna fetch over some dinner his wife cooked fer yuh. How yuh fixed fer readin'? This is right homelike. All yuh need is a phonygraph an' lace curtains, kid. Different from some uh the joints I bin in. Met Teton on the way to the ranch. She got in on Number One an' didn't know you was in the can. Said she'd be in tuh see yuh. She's home fer spring vacation. Seen the Great Falls papers? Shore looks like the ol' U.S. was a-goin' into the big scrap."

Pecos sat down on the edge of the cot and rolled a cigarette. Behind his grin was black worry that crept into his eyes in spite of his banter. Lance stepped to the barred door and looked down the short corridor. The jailer was in the outer office reading a paper.

"Did you see that lawyer of mine, Pecos?"

"Uh? The shyster? Yeah." Pecos gave Lance a searching look. "He tells me you don't want to get out on bail."

"No. Parsons has a fool-proof case against me. The stock association is backing him. I'm due for slaughter, Pecos."

"Looks that way," admitted Pecos. "An' we thought we was so danged wise. They're gonna haul yuh up fer a quick trial, too. Gonna make a example outa yuh. I bin moseyin' aroun', feelin' out folks."

"Then you know why I didn't put up cash bond to get out?"

"Well, I ain't plumb dumb, kid."

"I've written to the Helena bank, Pecos, transferring my account to your name. That'll keep things running. I drew out a thousand dollars. All I ask for now is a dark night and a horse staked out somewhere where I can find it. A couple of hack-saw blades beats a jack-knife."

"Hold on, hold on, hold on," grinned Pecos. "Yo're a plumb pilgrim at this jail bustin'. Supposin' you let yore Uncle Pecos handle 'er. You jest set here an' read yore magazines an' lemme do the thinkin'. Keep yore mouth shet an' let on like you knowed you was gonna beat yore case, savvy? Th'ow the jailer off his guard. We're about due fer some rain in a day er so. If yuh know ary prayers, try fer a nice wet night. Yo're gonna have a cell pardner about to-morrow that'll show yuh how tuh engineer one uh these can openin's."

"A cell-mate?" echoed Lance.

"Yeah. You do as he says an' ask no questions. He'll savvy plenty. He'll be pinched fer bein' drunk an' disorderly. You may recollect his face. He was down on the river the night you licked Dick Kirby."

"One of Dutch Henry's gang?"

"What'd I tell yuh about askin' no questions. He'll be a plumb stranger an' awful drunk. But he kin find his way acrost country on the darkest, rainiest night the devil ever made. An' it'd tickle him green if some gent like Lon Jimson er Zack Tanner was tuh cut yore sign. Which they might, fer Parsons is waitin' fer jest sech a move outa you."

"You mean he expects me to break jail?"

"Dunno. Lon an' Zack's in town. They kinda disappear after dark. I bin told they was seen coyotein' aroun' the jail. Parsons is shore foxy."

Pecos stayed for an hour or two; then left. At noon the bartender from the Last Chance brought a tray loaded with food. Also, in the way of liquid refreshments, there was beer — and a flask of red liquor for the bored jailer. Time was when this dispenser of drinks had been a top cow-hand.

He and Pecos had come to the country to-gether.

"Try that bread, Lance — some the missus made."

Lance broke open the loaf of French bread. Inside was a long, slim bundle wrapped in white cloth. The bartender stood by the cell door, his back to Lance, his big bulk darkening the narrow doorway. He carried on a rambling conversation with the jailer in the distant office.

"An' so I says to this high-tone shoe drummer, says I, 'Mister, I'd be right proud tuh mix yuh one uh them Manhattan cock-tails yo're askin' fer, but I ain't got a egg in the house.' "

Lance shoved the slim package under his blankets. He knew by the sharp feel of the edges that the white cloth contained hack-saw blades. When the heavy-paunched bar-tender opened a bottle of beer and winked, Lance thanked him with his eyes.

"Here's wishin' yuh luck an' plenty of it, kid." The big fellow filled a glass with beer.

Lance swallowed a lump in his throat. He had always thought this red-faced saloon man was just a sort of human beer-keg, loud of speech and rather a harmless braggart. But behind the liquor-puffed red face, the paunch, and bloodshot eyes he now saw something else — a something that was often found lacking among men of higher calling. Lance was to find that something in other men. It is what we find mostly in dogs, children, and mothers. It goes by the name of "loyalty."

Chapter XIX

Teton Kirby came that evening, just before sundown. She had ridden in alone from the Bench-K ranch. In the stilted little hour she was allowed to stay the boy and girl were oddly silent. "I'm looking after the dogs, Lance. I'm going to bring 'em over to our place."

"But you'll be going back to school in a few days, Tonnie?"

"School? Guess again, Lance. I'm all caught up with my education. What's the use of knowing how to use seven forks and four spoons on a cow ranch where the table-cloth is checkered oilcloth? I don't need French and Latin to talk to Pecos and Buck and Slim." She smiled gaily.

"Sure. But what's the real reason for quitting? Tell your old pard."

"You may not be aware of the fact, cowboy, but we've had a tough winter. Finishing schools cost money and money is getting as scarce as robins in January. Get the idea? I'd feel like a yellow pup, Lance playing lady with Dad out there learning to punch cows with one arm and a steel hook. I'm going to be one of these she-cow-punchers — cattle queen. I'll be owning my own iron by the time you get back."

"Back from the penitentiary?"

She gave him a swift look. The jailer went past whistling one of the new war tunes.

"Back from wherever you'll be sent," she said softly, "Deer Lodge, or Tipperary." She smiled at him. "Pecos was at the ranch to-day, after he'd been to see you. So I came *before it rained.*"

Now Lance knew that Teton had been let in on the secret. Moreover, she had read his intentions of joining the army. They stood by the tiny, steel-barred window watching the sun set. He held her close and she sobbed softly on his shoulder.

"Sorry, miss, but I'll have tuh ask yuh to go. No visitors after sundown."

Teton kissed him through the bars of his cell door. She was trying not to cry. Lance's smile, the twisted, wistful, whimsical smile that had been Tom Mansfield's smile, followed her down the corridor. He was trying not to act the baby.

Teton Kirby was gone. He would not see her for a long time — perhaps never again. He stood by the little window until dusk shadowed the sky-line. From beyond the rim of distant hills came a low murmuring rumble — thunder. A breeze stirred un-

easily. In an hour it would be raining —
raining and dark.

"Better eat before that supper gets plumb
cold, young feller," the jailer called through
the barred door. "Looks like we was gonna
have rain."

Lance ate absently. The jailer took away
the empty dishes. Lance heard him lock the
outer door and saw him go down the street
toward the Chinaman's restaurant with the
trayful of dishes. The boy brought out the
saw blades and set to work. He hoped the
jailer would linger at his own evening meal
and perhaps sit in a game of pitch with his
cronies at the Last Chance. It was possible
that the beefy bartender would delay the
return of the jailer. Lance whistled to cover
the noise of the saw blade as it bit into the
bar of steel.

It was two hours before the jailer returned. He was half dragging, half carrying
a man who would balk now and then to lift a
nasal voice in maudlin melody. Lance saw
him through the drizzling rain.

*"Parson, I'm a maverick, just
    a-runnin' loose an' grazin',
Eatin' where's the greenest grass
    an' drinkin' where I choose.
Had tuh rustle in my youth an'*

never had no raisin',
Wasn't never halter broke an' I
ain't got much tuh lose."

The jailer opened the door of Lance's cell. The cow-puncher weaved in, grinning foolishly.

"Company for yuh, kid. If he gits too noisy, knock him tuh sleep."

"That feller," confided the new-comer, who gave off a strong odor of stable and whiskey, "is shore crool. He's got a mean eye, pardner. What's yore name when yo're outa jail, anyhow?"

The jailer grinned. "He's all right but thinks he kin sing. He'll bed down directly."

Lance looked the man over. He was a tall, rangy man with gray eyes that laughed at one from under heavy black brows. Straight-featured, lean-jawed; his coarse black hair was uncombed and damp from the rain. His overalls and boots were service worn; his blue flannel shirt was faded from rain and sun. When he grinned, a set of strong white teeth showed against the deep tan of his clean-shaven face.

"Name's Fogarty, but the boys calls me Doc — Doc fer short. Have a drink." He brought out a quart bottle. "Then we'll sing . . . me 'n you, pard. Always sing when I feel

170

happy. Man orter sing more. Nice dry jail, ain't she? Drink, mister." He winked. Lance tipped up the bottle, but only a tiny bit went down his throat. The jailer left them, chuckling to himself.

"Church folks never branded me —
I don't know as they tried.
Wish you'd say a prayer fer me
an' try tuh make a dicker
For the best they'll give me when
I cross the Big Divide."

Lance saw him fish a saw blade out of his boot. He handed it to the boy, winked, and sang on without losing the thread of his melody.

At ten o'clock the jailer peered through the door. He had taken a few drinks with Lance and Doc Fogarty, who were apparently enjoying the evening.

Now both of them lay sprawled, fully clothed, on their cots. On the floor lay the empty whisky-bottle. He blew out the corridor lamp and went to his bunk in the outer office. Outside the rain fell in black sheets. The lights of the town were blurred, indistinct yellow spots.

An hour later three sawed bars were

171

twisted aside and the two prisoners slid into the rain-soaked night. Lance held to Doc's hand as they crept away. The mud was ankle deep. In a few minutes both men were soaked to the bone. They passed the last house at the edge of town and Doc led the way through the black night. They halted in a willow thicket. Two saddled horses stood tied to a tree, slickers over the empty saddles.

"Dunno as them slickers'll do much good now," chuckled Fogarty. He handed Lance a cartridge belt and holstered gun. "Let's drift, pardner."

They drifted. The wind at their backs swept them across the rain-drenched prairie.

"Swell evenin' fer ducks, eh, Lance?"

"You said it. Which way do we go?"

"They'll figger we headed fer Canada. Pact of the matter is, a couple uh fellers is gonna ketch sight of us goin' that direction, savvy? They'll tell the sheriff. But me'n you is gonna head south an' keep on goin' south fer a spell. They tell me there's a war goin' on somewheres acrost the big crick. I'm rarin' tuh look 'er over. How about Los Angeles fer a destination?"

"You're going to enlist, Doc?"

"Shore. I'd a heap ruther be a shot hero

than a hung outlaw. Bin aimin' tuh jine up with the Canucks fer a month, but I got in a ruckus with a mountie up near Calgary an' them boys is hell fer rememberin' faces. I hear they got a recruitin' office in Los Angeles, an' they ain't askin' a man's pedigree neither. They need men — especially men that knows squads east an' mules."

"You mean you've been in the army, Doc?"

"Cavalry. Have a drink?" He fished a bottle from his saddle pocket. "Pecos tells me you went to a military school. . . . Damn this cork. . . . Here yuh go." Lance drank but little. He was leaving Montana . . . leaving the Circle Seven . . . leaving home.

"Tanner an' Jimson musta got run inside the Dew Drop when the bottom fell outa that black cloud this evenin'," chuckled Fogarty. "Jest as well fer them two skunks that they didn't try tuh stop ol' Doc. I don't like them fellers."

They rode on through the mud and rain and darkness. It was getting daylight when they reached Dutch Henry's camp in the heart of the Little Rockies. The outlaw leader greeted them casually.

"Well, I see you boys made it." That was all, no mawkish sentiment, no inane question — just that casual greeting. The scalding coffee warmed Lance and he ate heartily of beef and biscuits, beans and fried potatoes.

"You boys better turn in," Henry suggested. It was still drizzling and they sat in a cabin that had a leaky roof. Only Henry and the cook were in camp. Lance got the impression that the rest of the gang were away somewhere. Probably holding a bunch of stolen horses. He wondered what Tom Mansfield would have said if he knew his son was accepting the hospitality of horse thieves.

Sleep came reluctantly, tired as he was. Fogarty was snoring gently. The rain dripped from the sod roof on to the dirt floor and spattered on the tarp of Lance's borrowed bed. The bed smelled of tobacco and horses. Finally he fell into a fitful slumber filled with chaotic dreams. He was surprised to find that it was late afternoon when he awoke. Fogarty's bed was empty. Men were moving about outside. It was still raining. Lance dressed and went outdoors. Fogarty and Dutch Henry squatted on their heels by the fire in the shelter of a canvas fly. The cook sloshed about in the mud, lifting Dutch oven lids with a long-handled hook.

"We'll pull out about dusk," said Fogarty as Lance came up. "We'll cross the river about daylight an' hole up at a 'breed camp on the south side. Sleep good?"

Lance grinned and poured himself a cup of coffee. He wanted to ask about the danger of a sheriff's posse following them, but the utter indifference of these men to law and its officers forbade it. They chatted aimlessly until supper-time. Then Lance and Doc saddled fresh horses and mounted.

"So-long, boys," said Dutch Henry. "Think uh me when yuh line yore sights on a Heinie."

Lance wanted to thank this outlaw for his hospitality, but somehow could not find the right words to say.

Henry stood there by the fire, a coffee-cup in one hand, a cigarette in the other — smiling a little, his eyes grave. It was the last time Lance ever saw the man. Fogarty told him later on that night that the gang had disbanded for good and that Henry talked of going to the Argentine.

"Can't make a decent livin' no more on account uh the country bein' so damn lousy with farmers an' fences," Fogarty explained the cause of disbanding. "They don't make 'em any whiter'n Dutch Henry. I tried tuh talk him into comin', but he 'lowed he was too old tuh learn takin' orders from any-body. Henry's crowdin' sixty-five, I reckon. Still, we had a gent in Pancho Villa's outfit that was close tuh seventy an' he was a machine-gunnin' fool."

"How old are you, Doc?"

"Mmmmm. Lemme see. I was twenty-one when I went into the Rough Riders. That was in ninety-eight. Reckon that makes me about forty."

"You were in the Spanish-American War?"

"Joined up with Bucky O'Neill at Prescott. I was deputy twice under Bucky when he was sheriff there. I was right behind him when he got his at San Juan Hill.

"Funny thing about ol' Bucky; a fortune-teller told him oncet that he'd never git killed by a bullet. Bein' superstitious, he believed it, plumb. Yes, sir, he shore believed that no bullet made could kill him. An' from the way he got shot at an' was missed, it shore looked like that fortune-teller was right. We're chargin' up the hill. Bucky's a captain then. 'Boys,' he says, in that don't-give-a-damn way he had, 'the bullet never was made that kin kill me!'

"An', by God, he gits it while he's speakin' — square through the mouth. Since then I ain't took no stock in fortune-tellers."

They halted at the Missouri River just at daybreak. The river was swollen and ugly looking — foam spotted, muddy, treacherous. Here and there a half-submerged tree floated with the current. They loosened their saddle cinches and took off their chaps and boots, which they tied to their saddles.

"I was takin' off my clothes once, tuh cross a river," said Fogarty with a wry smile. "Hoss quit me in the middle uh the river an' I come ashore on a log. My pony landed on the other side. I was sunburnt, scratched, an' mosquito bit somethin' scan'lous when I hit a Injun camp next evenin'. I'd ruther drown with my clothes on than go through 'er again. Let's hit 'er, kid."

The water was icy. The current pulled them downstream. Fogarty's horse acted badly and Doc landed on the far bank clinging to the animal's tail. Luck alone had saved both from a watery grave, for the Missouri River in the springtime is a river of undercurrent, snags, and swirling whirlpools.

"Some day when I git time," announced Fogarty as he poured water from his boots, "I'm gonna learn tuh swim."

"You mean you can't swim, Doc?"

"Like a rock. Couldn't swim ten foot if I was tuh hang fer failin'." He pulled a bottle from his saddle pocket. "Have a drink?"

Chapter XX

Lance Mansfield and Doc Fogarty hopped a freight-train out of Miles City. It took them ten days to reach Ogden, Utah. They saw streets decorated with flags and bunting. Somewhere a band played. A long string of empty day-coaches stood at the station. An engine chug-chugged as it waited. The station was crowded with men, women, and children holding balloons and little flags.

"Must be celebratin' some Mormon holiday," said Doc. They sat in the open door of a box-car, munching sandwiches and fruit. They had not seen a newspaper in almost two weeks and so they did not know that the United States was mobilizing troops.

"Gosh, look at the parade, kid. Must be Brigham Young's birthday." Doc called to a passer-by who was bent on obtaining a view of the parade from the top of a box-car.

"What's the holiday, mister? How come all the parade?"

"Say, who ya tryin' to kid, guy? Them's our Guard boys startin' fer France." The man climbed on to his box-car. Doc looked at Lance, smiling oddly.

"Now what do yuh know about that, kid? Uncle Sam's done spit in Kaiser Bill's eye an' the fight is on. Them's National Guard troops; look good, too. They seen service on the Mexican border an' got the rookie look off 'em."

"Doc, we're going to get a bath and shave and some clean duds, then ride the cushions out of Ogden, California-bound. We look like a couple of bums."

"You said a lot uh truth in that jawful, boy. Only that we look like cowboys, we'd uh bin vagged a dozen times. I got flat spots all over me from beddin' down on these board floors. Purty tune that band's playin'. We'll git into the cavalry — best branch uh the service. Savvy cavalry?"

"Enough to get by, I guess." Lance was thinking of his famous Black Horse Troop at school. "Let's get cleaned up."

"And we won't be back till it's over, Over There!" sang the crowd.

"Purty tune," mused Doc. "Gotta learn it. I'm right fond uh music." They found a barber-shop and bath. Each carried a bundle under his arm.

"You boys just in from the range?"

"Just in, mister. Give us all yuh got barrin' the finger-nail rasping'. We may look like we're lousy, but we got money tuh pay fer all we git." They had chosen a barber-shop not far from the stock-yards and the barbers were not unaccustomed to cow-punchers. When they left the place two hours later they looked like different persons. All that branded them as cow-punchers was the breadth of their Stetsons. They caught the next train for Los Angeles.

A movie or two, some extravagant meals, and they drifted with the crowds that buzzed with war talk. In a huge square filled with trees and benches and carpeted with lawn, the crowds surged about a platform. On this platform stood several celebrities of the films. An army officer and a recruiting sergeant lent color to the group.

"Gosh," said Doc in an awed tone, "it's Doug a-talkin'. Come on, boy, let's git a look at 'im. Mary's alongside him. Man, we're shore seein' country an' folks, ain't we?"

Speeches — cheers — bands playing — flags — perspiring, shoving crowds. And when the movie stars had been whisked away in expensive cars and the crowds had thinned, the two men from Montana found the recruiting sergeant. He wore leather-faced leggings and a yellow hat-cord.

"Have a drink, Sarge?" suggested Doc.

The brick-faced sergeant groaned. "Ain't allowed in saloons, but we might arrange to slip in a side door."

"Arrangements is under way. Lead the way, Sarge, us boys is strangers here." The sergeant led the way into a quiet little room at the rear of a saloon.

"What'll it be, gents?" inquired a man in a white apron.

"Beer."

"Three beers." Doc rolled a cigarette. "Us boys are aimin' to join up. Any room in the old Seventh?"

"You know the Seventh Cavalry? I thought you talked like a P.S. bird. Want to get back in, eh? You're a hound for punishment, bo. Take my advice and join the navy."

"I'll do my scrappin' horseback, thanks," grinned Doc. "I can't swim."

"Can you hike?"

"Meanin'?"

"Meanin', old trooper, that there's damn little ridin' done in this man's war. You can get into the cavalry — easy as shootin' fish. But the only horse you'll get comes in a can called corned beef. This ain't no goo-goo fightin' like the Islands an' Cuba, boy. Join the navy an' see it through a port-hole. The gobs is gettin' the cushy end."

"I don't like them funny sailor pants," insisted Doc. "An' I'd never be handy with no mop."

They finished their beer. "Well, don't say I never warned you. Come on an' the loot will look yuh over."

He led the way into a tall office building. They took an elevator to the sixth floor.

Inside the recruiting office was a line of boys and men. All sizes and apparently from every walk of life — more than a dozen. A corporal looked relieved when he saw the sergeant.

"The looie is inside havin' big fits an' little ones, Sarge. Where you been?"

"Who wants to know? Pull your ears in, kid. You got a lot to learn about this man's army. Stick to your typewriter an' you'll wear a sergeant's stripes maybe next year. Go askin' a lotta fool questions an' you'll be seein' that we break 'em easier'n we make 'em. Whenever you feel the urge to be back at Kearny doin' squads west, ask me again where I been. Button your blouse."

He looked down the line of men. He sniffed. "Somebody's bin usin' sashay powder." He fastened a keen eye on a slim-shouldered, slick-haired youth in a wasp-waisted coat. He sniffed and nodded again.

"When we begin issuin' silk pajamas an' a ration of cocaine in this army, we'll welcome such as you, sister. You an' me has met before. I was over at court this mornin'

when a blonde dame bailed you out on a
hop-peddlin' charge. Be on your way before
I carry you out to the elevator shaft an' drop
you. Git."

The sallow-faced youth edged out the
door.

"Dammit, Corporal, use your eyes. We
don't want men like that."

He turned to Doc and Lance.

"Fall in, boys. See you later. Think that
over about the navy. *Adios*."

The corporal assumed an attitude of dig-
nity when the sergeant had stepped into the
adjoining room. Galled by the harshness of
the sergeant, he looked up scowlingly at the
two men whom the sergeant had brought
in.

"You there with the ears, what name?"

"Ears?" said Doc softly. "Me? Name?
Isadore Iskowitch. Who are you?" He
stepped to the desk and looked down pa-
thetically at the red-faced corporal.

"Look here, little feller, me an' my
pardner is here to join the army. Judgin'
from what I make uh you, it's a different
army from the one I was a sergeant in once.
Ears, eh? Be yourself, feller. You ain't
springin' your rank on a green civvy. Lance,
if they're makin' non-coms outa such as
this, me'n you is gonna wear a general's

183

gold stars by Christmas."

The line of recruits tittered. They had all tasted the petty sarcasm of the corporal. Now they saw the corporal shrinking into his chair as the tall man in somewhat wrinkled blue serge suit and yellow shoes stood smiling down at him.

"Now if you're ready to act human, little feller, we'll talk about names an' so on. My name is John Fogarty."

"Birthplace?" The corporal's tone was sulkily civil now.

"Nome, Alaska," replied Fogarty. "December first, Eighteen seventy-seven. I'm all white. . . . Father and mother Irish. . . . Previous service in Spanish-American War. . . . Roosevelt's Rough Riders. . . . Rank of sergeant when discharged. . . . Reënlisted in Seventh Cavalry. . . . Served three years of my hitch; then cleaned up one pay day in a stud game and bought out. . . . Rank — stable sergeant. . . . Got that, Mister?"

"Yes, sir," came from the now thoroughly subdued corporal. The rest of the formal questions were voiced with respect.

"You're next." He looked at Lance.

Lance went in under his right name. He and Doc had talked that matter over. "Better take a chance thataway, kid. Fraud-

184

ulent enlistment ain't a easy thing tuh laugh off at court-martials."

The sergeant shoved his head through the doorway. "All right, you guys. This way. Into that room an' strip. The medico will give you the once over."

They stripped. A battery of doctors examined them. . . . Thumping, eye tests. . . . "Say ah." . . . The morning became afternoon. Finally they were again clothed and sworn in.

"Report here at eight in the morning for travel orders. Fogarty, I'll put you in charge of these men and you can attend to their meals and transportation. I want you men to be sober as possible, see? Get that? No drunks in the morning. Savvy? All right. Dismissed."

"When do we get our uniforms, Captain?" asked an eager-eyed recruit.

"Soon enough, buddy. Don't worry about that. You'll be drawin' an O.D. outfit at Camp Kearny — along with your vaccinations and inoculations. On your way, soldiers."

"Soldiers," grinned Doc when he and Lance were again on the street. "I swore when I got out last time that they'd never git me again. Funny world, ain't it, kid? Let's tip over a beer, then eat some more grub."

"You're in the army now;
* You're not behind a plow.*
Pull in your belly, shove out your
*   chest —*
You're in the army now."

Chapter XXI

Dust — red dust. . . . Bugles, horses, men — thousands of men, in olive-drab uniforms, in squads, in blue denim fatigue clothes; sweating, learning — thousands of men yanked from civilian life, being made into soldiers.

" 'What do you know best,' says this efficiency loot. 'Horses,' says I; and damned if he don't put me on K.P. I peeled all the spuds in California this mornin'."

"You got off easy. I been on latrine duty for ten days solid. That danged corporal is ridin' me, that's all."

"I'm goin' on sick report."

"Don't. They'll vaccinate you again and fill you full of C.C. pills. I know. I went on sick report yesterday morning."

"I put in for an Eastern camp. They sent me here. I wanted a change, see? Been in San Diego all my life and I got a girl in New Jersey. So I asks to be sent East."

"When do we eat?"

So they grumbled and grinned and cussed and sang, those overnight soldiers who still had difficulty in keeping their hands out of their pockets. They drilled. They listened to lectures on morale and trench warfare. They went to town on pass and came home grumbling because the gobs had all the girls. Their commanding officer was General Rumor.

Hat-cords of red and blue and yellow and red-and-white became sun-faded. The wiser heads learned the art of gold-bricking. Planes from Rockwell Field droned over the dusty parade ground. There were crap games and movies and Y.M.C.A. stationery. Their conversation was colorful with new words that roiled impressively. They stood guard and learned by heart, "To walk my post in a military manner." They were soldiers, in for the duration of the war. On the whole, they were a cheerful lot. They had youth. They bore up splendidly under the irksome monotony of training camp. They hated M.P.'s and gobs. Most of them envied the men in the air service but they labeled the air branch "Boy Scouts."

In three months Doc Fogarty had his sergeant's stripes. Lance was content to remain a buck private.

"Why don't you go to the officers' school an' get a commission, kid? You got education an' trainin'."

But Lance shook his head. He liked the cavalry; their swagger, their hard-boiled comradeship, their pride. Fogarty took his sergeant's stripes with the proper amount of seriousness. He had whipped the hardest buck in the troop.

"An' if any of you babies think that's scrappin', just try out my pard Mansfield. He fights."

It was Lance's ability as a boxer rather than a soldier that brought him under the scrutiny of his captain.

Captain Burke had won fame at West Point for his boxing. He and several other officers had been listed on a committee — an entertainment committee. He read the order and promptly exploded.

"What do they mean, entertainment? I suppose that after drilling a troop of green men in cavalry maneuvers, bayonet practice, gunnery, wireless, reports, what not, I can organize my outfit and teach 'em to sing songs about Cock-Eyed Katy and Over There Somewhere. . . . Lieutenant Sloane! Now where in hell's Lieutenant Sloane? Sergeant, hunt up Lieutenant Sloane and tell him to learn the words of 'Pap's a Soldier.' Wait, dang it, hold on. At ease. Lope over to I Company and tell the — wait. I'll send a note to the C.O. of I Company. He's on this death-list. Entertain, eh? I'm no Y.M.C.A. psalm-shouter."

"How about a little boxin' show, Captain?" suggested the top sergeant, who knew the way of a C.O. and felt fairly certain that the burden of entertainment would finally rest with him.

"How's that, Sergeant?" Burke looked up from his note to I Company's commanding officer. "Boxing?"

"We got some good boys, sir. Fogarty's no slouch, and this guy Mansfield is a darb."

Captain Burke grinned and slowly tore up the note.

The following morning a bulletin was posted. The top sergeant saw to it that Lance Mansfield reported with several others.

"Where'd you learn fighting, Private Mansfield?"

"At Culver, sir."

"You matriculated there?"

"I was there five years, sir."

"Then what in hell are you doing in the rear rank, may I ask? Hmmm. Eh?"

"I'm pretty much of a kid, sir, to be wearing officer's bars."

"I see. Wish some of these downy-cheeked shavies were of that very same opinion. Your modesty is highly commendable. You look to be well along in your twenties."

"But I'm not, sir."

"They tell me you can handle your mitts. You and Fogarty and the other boys who are interested are relieved from all duty for the present. Report at the Y after inspection. Culver, eh? Black Horse Troop?"

"Yes sir."

"Hmmm. Good. So was I, once. Dismissed."

A week later the boxing squad was in full swing. Lance fought his first bout and knocked out a corporal from the field artillery. Fogarty lost a four-round bout on points.

Burke poked a major in the ribs, as Lance dropped his man

"Give that big kid the once over, Major. He don't know it, but he's going to officers' training school next week. He has guts and I think he has brains. And, thank the gods of this man's war, the boy's blessed with modesty. Told me that he figured he was too young to be an officer. Can you beat that?"

"Can't even tie it, Jerry. Wish I had his build. Is he one of your Native Sons?"

"His service record says he was born in New York. . . . Orphan. . . . Cowboy by profession. Watch him at school, that's all. Just watch him, Pete."

The major smiled at Jerry Burke's enthusiasm. They had been classmates at West Point. They had played football together. Now they were to share the fortunes of war. Major Peter Foss smiled as Captain Burke rushed off to the dressing-room to see his protégé.

"The wild Irishman," Foss chuckled.

Burke was in the dressing-room, untaping Lance's hands.

"Great fight, kid. Keep it up and you'll be champ of the division, if you'll just quit leaving yourself open as you did three times to-night, You sure threw gloves, boy. And when you connected with his button, he went out like a candle."

So it came about that Lance's skill with padded gloves won him a second lieutenancy.

A month later Fogarty saluted smartly, then grinned. "You sure look grand, boy. . . . Boots, spurs, an' nice shiny bars. . . . Hair on yore lip too; makes yuh look older."

"That's why I grew the damn thing." Lance grinned and twisted at his mustache, which, in spite of its blond color, became him. It is not every man who can appear manly in a small, light-colored mustache. Later that same corn-colored lip adornment was cropped after the manner in which Tom Mansfield had worn his mustache. The resemblance between the dead father and the living son was remarkable and was destined to play a part in the life of the boy. But that time was distant. A few months and several thousand miles distant.

Lance, now Lieutenant Mansfield, detached, reported at the tent of Captain Jerry Burke — "Brimstone" Burke, to give him the name by which he was known from California to the Argonne.

"Well, Mansfield, you look like something now, eh? And if Pete Foss has half the drag at headquarters that he brags about, I'll have you in my outfit. There are times, Lieutenant, when you'll wish to heaven you were under some one else. I'm no sweet child, see? And if I don't get the brand of discipline I'm after, I'll skin somebody alive. There are a few shavetails that will fervently tell you that they'd rather be in hell with a case of hives than be under me."

He looked keenly at the newly made officer. Lance met the gaze, caught the hidden twinkle in Burke's Irish blue eyes, and nodded.

"So I've heard, Captain."

"Well, now's your last chance to step from under."

"If you'll have me, sir, I'd like to be with you."

"Well, don't tell yourself later that you weren't warned."

His men swore at and swore by Captain Brimstone Burke. His troop admitted that they were the smartest cavalry troop in existence. When that hard-bitten bunch of riders swung at a gallop past a reviewing staff, certain colonels and a brass-hat general smiled in approval.

Lance was a creditable addition to the crack troop. He sat his horse well and he knew drill. Also he was in line for the middleweight championship of the division. Burke was aware of this, even as he was aware, of the fact that his non-corns were old troopers, that his horses were the cream of the remount stables, and that his men could ride anything that wore hair. He was profanely proud of his outfit. When any of them were in trouble, he stood by them in a manner that endeared him to the roughest of the roughnecks in his troop. He cursed and praised in the same profanity, the difference being only in the manner in which he said it. And they understood.

Chapter XXII

One evening Captain Burke called Lance into his tent.

"Mansfield, take my car and go into San Diego. Here's a list of men off on pass. Bring every man back. Make the rounds of dance-hall, blind-pigs, and other joints. Then present this order to the M.P. station. There'll be a few in the hoosegow. Get 'em if you have to steal 'em. I want you to report your troop all present at midnight. God save your neck and your tin bars if you don't. Get that?"

"What's up?"

"Nothing, nothing much, boy; except that we entrain at midnight for some port of embarkation, that's all."

"You mean we're —"

"We're off for the big show, Mansfield — secret orders. Damn 'em, they've set us afoot to boot. Took our horses. God knows what they'll give us over there — shovels, probably; Boy Scout flags; God knows what. But we're going. Going, get that? And I don't want a man left behind. You're going on a forged pass, so use your bean. If you get in a jam, it's your neck, kid. Only staff-officers are allowed out of camp to-night. We're in quarantine for flu or some-thing, see? If you're caught, they'll bust you."

Lance grinned. "How about taking Sergeant Fogarty as chauffeur?"

Burke exploded like a bomb. He was still swearing when Lance took his leave.

On his way to the garage he halted at Fogarty's tent and called him out.

"How long since you've been given a pass to town, Doc?"

"Not since I mistook that fat major fer a buck in the dark an' bawled hell outa him. Brimstone saved me from court-martial, but he took my pass away fer a month."

"But that didn't keep you from getting to town."

"Hell, no." Doc winked broadly.

"Can you run the guard to-night?"

"I'll tell a green trooper I kin."

"Then meet me down the road. Go careful. The camp's in quarantine and under double or triple guard. When a car comes along with the right headlight dark, show yourself. . . . About a quarter of a mile past the outer guard line. Snap into it now."

"I'm snappin' right now, loot." Doc saluted, stepped between two tents, and dis-appeared. Lance got the captain's private car and drove out of camp on his forged pass. He knew the gravity of detection. It meant that he would face a general court-martial; that he would keep Burke's name and rank intact by silence or perjury; that he would be broken and perhaps be imprisoned as a suspected spy. This was wartime and punishments were severe. Yet he grinned into the night as he extinguished his right headlight and went on.

A quarter-mile beyond the last outpost he picked up Doc Fogarty.

"Is it bank robbery we're goin' on, er plain killin', Lance?"

Lance exploded his bombshell of information and silenced Doc's threatened joyful yelp with the palm of his hand.

"We're goin', eh? Man, oh, mister! Goin'!"

"If we don't go to Alcatraz for life," amended Lance. As the car sped along the dusty road, its headlights boring a white hole into the starlit night, Doc Fogarty took something from his pocket and caressed it lovingly.

"Hind laig of a rabbit. It's pulled me through some tights. It'll see us through this."

But before the evening was done it was apparent that Doc relied as much on his wits and fistic ability as he did on his luck charm.

For the infantry doing M.P. duty in San Diego were of the regular army. They were wise and sharp-eyed and they were carrying out certain special orders regarding certain troops. Doc and Lance ran into a sergeant and two privates. The sergeant halted them. An M.P. has rights. His tone was curt.

"What outfit, sir?"

Doc pushed between Lance and the burly sergeant. "Say, where do you get that stuff? One side, doughboy, or a leg off." Doc's fist shot out. The infantry M.P. sergeant dropped in his tracks. Lance hit a private as the man jerked his gun. Doc kicked the third man in the stomach. They were in an alley off Broadway. Doc's glance traveled to a knot of men grouped in a warehouse doorway.

"Hey, sailors!" he bawled. "Fight! Hey, sailors!"

They came at a run, a bulky wedge of blue-uniformed men. There is a saying that whenever you hit a sailor, the whole navy hits back. Gobs have a habit of sticking together.

"Me'n the loot is in a little tight," panted Doc. "I got twenty bucks that says you boys will ride herd on these lousy M.P.'s for half an hour."

"Let's look at the twenty, soldier,"

grinned a broad-shouldered sailor meaningly. Doc passed over the twenty.

"There's fifty more in it," added Lance, struck with a sudden desperate inspiration, "if two of you boys will rent your clothes for an hour or so. You can stay in a room some-where. You'd know about where. How about it?"

"What's the game?"

"Little party the sarge and I are throwing. Nothing you need be scared of. How about it?"

"For fifty smackers, Lieutenant, I'd do a lot. Eh, Brick?" He turned to a red-haired sailor.

"We're your huckleberries. We got a room, but no jack an' no booze. Come on."

"Who said we was goin' dry to-night," chuckled a sailor.

Lance and Doc followed four sailors to a roominghouse on lower Broadway.

The two conspirators emerged a little later in the uniforms of two sailors.

One by one they gathered in five of the seven men who were off on pass. As the men were gathered, they were ordered to go to the parked car and wait there. The car had been left in the private garage of a friend of Doc's. It was nearing ten o'clock when Lance and Doc got back to the cheap lodging-house. They changed back into their own uniforms, shook hands with the admiring gobs, and headed for the M.P. guard-house.

"This is the tough part of the program," said Lance as they approached the place. "One chance in a thousand."

"Then hold on a minute while we cut down them odds." Doc opened a mysterious bundle that he had gotten from the car. The bundle contained belt and side-arms and an M.P. armband.

"Pin on this M.P. band, savvy? Buckle on this gat. Then crash the gate. Gimme time to call up the officer er sergeant in charge there. I'm tellin' him that Lieutenant Mansfield, officer of the guard at Kearny, is due with an order for all prisoners there. Has he gotten them? No? Then what the ding-busted hell's he so slow about? When he gets there, tell him Colonel Umpty Stump said to shake it up. That Colonel Umpty Stump is going to rip the hide off his bones and hang his double-be-damned pelt to the flagpole. I ain't bin in this man's army for two hitches without learnin' how tuh cuss like a staff-officer. Git the drift, kid?"

"Do I? Doc, you're a genius."

"Just a sergeant, old-timer. Now step on 'er. Good luck. You'll need it. Gimme time tuh drop into that drug-store an' burn up that phone with a brigade commander's pet cuss words."

Lance, inwardly jumpy as a wildcat but outwardly calm and very military, swung into the guard-house. A serious-mouthed young second lieutenant returned his salute, looked at his order, and smiled a little patronizingly. For a moment Lance's guilty conscience made his heart thump.

"Boy, you're in for a lacing," said the M.P. officer. "Some shirty colonel phoned and raised hell on stilts. Near as I made out, he's going to bust you, skin you alive, boil your skinned carcass in hot pitch, then cut it into bits and feed the chunks to the rookies. Then he's going to hang you. After that he'll begin all over again. And he jumped down my neck because you'd stopped at the officers' club to pin on a few highballs. If I had what you seem to have coming I'd borrow a dull knife and cut my throat."

"The old boy was on his ear, eh?" Lance grinned.

"Was he? He was frothy." He delivered the two half-sobered troopers who stood at wabbly attention. "Anybody would know without asking that it was a colonel on the

201

other end of this line. Good luck, Lieutenant."

Lance marched his prisoners a block.

"Halt, men. At rest." Fogarty appeared from somewhere. "How sober are you birds?"

"Cold sober, sir," they lied like true cavalrymen.

"Then try to get this clear. You're my prisoners. No doughboy M.P. or group of doughboy M.P.'s can take you away from me. If they try it on, pick your man and rock him to sleep. Get that?"

"You bet!"

But fortunately they hailed a cruising taxi and made the journey to the hidden car in peace. It was a five-passenger car but it managed to hold its cargo. Lance kept to the side streets and they slipped out of town on to the road to camp. Lance unloaded his cargo before they reached the guard line.

"Sergeant Fogarty, you will see that these men get into camp and are in their quarters in half an hour."

"Don't worry, Lieutenant," spoke up a short-statured, bow-legged trooper, one of the two who had been in the guard-house. "We'll be there. That straight dope about us leavin' at midnight?"

Lance shot Doc a swift lock. Doc gazed at

the stars. Lance grinned and said nothing. The little trooper was almost tearful.

"An' to think I was almost left behind. Lieutenant, I hope I can square this some day. That goes for the gang. Eh, guys?"

"You said it," came the whispered chorus.

"Hit a lope, you rum-hounds. Burke'll kill the man that's not in ranks at roll-call. Scatter." The next moment he was alone. Doc Fogarty was leading them on the double-quick toward a certain spot where a man, by crawling a hundred yards on his belly, could wriggle past the guard unseen.

Lance reported to Captain Burke. Burke waxed affectionately profane. There was a dark bruise above Lance's left eye where the M.P.'s club had glanced. There had been a vitriolic phone call from headquarters demanding that all cavalry personnel be checked. That a lieutenant and sergeant of cavalry had assaulted and badly beaten, then stripped the clothes from an M.P. detail. The naked men had fortunately hailed a passing patrol-wagon. They had just checked in. What the ding-dong hell did Burke know about it, if anything? Were his officers and sergeants all present and in their quarters?"

"All present, sir," Brimstone Burke had

lied desperately, then added acidly, "Try G Troop C.O." The commanding officer of G Troop was one of Captain Burke's pet enemies.

"Some day, Mansfield," said Captain Burke, his blue eyes alight, "when we're far, far away from here, I'd be glad to listen to the tale of this evening's entertainment. Meanwhile, old son, I want you to know that I have a sort of sense of appreciation. Damned if I know of another shavie I'd have trusted with the detail. What the hell is it about you that makes me pin my faith to your judgment?"

"Perhaps," grinned Lance, caressing his new mustache, "it's the hair lip?"

"No," said Burke solemnly, "it's that damned smile of yours. I bet a pair of boots that if a Hun tags you with a bullet, they'll find that grin on your mouth."

When Lance had gone, Burke got Major Peter Foss on the telephone.

"Hell only knows how he did it, Pete, but the kid put it over. I'm all present at midnight."

"You're the *damnedest* fool alive!"

"Wrong. The honor and title goes to a kid named Mansfield. He's the — Hello! I say. Hello, hello! Hell, he's hung up."

Chapter XXIII

Mud . . . Mud, belly-deep to a tall camel —
black, oozy mud. . . . Rain and more of it.

". . . I tried kerosene, buddy, but it never
got me nothin' but a lotta raw hide.
Nawthin' can kill 'em, once they get a
healthy start. . . ."

The road was choked with trucks. Now
and then an ambulance slithered around
and past. Men stood in little groups or sat
on ponchos. Some slept. Guns were going
forward. Men, hundreds of men, gray-faced
from fatigue, were returning from the hell
into which fresh-eyed men were going.

Some of those men would return, even as
these utterly weary, soul-sick men were
coming back — with the eager light forever
gone out of their eyes and, in its stead, the
glaze of horror that is war; young men who
had lost something that is an essential part
of youth. They would never forget, those
men who returned. For God has somehow
neglected to bless men with that forgetful-
ness of war pain. He saves that gift for
mothers in childbirth.

"So this is the cavalry! Shanks' mare fer a
mount. Hey, Sarge, what we waitin' fer?"

"Hi, Sarge, what we waitin' fer?"

Sergeant Doc Fogarty plodded on through the mud. "Looks like rain," he halted, held out the palm of his hand, and cast a speculative eye at the gray sky that had been leaking steadily for sixty hours. "It'll be a good thing. Settle the dust," he said, and then trudged on.

A mud-spattered, harassed-looking man in the uniform of a second lieutenant stood swearing sullenly at a balky motor-cycle with attached side-car. An equally muddy, equally profane private tinkered at the motor.

"Anyhow," grunted Fogarty as he saluted, "we won't need worry about waterin' the troops."

"These boots set me back forty bucks," announced the second lieutenant. "Hell, eh? What's the good word, Sarge?"

"Keep movin'. The kitchens are comin' up. Horse gone lame?"

"Lame?" Lance Mansfield took three minutes to describe the temperament of the refractory motor. Doc grinned understandingly. A staff car roared past in second gear, showering the three men with more mud. They damned the lurching car as it went back along the line of crawling trucks.

Ahead, men labored at a bogged gun.

"Anyhow, give thanks we ain't in the field artillery," announced Lance.

The little motor suddenly came to life, roaring its staccato bark. Lance climbed into the side-car.

"Get word back to Captain Burke that I'll have the outfit shoved up where he wants 'em. The devil knows how, but we'll be there." And he wriggled up through the maze of trucks and stalled caissons and men.

Fogarty went back along the line. "All right, you soup-hounds, here comes the mess wagon. Fill yore bellies, you walkin' troopers. Fall in."

Lance came back on foot. He grinned at the muddy, hungry men who sucked hot soup and coffee into their chilled bodies. He saw them grin back and heard a man say, "Sailor's one regular guy, I'll tell the troops." It did not occur to Lance until later that the man referred to him. He did not know that the tale of his sailor disguise was now divisional property and that the colorful incident had not in the least hurt his popularity. He had gained the sobriquet that was to last so long as men spoke of war and soldiers and officers — "Sailor" Mansfield. Later he was to acquire another title.

★ ★ ★

". . . In this corner, Lieutenant Sailor Mansfield, champion of the ——th division. . . ."

"Champ" Mansfield. . . . That was later on — months later. To Lance it seemed years, those months under fire.

For the cavalry became scout and liaison troops. Weeks hardened them into seasoned fighters. Theirs was the job of prowling across that wire-strewn, corpse-dotted area — that strip of shell-pocked waste that was No Man's Land. . . . Listening-posts. . . . The never-to-be-forgotten stench of dead flesh. . . . Star-shells. . . . Machine-gun fire. . . . War Crosses; other war crosses of wood — each marking a hero. . . . Paid for — bought — with the blood of youth.

Lance looked older. He had gazed on things that left scars on one's memory. He had seen Brimstone Burke, after a terrific fortnight of battle, stand white-lipped while a French general pinned on his blouse the War Cross of France. Later that night he had found Burke alone in his room, lying face downward on the bed, sobbing horribly, the bit of bronze and ribbon crushed in his clenched fist. Lance had backed qui-

208

etly out of the room. Burke never knew that he had been there. After that, Lance never showed Burke the casualty list unless commanded to do so.

He had seen men who were horribly, terribly afraid, try to laugh. He had held a dying man who passed on with a careless jest on his torn lips. He had seen things like that, and the brand of them seared his soul. He had killed men. He had been wounded. He was twice decorated. In payment for this glory he gave something of his youth that could never be regained.

He had been there six months when Dick Kirby reported for duty.

"With all of the A.E.F. to choose from, some idiot assigned me to this outfit," said Private Kirby bitterly. "Believe me, Mansfield, I didn't do my own choosing."

The two were alone in Lance's tent back of the lines. Lance rose from his seat on an empty packing-case and rounded another packing-case that served as a desk. He held out his hand to Dick Kirby.

"Don't be a damn fool, Dick. You're thinking all wrong."

Dick ignored the proffered hand. "I'll try to get a transfer. Meanwhile I'm buck-private Kirby, and you're Lieutenant Mansfield. But I'll see you in hell before I do any handshaking, literally or otherwise."

"In hell is right," said Lance, smiling twistedly. "Ever done any scout work?"

"I've been stuck back in some fool camp or another. This is as close to the lines as I've come. That's why I tried so hard to get a transfer from the Limies. Now I'm into this mess."

"We're going up again in a week. If you're hungry for action, I guarantee you a bellyfull. Before we go up, it won't hurt you to get an idea of what you're up against. My top kicker is a man named Fogarty. You'll find him wherever they sell the best cognac. Hunt him up and he'll give you some pointers."

"Is this a command or a suggestion?" Dick's tone was sullenly defensive. He was accustomed to British officers whose sole contact with their men was a sergeant. British sergeants were very British and never forgot their rank. Dick had a hearty hatred for rank of any kind, commissioned or non-commissioned. Lance's suggestion was distasteful to Dick Kirby, fresh from the British forces.

"Call it a suggestion. You may remember Fogarty. He was one of Dutch Henry's gang. Dismissed."

Dick stiffened to attention at the curt

"dismissed." But a faint derisive smile twitched at his mouth as he saluted and went out.

More than anything in the world, Lance had wanted to ask Dick a few questions; questions about home, the Bench-K ranch, Big Jim, Bob, and — most of all — Teton. For he had neither written nor received a letter since he broke jail at Chinook. To question Dick in his present mood was folly. Yet Lance was almost sick for news — news from home.

"Well, Champ!" It was Captain Brimstone Burke who ducked into the tent. "How goes the strafing from the fat staff colonels? Don't take it too hard, old son."

Burke picked up a typed paper on the packing-box desk and grinned at Lance. It was a communication in the nature of a reprimand and cited incidents of misconduct of some of Lance's men while on pass in town. It suggested that lack of company discipline caused such misconduct and therefore suggested — *et cetera, et cetera, et cetera,* and so forth.

"Oh, that." Lance shrugged and rolled a cigarette. "Gas."

"Then what's biting your sweet disposition, kid? Is it a plain hang-over or are you lousy again?" Burke seated himself on the

211

improvised desk and reached for Lance's tobacco. "Don't your nice medals fit to-day? Or did that frog general bite you on the cheek? Hell, you act like a man in love. How about a bottle of real, honest-to-glory champagne? Pete Foss is giving a dinner at some château where he's billeted and you're on the list. Whatever's souring you will be cured by one dram of that wine. Grab your bonnet, Sailor."

Lance obeyed listlessly. That night, for the first time in his life, Lance Mansfield got drunk — quietly but unmistakably drunk.

Chapter XXIV

The deafening rumble of a heavy barrage lulled. Here and there a machine-gun rattled. Lieutenant Lance Mansfield stared at the luminous dial of his wrist-watch. Alongside him, in a front-line trench, four men waited his signal. Among the four were Fogarty, a bow-legged little corporal who chewed tobacco, and Dick Kirby. The fourth was a tall man named Pickott, who had been a telegrapher in civil life.

These five constituted a patrol. Their orders were to find out the damage done by the American barrage that had swept No Man's Land. It was Dick Kirby's first patrol. He was trying to hide the nervous feeling that was almost nausea. He fooled no man, for each of them had known that same horrible feeling just before his first patrol.

Lance grinned and borrowed a chew from the corporal. Dick mistook the action for pose.

"All set, boys?" the lieutenant whispered. "Then let's go."

They wormed their way over the top and crawled forward. It was drizzling and the ground was slimy. Machine-guns clattered crazily. Here and there the dim skeleton of a shell-blasted tree stood against a blurred sky. The place was snarled with barbed-wire, pitted with shell-holes that held pools of foul-smelling water. A star-shell illuminated the ghastly strip of desolation and the flattened men lay motionless. This brief interval of light that whitened the night seemed eternity to Dick Kirby. A dead man hung limply across some tangled wire. Then darkness, and through its thick blanket came the delirious calling of a dying man. They crawled onward once more.

Minutes stretched to eternity. Dick's groping hand touched the rain-washed face of a dead man. He recoiled with a choking gasp, then silently cursed himself for being squeamish. Another star-shell flattened them. But before darkness came, the muddy slime was spattered with leaden hail. A German machine-gunner had located them. Twenty feet ahead lay a shell-hole.

"Time we was duckin'," grunted Fogarty in Dick's ear, as darkness hid them.

The next shell burst as they fell into the inadequate shelter of the hole. It was occupied by three dead Germans. The machine-gun sprayed the edge of the hole. The nest lay somewhere ahead of them. Darkness again, while the gun still rattled.

"You men stay put. . . . Sergeant Fogarty in charge."

And the next moment Lance was out of the hole, running ahead. He pulled the plug on a grenade, counted as he ran, threw. It burst with a thudding crash. Another star-shell whitened the snarled wire, the dead bodies of men, the gaping shell-holes. Doc peered across the edge of the hole. He saw a huddled, olive-drab object beyond. From the machine-gun nest the scream of a man shrilled, then went silent in death. The gun was now silent. Again the sticky darkness hid them. "I reckon," said Doc, his face pasty white, "that the Champ got his."

"Damn 'em!" sobbed the little corporal. "Damn 'em!"

Then something slid into the hole and Lance's voice came out of the black slime. "All right, boys. To the left now."

And Dick Kirby was suddenly aware of the strange fact that he was fervently glad that Lance Mansfield was alive. In those tense seconds he had passed through an indescribable something. Lance Mansfield had become the Champ. Why, how, by what twist of reasoning, God alone knew; but they were no longer enemies. Moreover, Dick had glimpsed the drawn, white faces of

215

his companions and he knew that they also felt the icy grip of fear; that his own fear was not cowardice. And in him was now glowing that courage begat by fear. The next star-shell showed a game, ghastly grin on Dick's face.

"Sergeant, make your way back. Report to Captain Burke that the barrage was effective."

They crept on through the horrible mud. They had been out almost an hour. Then Lance whispered something. They were on the edge of a huge shell crater. Lance had crept forward, looking cautiously over its rim, then wormed his way back to his companions.

"There's a Boche listening-post in that hole — three men there. We get 'em quietly, see? Then you, Pickott, take this code sheet and send the message written below. Pickott stays back while we mop up in the hole. It's automatics and knife-work, boys. Play snake till we get to the hole. Then down and at 'em. Let's go."

"One apiece," whispered the little corporal. He was one of the two soldiers whom Lance had stolen from the M.P. guardhouse that night in San Diego.

They covered the torn ground along the edge of the shell crater. They crouched in the darkness, tense, gripping heavy automatics. Then they leaped down. A star-shell lit up the brief bit of combat. White faces, naked steel, and the crimson smear of blood. Fate leered grotesquely in those brief seconds. For the shell-hole held six instead of three Germans. Between Lance's first glimpse of the listening-post and his return, a relief party had come to occupy the position. Lance's gun jammed, its mechanism clogged with mud. He used it as a club. Three of them were at him with ugly trench knives.

The bow-legged corporal, with a snarl of fury, jerked his gun trigger. Bullets thudded into flesh at a range of mere inches. Lance felt a hot, searing pain in his shoulder, another in his groin. He felled a German officer with his clubbed automatic. The corporal killed two men in the space of two seconds. Then the little fellow crumpled, blood gushing from his mouth.

Dick fought like a madman, saw one man drop as he shot, saw a second man reel drunkenly; then he went down as a burly German charged like a bull. Dick saw Lance leap at the man, then darkness blotted out the two. In the slimy mud Lance and the big German fought like two beasts. Then the sounds of struggle lessened, a guttural voice croaked, "Gott!" Then silence.

"All right, Dick?"

"Okay, Lance."

When the next star-shell burst, Lance was sitting with the little corporal's head in his lap. The little corporal grinned through a smear of blood, a shudder swept his body, and so he died. Lance sat there, staring into the mud and blackness, forgetful of his own wounds, of the six dead Germans, of everything except the little non-com who had died for him.

Memory mocked him — memory of that starry night at Kearny, the little corporal's fervent words:

"An' to think I was almost left behind. Lieutenant, I hope I can square this some day."

The little trooper had squared his debt. He had paid with the only thing of value he had to give. Lance's eyes were hot with unshed tears. How mach better it would have been if the bow-legged trooper had been left behind in —

"Lance!" It was Dick's croaking whisper that brought him back to the reality of things.

"Here." His voice sounded flat, lifeless. He told himself that he must snap out of it. There was a war going on. There was a job yet to be completed.

"I want you to know," came Dick's voice, oddly thin and far away, "that I've been a lousy — a lousy —"

Dick's voice trailed into silence. Dick must be hurt. Lance pillowed the dead corporal's head with his own blouse; then, in his shirt that was slowly staining under the shoulder and across his chest, he crawled over the dead Germans and found Dick Kirby in a motionless heap. He was dressing a wound in Dick's thigh when the telegrapher slid into the hole.

"Okay, Lieutenant?"

"Yes. Find their damn instrument. If it's a key set, read that code with your flashlight and send it, being damn careful to shield the flash under your helmet. If it's a phone, lay off. Those Krauts'd get wise to our brand of their lingo."

"It's a key set, sir."

"Then shoot, boy — and code 'em this: That there's been some strafing out here; that the three men about to go off duty are dead. Get the idea? Then they won't get suspicious when the three birds don't show up after being relieved here."

The telegrapher could read and write German; could send and receive in that language. His father had been a German — a delicatessen storekeeper in New Jersey.

Lance finished bandaging Dick and turned to his own injuries — a trench-knife wound in his groin, a bullet hole in the muscle under his armpit. He adjusted a crude bandage and took a pull at his water bottle that held brandy instead of water. Water is not good for wounds, but there are times when a strong stimulant is a godsend. This was such a time. The sending key stuttered out its code message that was to convey certain false information to the enemy. Fifteen minutes later the key halted.

"Finished, sir."

"Then give me a hand with Kirby. We've just time to get back before our artillery lays down a barrage. You've just sent word to the Boche that things are ripe for a raiding party — a big one. We've got to move right along or we'll be caught between our G.I. cans and the Kraut raiders."

Between them they got Dick out of the hole. Lance halted and consulted his watch.

"Late! Strap Kirby on my back, then streak it for our line. Tell Captain Burke that we've put the message through that she's all set. Hurry, man."

"But you'll be caught in —"

"Hurry, damn it. Use this belt . . . tighter . . . good. Now slide for home base. Go, boy, go!"

Chapter XXV

In war-time an order is a sacred thing. To obey without question, without compromise, that is the duty of a soldier. Pickott, the telegrapher, was a good soldier.

"There will be a German raiding party coming over, sir," he reported to Captain Brimstone Burke. "Lieutenant Mansfield says it's all set for the barrage."

"What's keeping Mansfield?"

"Kirby's wounded. Mansfield's carrying him in. I'd like to be getting back now, Captain. He'll need help with Kirby. He's wounded himself."

Burke, white-lipped, stared at the soldier. A mud-caked, lanky form shot past them in the narrow trench, slid over the top, and was gone.

"Fogarty beat you to it, Pickott. That doesn't keep you from being a hell of a brave man. Report to Major Foss to lay down a barrage. May God help those three men out there. Step on it, soldier."

Burke, the firebrand with the Irish heart of a child sometimes, stared with red-rimmed, bloodshot eyes out across the strip of wire-tangled, shell-plowed land that held his friend. He felt like a man condemned to murder a brother, albeit he was but doing his duty as an officer. To hold up the call for barrage meant that the Boche raiding party would be in on top of them; that if he withheld the order many lives would pay the penalty.

Suddenly the guns went into action — a thundering, roaring, belching hell that ripped and tore and screamed. Machine-guns clattered their puny hail. Shrapnel burst. And still Burke stood there, motionless, hard-eyed, staring out over the stark desolation that held three Americans.

A star-shell lit up the gray horde that came from the front-line trenches of the enemy — a gray line that staggered, fell, rose and fell again, nevermore to rise. The Boche raiding party was being ripped to bits and thrown back, maimed and killed, across their own barbed-wire entanglements.

Back in the P.C. dugout a major of the intelligence department impatiently waited for the return of Captain Burke. The major was a thin-lipped man with ferret nose and eyes. He chewed a cold cigar stump and wished with all his might that he was back in town at his desk. The ground shook with the heavy gun-fire. Then the firing lulled to a shuddering silence. Some men were coming down into the dugout. They moved slowly, making grotesque shadows in the light of the guttering candles.

Two men, supporting — carrying — another man between them. Behind them came Captain Burke, white and grim and terrible. Then the I.D. major caught a glimpse of the face of a man who helped carry in the badly wounded private. This man wore the field boots of an officer. He was mud-caked, blood-smeared, and wore no blouse. His face was a horrible mass of bloody mud, his nose was a red pulp, a cheek was torn away and the raw flesh smeared with dirt.

"There," croaked Burke in a terrible voice, pointing to the officer who, with the tall sergeant, deposited the unconscious moaning private on a blanket, "there's the man you want. But, damn you, try and take him! Try and take him, you desk-riding, swivel-chair M.P. herder. That's Mansfield! He's worth the whole damn department you serve. Get to hell out of here before I —"

Burke caught the swaying form of Lance Mansfield in his arms and laid him gently down alongside the moaning Dick Kirby. "You better be goin'," Fogarty said to the red-faced major, "while the goin's possible."

"Burke, you will hear more of this," muttered the ferret-eyed major, and took his leave.

"That damn skunk has an arrest warrant for Mansfield," cursed Burke. "Some damn civil charge from the States."

"The hell he has! Any way uh hidin' Lance?"

Burke looked up from the wounded officer. "The kid's all shot to pieces, Fogarty. A hundred to one he'll never live till they get him to the base hospital. Know anything about his folks, sergeant?"

"Not much. His father's dead. No other kinfolks that I know of. Kirby, here, comes from the same place. There's a frame-up cow-stealin' charge against the kid. Him and me quit Montana together. We busted jail together up there. God, his whole face is gone!"

"You got a hole in your shoulder, Fogarty. Get it tied up and go on back with these two men when the stretchers get here. If Mansfield dies, do what you can about letting his friends know. Kirby's also in bad shape. I don't know what you were in civil life, Fogarty, but you've been a man here. I saw you go out after these men."

"Lucky I went. Lance was crawlin' with Kirby strapped on his back. The kid's face was like that. He was blind with blood, an' crawlin' toward the Boche lines — crawlin' the wrong direction, blind! Didn't know me when I spoke. He tried tuh shoot me but his gat was fouled with mud. Batty, clean out of his head."

"And that brass-hat fly cop was waiting to pinch him — waiting down here where it's warm and dry and safe. I wonder why I didn't shoot him?"

"Now why didn't I think uh that," said Fogarty. "Gosh, I'm gittin' thick-headed. This war's got me rattled, I reckon."

The stretcher-bearers came and went away again. Fogarty went with them. At the dressing-station he fastened himself to a red-armed, tired-eyed surgeon.

"You gotta look at the lootenant, sir. You gotta!" He towered over the surgeon, who nodded and smiled wearily.

"All right, big boy. Keep your shirt on. I'll have a look at your lieutenant. You keep an eye peeled for the next ambulance. I can't do much."

"Will he live, sir?"

"Hard to say. I doubt it."

Lance, in a semi-coma, heard. He tried to open his eyes. He tried to tell them that he was going to live. He did not know that his eyes and face were heavily bandaged; that

225

only his mouth showed. Dimly he heard Doc's voice. His whole body was burning with pain. He felt weak and giddy and sick. Doc's voice came as from a long distance.

"He was crawlin', Doctor — strapped to his back. . . . Blind as a bat an' loco as a sheep-herder. He taken me fer a Boche. He'd got me only his gun jammed. Me, I use a single-action gun — damn automatics can't be trusted. Here's the ambulance. I'm shore obliged, sir. How about Kirby?"

"He'll be out and back in the scrap in a month. And by the way, Sergeant, when you get to the hospital, try to get Colonel Crowther to take a look at your lieutenant. He'll be busy as hell and hard to get hold of, but you have wonderful persuasive powers, especially when you have a hand on that single-action Colt's you pack. Good luck to the three of you."

Lance felt himself lifted into the ambulance. . . . Doc's voice again, either praying, or swearing at the driver. . . . Then the jolting sent the wounded man back into a pain-racked nightmare of oblivion.

He awoke to stare at a white ceiling. His face and head were swathed in bandages. Only one eye showed. He tried to rise, but a hand held him back, and a woman's voice, cool, sweet, yet with a note of authority, spoke:

"Just lie quietly, won't you? You must anyhow. You're tied down. Be a good chap and don't wiggle. You're all done up in yards of fancy bandage. That's a good chap."

"Where's Dick?" mumbled Lance. He caught sight of the woman now. All in white, she was, with large, heavily fringed gray eyes. Her hair was the color of copper.

"Dick who?" she asked.

"Dick Kirby?"

"The tall cowboy chap who threatened to shoot Colonel Crowther if he let you die?"

"That was Doc Fogarty, I reckon," said Lance. "Dick was wounded out in the shell-hole." He smiled twistedly.

"Quite so," the nurse lied bravely. "He's coming on splendidly. Now, no more talking."

"The doctor back somewhere along the line said I was going to die. He's all wrong." Lance went back to sleep after that. The nurse tiptoed away.

A tall man in the uniform of a British colonel met her. He jerked at an end of a mustache and scowled down at her.

"My dear Lady Janet," he told her sternly, "I must forbid this being on duty after hours. One can't stand up under it, you know."

"But this case, Herbert, is quite an exception."

"I quite agree with you, my dear. Fancy having a gun poked into one's ribs by a wild man from America — being ordered to attend to a wounded man."

"But the wild cowboy won his point."

The colonel smiled broadly. "Rather. But it was the chap's utter disregard for his own injuries, his splendid loyalty to his comrade, that won the day. How is the Kirby chap coming along?"

"You discovered his identity, then?"

"After quite a struggle. His name is Richard Kirby, private. The other chap is a Lieutenant Somebody. The tall chap had their identification tags. He's a rum one, that cowboy. Gamey sort. Refused anesthetic on the grounds that he might talk too much while under. Sat like a brick while I dug shrapnel splinters out of his arm; then asked what sort of grub we fed our 'prisoners.' Fancy."

"And this lieutenant, Herbert? What was his name?" The gray eyes of the nurse held the British colonel's eyes with a steady grip.

"His name," said the tall surgeon slowly, "is Mansfield — Lance Mansfield. But, my

228

dear lady, there are many of that name Mansfield. It's rather impossible that —"

"No, Herbert. It's Tom's boy." She passed a white hand across her eyes and smiled wanly. "Odd, but this man who is so terribly wounded was asking about a Dick Kirby. There was something about his voice, the smile on his poor lips, that — that was like Tom's. You are quite positive that the other chap is Lance Mansfield?"

"Well," smiled the officer, "I've only the wild Yankee's word for it, but he was quite positive. He and the Mansfield chap have adjoining cots and are awake, so you might go see for yourself. But I warn you, make your visit brief. You need rest and a great deal of it."

"Who was it that said somewhere that the wicked cannot rest?"

"Tut, tut. None of that."

"One pays for one's sins, Herbert, here on earth. I fancy my payment must go on, and on."

The colonel took her by the shoulders and for a long moment looked down into the gray eyes that seemed dark with pain.

"Don't cultivate a martyr complex, Janet; and don't hint to the boy that you're his mother."

"Hardly, my dear Herbert. He won't

229

know, ever. As for the martyr rôle, don't let that upset you. In all my stage career I could never have played anything so heavy. I prefer to remain in character — light comedy, rather. Cheerio, Herbert. And I'll make my visit short."

The tall colonel watched her out of sight. Even the shapeless white uniform could not conceal the superb grace, the queenly carriage of the woman who had once been the wife of Tom Mansfield. Two continents had once applauded her as a great actress. Her marriage to the British army officer had blighted a promising stage career. She had dropped from public view, then had stood for a brief month in the pitiless spotlight of scandal. That was in British East India.

The affair had been smothered, facts withheld — then divorce. Tom Mansfield had resigned from the army and gone to America. Janet Mansfield had disappeared. Now and then she was seen. . . . Paris . . . Russia . . . Monte Carlo. Always alone — always the gay comedienne. Men flocked about her. And when the war dragged Great Britain into its bloody meshes, Janet Mansfield had offered her services. This hospital was her donation. Her estate on the Riviera was a convalescent station. Colonel Herbert Crowther was one of the few men who saw the real woman beneath the actress.

Crowther now moved to Lance's cot and stared broodingly at the twisted smile that showed from the bandaged face . . . Tom Mansfield's smile . . . Crowther had been in India with Tom Mansfield.

"For some fool reason," mused the surgeon, "that Yankee sergeant lied about those identification tags. So be it."

As he stood there Lance's one unbandaged eye opened. Crowther smiled.

"You've been badly shot up, my boy, but you'll come around in a few weeks. Name's Mansfield, is it not?"

"Lance Mansfield."

"Quite so. Better go back to sleep now." Crowther moved away.

Lance, his sense numbed from opiates, drowsed again. He did not know that those facial bandages hid a horrible mass of raw, beefy flesh. That even the service-hardened surgery nurses had shuddered when Colonel Crowther sewed together the torn flesh from which the skin was gone. And when the bandages were wrapped, the surgeon had shaken his head.

"It would have been better if the poor devil had died," he'd heard an interne mutter.

Chapter XXVI

"You win, Colonel," said Doc Fogarty. "Mansfield is the gent that got it in the face."

"Then may I ask why you lied?"

"You kin ask, sir, but there ain't nothin' in my I.D.R. that kin make me answer. Mebby so I was just kinda goofy. Mebbe drunk. *Quién sabe?* How's the loot comin' along, sir?"

"There's a French surgeon who has done miracles in plastic surgery. He's going to have a look at Mansfield."

"I bet that's Lady Janet's doin's," said Doc. She was known to those occupants of white cots simply as Lady Janet. "Gee, she sure is one swell lady. I always thought these lords an' ladies was high-toned as hell. Shows how danged ignorant a cow-hand is, once he's shipped off his home range."

"There's some letters I wish you'd send to Mansfield," said Dick Kirby.

"Letters for him?"

"Well, they come for me, but they're about home. I reckon he'd be glad tuh hear from the folks. Lance is kinda stuck on my kid sister. The letters is from her. Dad's

232

writin' arm got shot off an' Maw ain't much of a speller, so Teton does the writin'. Teton's the kid sister."

Dick handed over a little pile of letters addressed in Teton's vertical, round-lettered handwriting. Crowther took them. In the hallway he delivered them to Lady Janet.

"Fancy Tom's son engaged to a girl whose father's writing arm got shot off and whose mother can't spell."

"Don't be a snob, Herbert. Did you learn anything from the cowboy?"

"Questions pass off the fellow like water from a duck's back, worse luck. But I rather think he'll talk to you. For all his professed ignorance, the chap is shrewd. True example of Yankee wit and all that, I daresay."

"I'm quite fond of Sergeant Fogarty. I'll go and see him."

"Do, please."

"After I've taken these letters to — to Lance, my boy . . . my own son, Herbert!"

Lady Janet spent a long hour reading aloud from Dick Kirby's letters.

"— and if you run across Lance, be decent, Dick. He has but few friends left now. And I hear that Jack Parsons has gotten a captain's commission and is stationed at Helena — the intelligence department. He told some one that he would bring

Lance back if he had to go to France. He is a dangerous man. He is after the Circle Seven ranch."

The reader paused. Lance's unbandaged eye was closed. He might have been asleep, save for the twisting of his lips. Lady Janet went on reading.

"Daddy Jim is practicing shooting with his left hand. He says it is just to be doing something, but I'm afraid it's something more serious. Bob is worried about him. Poor old Bob, he's doing ten men's work.

"Bridget has ten puppies. She brought them in from the brush and insists on bedding them down in the front room."

Lance chuckled and his eye came open. "She's always brought her pups into the house. She's an Irish wolfhound. If you don't let her, she howls like the dickens."

Lady Janet smiled; began another letter:

"— Pecos was over yesterday. He was cheerful and all that, but you can see he's worried about Lance. He and Bob have pooled the two outfits. That's all that's saving us. I was round-up cook. Had a little trouble driving four horses. They ran away once and tipped over the wagon. After that I let the horse-wrangler drive and I took care of the remuda. Only that Bob needs me, I'd go in as nurse in the Red Cross. But I save

234

the outfits cook's wages. Jim and Bob and Pecos all try to bully me into quitting, but they can't win much.

"Pecos painted three service stars on the mess wagon. One for you, one for Lance and, despite all my coaxing, I could not find out who merits the third star. Bob and Pecos just grin. I think it is for the man who quit the country with Lance. We're all proud of you both. Pecos says the war would be over in a week if they'd ship a troop of Texas Rangers over. Bob says to run the Parsons iron on Kaiser Bill when you get him roped and hogtied; says Parsons and Bill must be kinfolks — land grabbers."

Lady Janet finished the letters. The ugly twist was gone from Lance's lips.

"Teton must be a remarkable girl, Lieutenant."

"You bet she is," came the quick reply. "The Kirbys are real folks, all of them. I'd like to have been there when Tonnie had the runaway. I bet she was mad."

"And horribly frightened."

"Mad, mostly. She has Dick's temper. She'd give her eye-teeth to be over here." Lance smiled.

Lady Janet was looking out the window, her eyes misty with thoughts. There had been a P.S. at the end of one of those letters. She had not read it aloud to the wounded man — a short little postscript: "If you see Lance, tell him that I am caring for his father's grave."

Somehow Lady Janet had not trusted herself to read it aloud. It was an answer to the question she had wanted to ask about Tom Mansfield. It told her that he was dead. She roused herself from her memories and smiled.

"Some day you must tell me all about your Montana and your life there, all about Teton, won't you?"

"I reckon it'd bore you."

"Bore me? Hardly. You'll tell me about it all?"

"I'd like to, if it wouldn't be a bore."

"I'll consider that a promise and hold you to it." And she left him then.

He wondered vaguely why she seemed so starry-eyed. He could not know that it was mother-love that lighted her eyes — gray eyes that were usually so shadowed with pain that belied her gay smile.

They brought in Brimstone Burke that night. There was a soggy cigarette in the corner of the captain's stiff lips. His face was drawn and gray with pain.

"This man was wounded hours ago,"

snapped a surgeon. "Why wasn't he brought in sooner?"

"He wouldn't let us move him till his men were all loaded and sent in first. He lost a lot of his outfit to-day," said the ambulance driver. "He sat all afternoon with his back against a tree, smoking and cussing and running his end of the war. You see, Major Foss got killed this morning and Burke wouldn't let anyone else handle his men. He blessed out every man, officer, or non-com that crossed him. Hung on to that field phone like grim death. He knew every foot of No Man's Land by heart, directed patrols and liaison work, cussed out every stretcher-bearer that came near him. When it got dark, he let us load him in and fetch him here. I heard a staff colonel say that Burke saved his division."

"Well, he'll lose that leg — maybe his life."

"Do you think he don't know it? Do you think he gives a damn? Hell, he's an officer, that guy. If you don't want to take my word for it, ask his men — or General Pershing."

They amputated Captain Burke's leg at the knee. But no surgeon's knife could cut away the smile from his lips. When the pain got too severe he would wave away his nurse.

"An act of Congress made me an officer and a gentleman. What I'm about to say is not for a lady's ears. I'd suggest an orderly retreat, lady." And for some minutes he would delight the ears of fellow-patients with an amazing vocabulary of profanity.

One day he detained Lady Janet. "There's a shavetail of mine here somewhere. Lieutenant Lance Mansfield. They tell me his face is half gone. If it's a question of money, I have something like a couple of million in the bank at New York. Whack away at it. Get the best plastic hide carpenter in the business. Get that kid fixed up. Dammit, he has a girl waiting for him back home. He'll never go back as he is, because he's as proud as Lucifer. There's a Frenchman that they claim is a wizard. Can't we get him?"

"We've been trying to, Captain. It is not a question of money. But Dr. Dufresne is overworked at his own hospital in Paris."

"Hmmm. Then we'll use military tactics. Old General Rumor tells me that we're due for some medal-pinning here about tomorrow. Marshal Foch himself. I'm booked for some sort of citation. So is the Champ. Here is where we cash in on our glory, Lady Janet. Will you join my conspiracy?" Burke's eyes twinkled merrily.

"Indeed I will, Captain."

"Good. First move is to have a man named Fogarty moved in here alongside my cot. You may recall Sergeant Fogarty — a cow-puncher to whom generals of any country's army mean nothing. And he has the gift of gab peculiar to the Irish. Just move Doc Fogarty in here and we'll pull a flank attack on these medal peddlers that will be worth the price of admission. I hope Black Jack Pershing is along, that's all. Lady, if we don't put it over, you can saw off my other leg. Speaking of legs, my afternoon strafing is about to begin. Would you mind leaving now while I sound off?"

Burke was still swearing beautifully at his leg when Fogarty came in. Fogarty was a "walking case." It was Doc's first trip from his own ward. Two white hands gripped in silence. It was their first meeting, dramatic in its very silence. Lady Janet walked quickly away before these two men saw her tears.

"Doc, you damned old horse thief!"

"Brimstone hisse'f. Howdy, Cap'n."

Doc was seated on the adjoining cot, his lean face beaming, when Lady Janet came back.

So it came about that when, on the following day, an impressive group of gold-starred generals came through the hospital, they were delayed for several minutes when they halted to decorate a Captain Burke A.E.F., who had saved a division.

"Jest a second, gents," one Sergeant Fogarty grinned. On his nightshirt was pinned the Croix de Guerre with two palm leaves. "Jest a second, beggin' yore pardon fer bawlin' up the deal, but me'n the skipper here 'ud like fer tuh make a sorter dicker. We're both prideful as hell concernin' these decorations — proud as a kid with his first pair uh red-topped boots. But we'll swap 'er all an' give plenty to boot if you kin kinda arrange tuh herd Dr. Dufresne over to'rds our corral. We got a buddy with his face half tore off. He got it savin' Dick Kirby's life. There ain't a hell of a lot uh shavetails as 'ud risk their bars an' looks fetchin' in a buck private that hated his guts. He was wounded twice when he started back. Shrapnel tore away his face. When I found him, gents, he was crawlin' fer the German lines. Blind as a mole in the sunlight, clean outa his head. He taken me for a Boche, an' he'd uh got me only his gat was clogged with blood an' dirt.

"I know I ain't supposed tuh run off at the head like this. Bust me, take back these medals, slough me in the hoosegow — do what you damn please, gents, only get that

French doctor tuh fix up our buddy. Hell, generals, that boy was middleweight champ uh our division, the same division the skipper here give his laig tuh save. What the hell do these medals mean to us when we know the Champ will get sick to his stummick when he looks into a mirror when he realizes that he can't never go back home to the purty li'l gal that's waitin' fer him. By God, he'll blow his brains out, that's what'll happen!"

Doc lay back, white-faced, his eyes hard and shining. Behind the group of officers, Lady Janet Mansfield sobbed softly, her face hidden. The officers eyed one another with sidelong glances. This was not on the program.

"I had a similar speech rehearsed, gentlemen," said Captain Burke huskily, "but Sergeant Fogarty has left nothing for me to say except this: I wish I could have spoken as well and as unselfishly in behalf of a friend."

The tall, military man in the uniform of commanding officer of the American Expeditionary Forces nodded, smiling oddly. One of the French officers blew his nose.

"It shall be as the sergeant wishes," said the little gray man in sky-blue uniform. "I salute you both."

They moved on down the line of white cots. The American general was explaining. A word floated back, "Cowboy." There was a note of pride in the American's tone. For had not this tall officer known the breed? The backbone of that other army that charged San Juan Hill in '98?

No more picturesque body of troops ever lived than Roosevelt's Rough Riders. More than a few empty saddles now gathered dust on pegs, back in the cow country. The West had given its hard-riding, hard-fighting cowboys to the A.E.F. This was one of them who had spoken.

"God," said Burke softly, "you put it over, Doc. Oh, man, you did it. Not a false note in the speech. God!"

"I reckon I meant it, skipper, if that's what yuh mean."

There was the rustle of starched white skirts. Lady Janet stooped, kissed Doc Fogarty hard, then — with a shaky little laugh — followed the officers.

"Man!" said Doc, his face full of color now. "Man! Kissed me. . . . *Me!* An' her one uh these she-dukes!"

Chapter XXVII

The great Dr. Dufresne had come and gone. Lance now knew what that series of trips to the operating room had meant. But he said nothing to anyone of those thoughts that kept him awake sometimes at right. He had seen one or two of those men who should have died, men with covered faces. He smiled bitterly.

Doc Fogarty came in one day, dressed in a new uniform.

"Two days in gay Paree, then I'm goin' up an' stop the war, kid. It'll be kinda lonesome up there without Burke's cussin' an' without you to look after. Wish you was comin', Champ."

"Wish to God I was." Something of the earnest harshness in Lance's voice made Doc quit grinning. He looked hard at Lance's bandaged face.

"I get yuh, kid. I get yuh, plenty. But the joke's on you. I'll tell the A.E.F. you was a mess when you come here, but I seen that mug of your'n when they had that Frenchie workin' on you the last time. You was homely as hell before, but he made a matinee boy outa yuh."

"You don't need to kid me, Doc. I know."

"You know nothin'. Wait till them bandages is off."

"Wait, hell!" Lance's voice was cold. Deadly cold. "Get me a mirror, Doc."

"Say, be yorese'f kid. You monkey with them face rags an' you'll git us both hung. Mirror, hell!"

"Then I'll rip off these damned rags anyhow!"

"Not while I kin still sock you to sleep, yuh won't," snarled Doc. "After all we done, gettin' that doc here to patch yuh up, givin' hunks uh hide tuh graft on to yore map, you think you'll spoil it, eh? Rippin' off the bandage before it's time, eh? Not while Uncle Doc kin slap yuh to sleep, yuh won't. Yo're actin' like a baby. Worse'n that, yo're actin' yaller. Pecos told me you was game. Show yore gameness, then. Be a man. You don't hear Burke holler because he lost a laig. Nary whimper outa him. Says he never was much of a dancer, nohow. There's a buck nigger in my ward that'll never see no more. But he sings coon songs while he's learnin' tuh read without eyes. If you got guts, prove it."

"Guts, eh?" snarled Lance, "why damn you, Doc Fogarty, I —"

"Atta boy," chuckled Doc. "Now you're

snappin' outa it. I told Burke they orter tell yuh how things was goin'. I knowed you'd ketch on. Bound to. But, thank God, kid, that doc knew his saw-blades. He taken a few hunks uh bone an' hide an' jest nacherally built you up a fresh countenance, that's all. Saved yore eye, to boot, but yuh may have tuh wear specs awhile. When I git home I'm gonna make over some uh them ugly-lookin' cow-hands at a hundred bucks a throw. All a man needs is a good hunk uh rawhide an' some sheep ribs. Take it from ol' Doc, you kin write Teton Kirby that yo're comin' home, if yuh don't stop a Kraut shell with yore name on it. You bin layin' awake thinkin' too much. I want yuh tuh gimme yore word uh honor you'll write home. Dick'll put it in with his letter. If I thought yuh wasn't goin' tuh look okay, I'd tell yuh so. See?"

"I'm sorry I was so damned yellow, Doc."

"You better be. Now I gotta lope along. Good luck, Champ. There's a bocoo purty ma'amzelle waitin' fer me in Paree. See yuh when I git back with some more medals."

"So-long, Doc. God bless you, old boy."

It was two weeks later that Burke hobbled in on new crutches with the news that Sergeant Fogarty was killed in action.

Lance wrote to Teton that night. Into the

letter was written all the ache of his grief. For the third time in his life he turned to Teton in his hour of sorrow and loneliness.

Her reply came many weeks later. "Pecos covered the third star on the mess wagon with gold paint."

Lance showed that part of the letter to Lady Janet. They had removed Lance's face bandages and he, together with Burke, Dick Kirby, and some other convalescents, was at Lady Janet's country home in Devonshire.

"Who *was* Doc Fogarty?" she asked gently. "I mean, was he just a cowboy?"

"Just a cowboy," echoed Lance. "There is a range song that Doc used to sing. It seems to fit him:

"Tell 'em I'm a maverick a-runnin'
    loose unbranded;
Tell 'em I shoot straight an'
    quick an' I ain't got much to hide;
Have 'em come an' sire me up as
    soon as I git landed,
For the best they'll give me
    when I cross the Big Divide."

Lance sang the song in a soft baritone. When he had finished, they sat in silence for a long time. She sat beside him on the lawn, one of his hinds gripped tightly in hers.

Lance told her then what he knew of Doc Fogarty, how they had met, and, in a rambling, musing manner, he told her of his home; of Teton; of the dogs and horses, and of Pecos — of Tom Mansfield. Only when a hot teardrop wet his hand did he quit speaking.

"Why, shucks, I didn't aim to make you cry, Lady Janet." He was startled to see how much gray sprinkled her copper hair. He had never noticed until now.

"I cry so easily," she said. "You must have loved your father a great deal."

"I think I respected him and rather worshiped him," came Lance's frank reply. "I never had the love for him that some boys have for their father. Like Dick and Bob Kirby, for instance. They called their father Jim. Dad never was like that to me. He was kind and everything, but he always kept me at a distance, if you know what I mean."

"Dignified. Stern? Aloof?"

"That's it. Sort of aloof. And he drank heavily — alone — night after night when he thought I was asleep. He never knew I saw him like that. It came about quite by accident. I'd gone to bed and remembered I'd left the dog kennels open. I woke in the night and thought of it. So I slipped downstairs in my bare feet. He was in front of the fireplace, staring into the dead coals, his face gray and terribly sad. He didn't see me as I crouched on the stairs, afraid to move. I was just a kid, but I knew he was ill or something. Then he reached for the whisky bottle and his unsteady hand knocked it over. He staggered over to the table and got a fresh bottle. I knew then that he was drunk."

"Your mother?" she asked in a whisper — "did he ever speak of her?"

"Only a few times. He said he had done her a terrible wrong. Something that could never be repaired. I never knew just what it was all about. I've always thought I'd try to find her some day, if she were alive. Find her and tell her that, whatever wrong Father did, he paid for it. There was a stubborn sort of pride, I think, that kept him from letting her know."

"Yes. I understand. You missed that mother's love?"

"Horribly, at times. When he died; when Judge Truman died, and now, with Doc gone. You've been great to me, Lady Janet — sort of motherin' me, letting me talk like this. As if — well, as if you were my mother."

"I'm glad if I've helped. You've made me very happy this evening — sadder and happier than I have been in many years. But you've made me feel old — as old as my age. I'm forty-seven, but that's a secret. Old enough to be your mother, Lance. So as a penalty for so revealing my gray hairs, I'll kiss you good night, then leave you with your pipe and the sunset."

She kissed him almost gaily, then went away. Lance followed her with his eyes. She had changed her white uniform for a black gown. Lance told himself that she was the most beautiful woman he had ever seen.

Captain Burke, sighting her, halted on his crutches and saluted. "I thank you, Lady Janet, for bringing sunshine into the heart of a man who was being ridden by blue devils. You've driven 'em away. May I tell you, without seeming impertinent, that you are the loveliest vision that ever blessed the sight of a soldier of the wars?"

"A pretty compliment, Captain Burke. But one that hints of the Erin ancestry. However, I'm taking you at your word. I have just been made to feel very old by a certain young lieutenant. I can now go to my dinner-party without the aid of a face-lifting."

Burke's keen gaze was searching her gray eyes. "Lady Janet, I'm going to be rude. But it's because I love you as every man in the hospital loves you for your gracious hospitality — even as Lance Mansfield loves you."

"I don't quite understand, Captain Burke?"

"You and your son need each other. Why, in God's name, don't you tell the boy so that you can both be happy?"

"But how did you know — how can you interfere in the — ?"

"I know nothing except that he is your son; that he needs you as you need him; that I've been watching a terrible tragedy and had no power to help two people whom I loved. I am sorry because I've now hurt you."

"But supposing I were to tell him what I must tell him some day were I to claim him as son? Supposing he should then hate me? What then? Would it not be better to let him leave here knowing me only as Lady Janet? Caring for me as you and the other boys care? Rather than risk the chance of his hatred?"

"I think you underestimate the depth in manhood of that boy who is your son. He is a man, a real man. I know that if I were he, you could not malign yourself in my estimation. Nothing the world could say would keep me from loving you. Lady Janet, I don't give a damn what you say, what the world says, what anyone could say, you could not shake my faith in your goodness. You could not mar the love in my heart for you. Lance Mansfield would not be worthy of love if he would not feel that same way."

Lady Janet put a white hand against a tree to steady herself. Captain Burke, his eyes bright, his face now settled to a whimsical, wistful smile, waited for her to speak.

"I shall think it over, Captain. You've — sort of shocked me. Oh, God, if only you were right!"

"Steady," came Burke's voice, now calm again. "Take it steady. Can't you tell me enough, some day, to let me help you? If I could only be of some value, I'd feel a little bit as if I'd repaid some of your kindness. Why, faith, it can't be so bad as you see it! And I'll vouch for the boy. Let me help you, won't you?"

She smiled again through her tears. "What a loyal person you are! What a friend! You've made me hope to-night. If those hopes can ever find fulfillment, I can never in this life be able to repay you."

"Repay, eh? Be off with you now. Powder your nose and run along to your party. And bet on this, we're going to talk this out. You've had too much of this double-be-damned British conservatism thrown at your pretty head. Now trot along and smile and have a grand time. I'll go borrow some tobacco from that lieutenant son of yours." He saluted and hobbled on slowly, whistling an Irish jig.

Chapter XXVIII

Dick Kirby had gone up to the front again. Lance and Burke lazed through the long weeks of convalescence. Lance made several trips to the operating table for further work on his badly scarred face. He would always carry those scars, but he was not in any way repulsive to look at. The long scar from temple to mouth gave him the appearance of one of those Heidelberg officers marked with their coveted saber slash. It made him look older. He had grown his mustache again. He looked more than ever like Tom Mansfield.

"A soldier of the wars," Burke called him. "You were too damned handsome anyhow, Champ. How do you like me on my newly padded sticks, kid?"

Whatever bitterness over his loss Burke might have felt, he hid it well. He cursed the pain of the healing stump, but he did it so well that it was comical. He visited with those of his men who were wounded. He personally wrote letters to the parents of those killed. He laughed and joked and wrote out checks that went to needed places. And few guessed that his disability had robbed him of the one thing in life that he loved — namely, his soldiering. Wealth, society, position meant nothing. He had given up his clubs, his yacht, his all, to become a West Point man, an officer. Because he loved the life, he had won recognition. His men worshiped him. His brother officers envied him. Now he would be invalided home, given a discharge. His life would be empty.

"I'd gone as far as I could, Lance," he said one day, "a captain of cavalry at fifty. As the world takes it, I was a failure. But hell, I couldn't be bothered with garrison schools and learning new tricks. I can handle a troop, but I'd be in a blue funk with anything like a brigade." He rolled a cigarette. "No brains, see."

"No?" smiled Lance. "How about the day Jerry smeared your leg and you ran the show? I hear that a brigadier-general took Brimstone's order that day."

"Oh, that — a flash in the pan. I happened to know my blue-prints that day. Anyhow, I was half-lit. Remember the Scotch we had hidden in our bedrolls? Well, Pickott dug it up for me. I was plastered all afternoon. But don't let it get out. Wouldn't sound well. As it is, some of those pot-bellied staff-officers are rarin' to prefer charges of insubordination. I talked to 'em kind of rough. Pull in your ears, here comes Lady Janet."

She was still just Lady Janet to Lance, as she was to most of her wounded men. One would as soon think of asking the full name of a sister of mercy. But Burke knew and Lady Janet knew that some day Lance would learn her full name and wonder. She brought the mail. Lance had two letters. One from Teton, the other from Pecos.

Burke glanced at his mail, made a wry face, and then grinned. "Bills — just bills. One has many acquaintances, but his friends are to be numbered on the fingers of a one-armed man. If you'll sit awhile, Lady Janet, I promise not to cuss once. Moreover, I'll make this young man tell us the little yarn that has to do with a nickname the boys gave him. Tell us the sailor story, Champ, or I'll bust you. I'm still your C.O."

"He told me yesterday he was arrested for being a cow-thief," laughed Lady Janet, eager for a chance to linger near her son. "Is this another tale of dark crime?"

"Crime is not in the deed but the discovery of the deed. Fortunately, we were never found out." They chatted while Lance read his letters. These three people had fallen into the habit of spending the sunset hour together — out on the lawn when the weather permitted, at other times inside — the two men smoking, Lady Janet knitting. Burke had contrived these daily chats so subtly that neither Lady Janet nor Lance suspected. He loved to sit back, watching the play of emotions on the woman's face and in her eyes. . . . Lance's boyish heart spilling out its confidences. . . . She listening. . . . Burke smoking and watching — their hour. And into the Irish heart of Captain Brimstone Burke there crept a feeling of contentment.

He found himself looking forward to this quiet hour when the perfume of Lady Janet's nearness filled his senses. At first he had fought against this feeling, for he was afraid of its growth. For he knew that this contentment might easily become love.

"And me a damned peg-leg cripple!"

Yet he never missed that hour with her, watching her face with covert glances, listening to the soft music of her voice, lifted to glowing pleasure when she laughed. But a few evenings ago she had called him "friend." He took it that she rarely used the word in its true sense. That she was terribly alone, somehow.

They chatted idly now, he and Lady Janet, while Lance devoured his letters.

The letter from Pecos was short, misspelled, but pithy with news. "The outfit is goin' O.K. Zack Tanner is dead. He musta aimed to steal Sultan the stallion or burn out the ranch. We was all away that night. When I come in the barn I knowed somethin' was wrong, because Sultan was raisin' hell in his stall. Then I seen somethin' kinda tromped down under his feet, an' when I drug it out, it's Zack Tanner, dyin' an' bin that way fer hours. Good thing we kep' that stud, hey?

"Who is Captain Burke? He sure spiked that damn Parsons's guns some way. They can't touch you till the army turns you loose because this Burke gent says so to the big moguls at Washington, because you got shot to hell an' got medals to show fer it. You never told us you was shot. But this Burke feller told it sure scary, I guess. Our governor wrote me about it, and the Chinook paper give you a write-up. Teton like to bawled her eyes out, then run me outa the house when I ast her how come she was feelin' bad. She said she was bawlin' because she was happy. Now ain't wimen hell to figger out? Jim Kirby is packin' a gun fer somebody, but he won't say who. Rode a bronc to-day an' he throwed me. Sign I ain't so young no more. Say, that Burke must be a sure war-hog. Fetch him home with you.

We are goin' to need some fightin' fools before many moons, because Parsons is after our hides. Things is gonna tighten some day so don't throw away yore gun when the war is over. You'd orter be good with it, gettin' so much practice. Bring me home ol' Bill's whiskers, kid. So-long.

"P.S. So Doc got killed, hey? He mighta bin a horse-thief, kid, but he was a sure enough white man. I bet he gits a square deal Over Yonder.

"Yrs. Pecos."

Teton's letter was more lengthy; a girl's letter in its cheerful chatter of dogs and horses and cowboys — a woman's letter, inasmuch as she hid her heartaches until one read between the lines. Lance put the letters away and grinned.

"So you wrote to Washington about me, eh?"

Burke grinned uneasily. "Just a line or two, son. I don't think you ever knew that there was a major from the intelligence department waiting for you when you brought in Kirby."

"No!"

"Sure. He trotted up to the P.C. dugout right after you boys left on patrol. He was all for taking you back. I told him I'd show him where you were. I led him along the trench, then pointed over the top, but he lost all his zest for following you. Said he'd wait till you got back. The damned cootie was there in the dugout when you and Doc came down in with Kirby. But he didn't stay."

Burke chuckled. "They could bust me for what I called him. I was afraid they'd move again, so I beat 'em to it. I have a drag at the White House that comes in handy now and then. Now tell Lady Janet about the sailor story."

Lance told the tale. When he had finished, Burke proposed that the three of them have dinner at a quiet little tavern. His invitation was promptly accepted. When Lady Janet went to dress, Lance tried to thank Burke for what he had done.

"I'll bend a new crutch across your new face, kid. Forget it." He chuckled over the letter from Pecos. "And are you going to invite me to that cow ranch of yours, boy? Or do I come without a bid?"

"You mean you'd like to come, skipper?"

"You tell 'em!"

"You'd like Pecos and the Kirbys and the hounds and all. That leg won't keep you from riding. Darn it, skipper, I wish we — I know it sounds silly, but I wish Lady Janet could go along. But of course she can't."

"There's no crime in asking her, kid. And she might take you up on it. You like her, Lance?"

"Like her! Why damn it, man, she's an angel! Hasn't she sat by the hour listening to my darn fool babbling? Hasn't she pulled us all through hell? Like her? Why — why —"

"Exactly, kid. You ask her to-night. See what she says."

"You don't think it would sound goofy?"

"I think you'd seem ungrateful if you didn't ask her."

Lance shot Burke a searching look.

"Ain't love grand, skipper?" Lance grinned at Burke's sudden flush.

"Don't be a damn fool, Mansfield."

"You're as guilty as a chicken-stealing hound pup."

"One word out of you," sputtered Burke, "and I'll —"

"Guilty, old war-horse?" persisted Lance.

"Guilty as hell, kid. But don't let her know it."

Lady Janet came toward them. She still wore her white uniform. Burke saw that she was pale and tense with some emotion. She met his eyes. In them she read a message, "Steady, steady." She nodded briefly and forced a smile.

"I'm afraid our little dinner-party is off.

I'm more sorry than you can possibly know. Some people have come to see Lieutenant Mansfield. A Colonel Sir John Mansfield of the British army, your uncle, Lance. Some others, his wife, a couple of cousins."

"Well, I'll be darned," said Lance. "Dad's relatives. I've never met 'em. Wonder how they found me?"

Burke rose. "I'll leave you, son. I'm not accustomed to meeting royalty. One moment, Lady Janet, and I'll hobble along with you."

"Gosh, skipper! Lady Janet! Don't desert me!" But they smiled back at him as they crossed the lawn.

"I'll make a guess who sent word to the boy's folks," said Burke. "You broke faith with me, Lady Janet!"

"I sent for them, though they didn't know it was I. Colonel Crowther told them Lance was here."

"And you're giving them a chance to condemn you in the eyes of that boy?" guessed Burke. They halted for a moment beside a sun-dial.

"Some day he was bound to know what the world knows, Captain Burke. I would rather he heard it from the lips of Sir John Mansfield, his uncle. Sir John has never forgiven me for — for what happened one night at Rangoon — a silly girl's prank that wrecked two lives, mine and my husband's. Yes, I'd rather Lance heard it from Sir John. Then, if he can find it in his heart to love me, I will find happiness. You have been more than kind. I think you are the kindest person I have ever known. I must leave you now."

So a man in love saw the woman of his heart go away to be alone in the misery that he wished to share. And he was helpless to aid her.

Chapter XXIX

Even afterward, when it was all over, Lance Mansfield's impression of that meeting with the Mansfield family was a bit hazy . . . their abrupt coming, what they said, the manner of their saying the things they had to say — their visible sizing-up of Tom Mansfield's son as if he were a breed of strange animal. All was a bit hazy, undefined. From out of a background of smartly gowned cousins, a sallow youth in the uniform of lieutenant, an atmosphere of haughty disapproval — from out of this background stood the tall, stern-visaged form of Colonel Sir John Mansfield.

Their greeting was one of formality. "Dear Tom's boy. I say, Julia, can't you see the resemblance, what? Cousin Lance, so sorry to hear of your being wounded."

Tea was brought by a servant. Lady Anne, Sir John's wife, poured. Lance was plainly ill at ease. He felt like something that had been taken in on approval — that they each, in their own peculiar way, were looking him over in the hope of discovering flaws. When Lady Julia mentioned that Lance "has his mother's nose," he quickly caught the inference. In "having his mother's nose" he had committed the unpardonable sin.

He got no little satisfaction in explaining that a bit of shrapnel had taken away his original nose — that the present one was a synthetic product. For the time being the guns of Lady Julia were silenced. Lance inwardly grinned at their unmistakable horror as he rolled his own cigarettes. But his inward mirth was short-lived.

"You will, of course, return with us to our country place," Sir John had been saying. "I've already begun arrangements for your transfer."

"Thank you, sir," replied Lance, "but I'm doing splendidly here. My buddies are here. Captain Burke is here, and Lady Janet has been an angel."

They stiffened, visibly chilled. Lance saw them freezing like so many statues. He took their frigid attitude for pique at his refusal. "It is as I feared, Sir John," spoke the hawk-beaked Lady Julia. "I fancy you and Lance would enjoy a little chat alone. Come, children."

Sir John settled himself in the chair where Burke usually sprawled. Lance braced himself for some sort of ordeal.

"I fail to understand, Lance," rumbled Sir John, when his cigar was going well, "how you can accept the hospitality of that woman who killed your father."

"I beg your pardon, sir," smiled Lance in a puzzled manner. "I don't quite follow you."

"Not literally, of course. And I hear they called Tom's death accidental. But I knew he'd committed suicide. And it was because of that woman. By gad, sir, I can't and won't call her by name. She pulled the wool over Uncle James's eyes. She got all he had, even the title that Tom ignored. Lady Janet Mansfield! Bosh and rubbish! A woman of the stage, by gad, sir! — and I add, a woman of the streets!"

Lance, white as chalk, gripped the arms of his chair. The name Lady Janet had struck him like a blow across the eyes. In that instant he knew without being told that Lady Janet was his mother. Oddly, it was as if he had known it from the very beginning. His mother, Tom Mansfield's wife — the woman whom his father had forgiven for something Lance never understood.

"I repeat it, sir," rumbled Sir John's voice, "a woman —"

"Stop it!" Lance's voice, cold, terrible, even-toned, cut into Sir John's rumble.

"You are speaking of my mother, sir. Because you are my father's brother and an old man, I can't knock you down. But I can tell you this: when you say my father killed himself because of her, you lie. And when you seek to defame the character, the name, the virtue of Lady Janet, you are doing a low-down, cowardly thing. By God, sir, Burke would kill you for what you've just said. So would any man inside that house or in the hospital. You'd better go, sir, before I've said a lot I'll be regretting. I'm doing my damnedest to be respectful."

Lance was on his feet now, fists clenched, his scarred face white and set. Sir John Mansfield rose, saluted grimly, and stalked off. Lance, a twisted, bitter smile on his lips, saw the colonel gather in his family and march them to the waiting Rolls-Royce.

Half an hour later Lance found Burke smoking in the shadow.

"Where's Lady Janet, skipper?"

"Dunno, son. She left when the nobility came. They didn't stay long."

"No, damn 'em!"

"Sit down, kid. Sit down," he said. "Tell the old man all about it now. I'll help you strafe 'em. I take it that they tried to sling mud at your mother and you got shirty. Eh?"

"Yes. Burke, Lady Janet is my mother."

"And her in-laws don't like her, eh?"

"But you don't seem to get me. My mother is our Lady Janet!"

"Sure." Burke puffed at his pipe. "And the big walrus they call Sir John thinks she ain't good enough for his outfit."

"Them you knew that she was my mother?" persisted Lance.

"Hell, yes," came the laconic reply. "And I bet a new pair of boots that you piped the walrus down when he began his strafing."

"I'd be a fine egg if I didn't. Why, damn it all, skipper, Lady Janet is the finest woman in the world."

"Agreed. Now light up and smoke on it while you get calmed down. You're all a-flutter, kid. Light a pipe. Here's some good tobacco."

Lance's match lit up two faces. Burke's square-jawed countenance fairly beamed. Lance paced to and fro puffing clouds of smoke.

"You're getting on a man's nerves, kid. Go on down the walk to the sunken garden. Tell Lady Janet, when you find her, that Captain Burke would be tickled green if she'd wear that black gown to dinner to-night. I'll give you two half an hour. Step on it, Champ."

When Lance had gone, Burke smiled into the dusky shadows.

"If only Fogarty had been here to listen in while the kid blessed-out the nobility. Whew! As neat a job as a man could ask for. The boy came through like a champ and no mistake."

That evening as the three had dinner at the quaint little tavern, Burke seemed the gayest of the three, if such a degree of happiness were possible. And when Lance went to fetch cigarettes, Lady Janet held a hand across the table to the captain.

"My friend! God bless you for your wonderful understanding."

Burke kissed the slender white hand, holding it for a long moment.

"You have made me the happiest woman alive. Your confidence gave me the courage to do what I did in sending for Sir John."

"It was a cinch bet from the start." He was looking into her eyes, his own shining with a soft brightness. A rather handsome man, Burke, in a blunt-jawed, short-nosed way. His gray hair was crisp, close-cropped. His head was well shaped, set on a solid, muscular neck. Straight-browed, a little wide of mouth, he smiled well. He was smiling now.

And this was Brimstone Burke of the cavalry, who had lain for hours with his leg shattered to a bloody pulp, smoking, swearing, swallowing whisky as though it were water, directing his troops. He had won the war cross of three nations. He was maimed for life. His life as a soldier was finished. Still he smiled. And because Lady Janet was a woman, she knew that only his crippled leg kept him from declaring his love.

Lance returned with the cigarettes. Suddenly Burke cocked his head sideways, listening. Lance now caught the drone of airplanes. Somewhere up in the black sky German bombers were crossing the village. Now came the shriek of the village alarm siren. Lights were blotted out. People rushed for shelter. Lance snuffed out a candle. Burke reached to extinguish the other candles. At that instant the earth rocked, crashed, thundered. The little tavern was a mass of wreckage. Dust choked Lance as he picked himself up from the floor.

"Lady Janet! Mother! Burke, old man!" The boy's voice was harsh with alarm.

"We're all right. Quite all right. Eh, Lady Janet?" Burke's voice was trembling oddly.

"Quite — quite all right." Her voice broke a little.

"You're positive that it's — quite all right?" — Burke's voice again.

"Quite — dear."

"You heard her, Lance. It's quite — quite all right."

"Say, is this 'Quite all right' business a password to some lodge?" called Lance.

"Lodge? That ain't the half of it. It took an earthquake to do it, old son, but it happened. You need a hard-boiled step-dad. God bless that Boche flier."

"Well, I'll be gosh-darned," muttered Lance. "Nothing like a little bomb to promote happiness. Can you dig out all right? Then I'll be waiting at the car. The inn-keeper is out there weeping. I'll have to parley-voo enough of this tin-can French of mine to explain how we'll get him a new tavern and another barrel of dago red. If you're still listening, you both have my blessing. See you later." Lance climbed over the wreckage, whistling softly.

"It's a great old war, after all."

Chapter XXX

The eleventh day of November, the year of Nineteen Hundred Eighteen. Who in America, in England, in Belgium and France, in Germany, or in the entire world, can ever forget that day? That day when the big guns went silent. When men, gray-faced, haggard, war-torn, looked across the desolation and went wild with the joy of peace. Shouting, laughing, sobbing. Hysteria gripped them. The war was over!

Men got drunk. Women prayed. Children sang. And there were the white crosses, row upon row. Yes, the war was over. The price of peace was there for all to see. Some day vineyards and gardens would again grow from soil now consecrated. From the ruins would again rise villages. Men and leaders of men and nations would pay homage to the grave of an Unknown Soldier.

If Mars, the war god, smiled that day, they did not know it, those men and women and children. Perhaps those who had died, those whose blood had reddened Flanders and St. Mihiel and the Argonne, knew the mockery of "A war to perpetuate peace."

A bunch of doughboys, fresh from the red

271

mud of the Argonne, swung along the road singing, "I Love You, California." They stopped to give a drink to a black-faced zouave. They trudged on, singing once more.

Equipment lay strewn along the road where men had thrown it. Up on the edge of the front lines a burly, red-faced sergeant turned to four prisoners he had taken.

"Beat it fer Berlin, you guys. You there, you kid with the scared eyes, take these francs and buy yourself a haircut. So-long, birds. I'm in too much of a rush to get back to Hoboken to fool wit' prisoners."

In Paris a week later Captain Brimstone Burke sat at a battered table. In front of him lay a pile of typed orders and counterorders. A sergeant pecked out some sort of bulletin on a badly used typewriter. An orderly bustled in and out of the room. It was one of several rooms that had been hastily converted into divisional headquarters.

"Pickott?"

"Yes, sir." The pecking sergeant looked up from his labors. "Send somebody out for Lieutenant Mansfield. I hate like hell to tempt luck by being prepared, but there's a slim — a hell of a slim — chance that our outfit will be getting out of here soon. And I don't want any of my boys left here in jail.

Get Mansfield on the job."

"Yes, sir. The Sailor can round up the gang, if any man can. The boys are so tickled to get you and the lieutenant back, they'll come without too much fuss."

"If they wreck any more of these cognac joints, they'll wish to heaven I was dead. It cost me a month's pay squaring it with that Frenchman. These people have enough on their minds without you birds finishing up what the Germans were too busy to wreck. Now trot."

Pickott grinned, saluted, and was gone. Burke rose, hobbled over to the window on his new artificial leg that squeaked dismally, and stood looking down at the crowded street below. Cars, trucks, men, like a swarm of ants. He had been back with his outfit two days. Lance had come with him.

"And me married just five days! Janet back in her hospital. The fortunes of war." But a grin twitched at his lips, for Brimstone Burke was happy. Or as happy, at least, as Brimstone Burke could be, with a third of his troop marked on the casualty list. At roll-call that morning he had made a miserable failure of the little speech he had wanted to make to the men who expected it. He had choked in the middle of the opening sentence. They had understood and they had cheered with aching throats.

Anticipating a belated pay-roll, Burke had drawn funds from his personal account and sent the money to the troop commander. Such an understanding of a soldier's heart needs no carefully prepared speech.

"Get this, you birds," he had barked before he dismissed them. "Tone down on the hell-raising. Any man that gets in the can stays there till his clothes rot. We're going to be shoving off in a few days. Drink your liquor like men, not like hoodlums. Sergeant, dismiss the troop."

Lance reported. Burke grinned a welcome and handed him a list of names.

"These men are A.W.O.L. Round 'em up. Some of 'em are replacement men. Others on the list are men you know. Glance down along the K's and you'll find Dick Kirby's name. He's a sergeant now, but he won't be when he gets back. I'll show him we bust 'em easier than we make noncoms in this man's army. Use diplomacy, bribes, brass knucks or what have you, but don't check in until you bring those troopers. Vamoose, Champ. Good luck."

"I'll need good luck. This is Paris, not San Diego. Some of these gents will be in the hoosegow."

"Do tell!" gasped Burke drily. "Impossible, Lieutenant!"

Lance grunted, swore softly, and took his departure. Out on the street he paused uncertainly for a moment, then marched off, the list tucked in his blouse pocket.

In groups of twos or threes he located his men scattered about the city. They trailed along behind him, joking, smoking, singing. Some bore marks of recent fistic conflict. One or two marched unsteadily.

"That's Sailor Mansfield, you birds," said a tall trooper. "He's a go-getter. He was middleweight champ of the division when he got blowed to hell bringin' in Kirby. Wasn't I in San Diego that night when he trots into a dance-hall wit' a black eye an' wearin' a gob's uniform? I'll tell the troops I was. Him an' Doc Fogarty had mopped up a M.P. detail an' skinned the sergeant outa —"

"Squad, halt!" snapped Lance. " 'Tention. Private Jones, you're in charge. File your men into that church. Inside, sit down and sleep till I get back. Don't forget for a second that it's a church, not a barroom. You'll report any misconduct. Take the name of any man that speaks above a whisper or pulls a bottle. I'll take care of him personally. Get that, Jones?"

Jones was the tall trooper who had been

interrupted. "Yes, sir." He saluted. Lance returned the salute and went on down the street.

"Cripes!" growled one man. "A church!"

"Good place to sleep," snapped Jones. "In you go, soldiers."

Lance hunted the town from one end to the other. He picked up a French sergeant and a marine with a cauliflower ear who had halted him with a "Ain't you Champ Mansfield? Remember me, Lootenant? Spike Nolan? I done a prelim at the boxin' show when you won the belt. I thought you was dead."

"I may be by night. Got on your drinking clothes?"

"Aye, sir."

"Then lift one with me and Sergeant Laverne. I'm gathering in my A.W.O.L.'s. I could use a good marine."

"I'm your leatherneck, Lootenant. I know every barkeep in town. An' I set good at M.P. barracks."

Spike Nolan, marine, knew his Paris, it was more than evident. In an hour the cathedral held six more cavalrymen. They then picked up a captain of marines who, according to Spike, was "the saltiest skipper afloat or ashore."

"Got some men in the brig, Lieutenant?

Hmm. Let's crack a bottle, then cruise over that way. I got a couple of birds in there I'm going to spring myself. Some of these babies can't get it through their nuts that the country's gone peaceful. Only by the way they choose sparring mates, you'd think we'd been at war with Great Britain. Can you parley-voo this sergeant's lingo? Then ask him where there's good vino. Then we'll spring our babies outa the can. Then I gotta look up a naval officer that got bocoo sarcastic last night."

They found some champagne, then paid a call on the M.P. officer. They left the place with their men but with lighter bill-folds. The cathedral gained six more sinners. Lance looked at his list and scowled. But one name was left: Sergeant Kirby, ten days absent without leave. Lance cracked a farewell bottle with the French sergeant, Spike, and the marine captain. Then he sent his men under Private Jones to report to Captain Burke.

Filled with foreboding, he trudged on in his hunt for Dick Kirby. His mind was filled with a hundred black doubts. He saw Dick dead; in some jail; in some dark alley with a crushed skull. His wandering led him aimlessly along a road that led out of the city. Finally, leg-weary and disheartened, he sat down beside the road on a stone wall. Cars, trucks, and motor-cycles roared past. Men came along in straggling columns — prisoners who laughed with their jocular captors, French troops, Belgian troops, English troops; weary to the point of exhaustion, but going home; Americans, more fresh than the other allied soldiers, singing and calling out to every one; harassed looking officers.

Lance, rolling a listless cigarette, suddenly stiffened. Paper and tobacco spilled from his hands. From out of that moving, somehow orderly chaos, there drifted a voice raised in somewhat nasal song.

> *"Parson, I'm a maverick, just*
> *runnin' loose an' grazin',*
> *Eatin' where's the greenest*
> *grass . . ."*

Lance was on his feet, running, shoving past cars and trucks, pushing through men, shouting at the top of his voice.

"Doc! Doc! Doc Fogarty!"

The clattering roar of a motor had blotted out the song. Lance found himself lost in a maze of gaping, staring men, who plainly thought him crazy or drunk. There was no sign of the erstwhile singer. But only one man alive could have sung that song in that voice. That man was Doc Fogarty.

"God, have I gone bats? Was I dreaming?" Lance asked himself, his eyes searching the throng that was crowding him off the road. It was then, when his heart was pounding like a trip-hammer, that Lance sighted Dick Kirby.

A bloody bandage was wrapped under Dick's rakish helmet. His uniform was stained and mud-caked, and his face wore a stubble of whiskers. Dick's arm was supporting a hollow-eyed, bearded scarecrow in German uniform. Not until he came close did Lance recognize that German scarecrow as Doc Fogarty.

"Thank God, Lance," whispered Dick huskily. "Between us, we'll get him there. I'm about all in. Damn those cars. They been passing us up for a week. Doc's cuckoo. He's not so hard to handle when he sings. But when he fights, he's tough. Sometimes he knows me. Mostly, though, he's clean outa his head."

"Fever, Dick — fever and, I'd say, starvation. Hold him a second. Here comes a car." The car held a chauffeur and two lieutenants of infantry.

"We have a sick man," Lance explained when the car slithered to a halt. The officers

279

glared. The driver lit a fresh cigarette and apparently was about to go to sleep.

"This is not an ambulance, Lieutenant," snapped one of the officers. "It's a staff car and we're in a rush!"

"But this man is dying!" Lance stepped up on the running-board.

"Sorry. Call an ambulance. Get under way, Corporal."

"One minute, Corporal. Gentlemen. I reckon you didn't get me. My sergeant is damned sick. He's just from a prison camp and has fever."

"Sorry. Corporal, get going!"

With a quick leap, Lance was in the tonneau of the car. He kicked the door open. Then, with a grunt and a heave, he literally threw two second lieutenants over the side and into the mud. A faint cheer went up from some mud-spattered soldiers.

"Come on, Dick!" barked Lance. Then he leaned over and growled at the driver.

"Drive like hell when I tell you." He turned to swing at a face that popped up. One of the recently evicted officers went down again into the mud. Dick lifted Doc into the car.

"Step on it, Corporal."

"Paris-bound, Lootenant." The car leaped, showered mud into two wrath-distorted faces, and skidded around a line of trucks.

"Them damn shavies didn't belong, nohow, sir. They hopped the car a ways down the road. They was off for Paris to party for a day er two. Will a shot uh coneyac help that sick guy?" He passed a water-bottle back over the seat, driving recklessly with one grimy hand the while.

"To tell the truth, sir," he called back, "I found this can along the road. My motorcycle had gone blooey. I got the bus workin' an' come on. Got some orders fer headquarters an' I'm in a rush. Them shavies got their needin's. Bocoo jack on 'em, but not a franc come my way."

Lance passed over a handful of francs. Dick held the water-bottle to Doc's mouth. Doc swallowed once or twice, his eyes opening, then his grimy, clawlike hands clutched the bottle.

"It can't hurt him, Dick. Mebby do him good. Doc, old-timer, it's Lance. . . . Mansfield, old cow-hand, get me?"

Doc quit drinking. Sanity came into his hot eyes. "Lance, you damned old cow-thief. Tell me I ain't loco, Champ."

"You're sick, Doc, that's all."

"Yeah, sick, son — sicker'n hell. Kin yuh make out tur roll me a smoke of some kind?" But the next moment he was asleep in Lance's arms.

"God knows what he's been through," said Dick. "I found him the other night in No Man's Land, in a hidden listening-post. He was handcuffed to a German. Two more Germans were in the hole. Doc had killed the three of 'em. They must have taken him out there to interpret our code or something. He got hold of a gun and cleaned up on 'em. Then was too weak to get to our lines. I didn't know him at all till he began babbling about cow-hands and trying to sing. I was shooting off the damn handcuffs when a hunk of shell knocked me out. When I woke up the war was over, but the damn fools were too busy celebrating to pay any attention to us."

"The top kicker has you down as A.W.O.L., Dick."

"He would," said Dick with a snarl. "The first thing I do when I get out of this man's army is to knock that top kick for a loop of latrines. I bet he wouldn't last long with Burke as skipper."

"You win the bet. Pickott's acting top. Burke's running the troop again. Seems like this top sergeant got sort of beaten up Armistice night. Burke put him on as mess sergeant."

"Hope he don't find any arsenic to

season our grub with. Think Doc'll die, Lance?"

"I'm betting he'll be on his pins in a week. He's running a fever, but it's from exposure and bum food and not enough of that. All he needs is a bath, good grub, and rest. He'll get that at my quarters. He'll want to go home with the outfit, so we won't put him on official sick report."

Burke and Lance shared quarters in a private home. The corporal took them there. Lance and Dick carried Doc into the house, followed by the landlady and her daughter.

"What the hell —" Burke met them at the door of his bedroom. "Fogarty or I'm a Swede!"

Doc straightened, stood alone, and saluted weakly. "I'm weaker'n a bogged cow, skipper, an' lousy as a pet coon. But I kin draw you a map uh them Boche lines an' I don't mean mebby. Give yuh figgers on guns an' men to boot. Get me pencil an' paper."

For Doc Fogarty the war was still on. He was close to the cracking point of sanity. But when he went aboard the transport with his outfit he was well enough to smuggle six quarts of champagne aboard. Moreover, he sang as he came up the gang-plank.

"Tell 'em I rode straight an'
square an' never grabbed
for leather;
Never roped a crippled steer er
rode a sore-backed horse."

So they came back, those men who had
gone to the war, came back to adjust themselves once more to the mundane things of
civilian life. They lined the transport rail,
waving, cheering, calling back. A tightness
in their corded throats, a mistiness in their
eyes. There were some who would always
be crippled, or blind, or suffering from gas
and shellshock. And there were those who
would never return.

That night an ensign with a voice like an
angel sang for them. Some one said he had
been a vaudeville headliner for years.

"Oh, how I miss you, dear old pal of
mine —
Each night and day, I pray —"

"Let them as kin sing, sing," announced
Doc, making no effort to hide the tears in
his eyes. "Me, I know when I'm out-
classed."

Chapter XXXI

Number three was due at Chinook in half an hour. The Kirby family sat in their battered flivver, despite the chill zero weather. Buck and Slim paced the platform, their eyes on the clock inside the waiting-room.

Pecos, in chaps and coonskin coat, was inside the baggage-room, talking to the sheriff.

"The kid's due in on Number Three, sheriff, and while I ain't rarin' fer trouble, still, us boys has a kinda party planned out at the Bench-K ranch — sorter welcome-home proposition. Dunno how we'd take it if anybody was tuh kinda cut in on the deal."

"I got a warrant fer Mansfield some-wheres around the office. It's bin gatherin' dust fer nigh two years. Dunno as I could find it inside of a week. Come tuh think about it, the missus told me tuh git some darnin' cotton at the Mercantile. Dunno as I'll be here when the train gits in." He winked at Pecos and departed. Pecos heaved a sigh of relief.

A whistle shrieked warning of the train's approach. The Kirbys evacuated the an-

cient flivver. Maw Kirby was already snif-
fling. Big Jim swallowed hard. Teton
gripped Bob's arm tightly. Buck, Slim, and
Pecos became suddenly, awkwardly diffi-
dent — afraid to appear emotional.

The train ground to a halt. Dick swung to
the platform before the train fully stopped.
He looked up and down the platform with a
swift glance, then called over his shoulder.

"No posse waitin'. Light, outlaws."
Lance and Doc heaved bags out, then
jumped to the platform. Teton was the first
to reach them. Dick side-stepped neatly and
thrust Lance into her arms. Then he gathered his father and mother into an embrace
that made even big Jim grunt.

"And Bob! Boy, I'm glad to see you."

Pecos, Buck, and Slim shuffled up. Doc
looked on, a wistful twist on his lips. Then
Pecos and the two cow-punchers mobbed
him.

"I spent five bucks on gold paint, yuh
danged walloper! Did yuh fetch back Kaiser
Bill's whiskers fer me?"

"Brung yuh five Luger pistols an' a swell
Dutch uniform," grunted Doc. "You kin
wear my tin hat on Sundays."

"Is that Doc Fogarty, Lance?" whispered
Teton.

"That's the notorious Sergeant Fogarty of

the dehorsed cavalry, Tonnie."

She slipped from Dick's arms and ran toward Doc. The next moment he was unmistakably kissed — twice.

"One for myself, the other for the family," she explained. Doc, red-eared and grinning, gulped and nodded.

"He didn't act so darned dumb when that French ma'amzelle manhandled him," chuckled Dick. "Great guns, what's that comin' down the street? Looks like a parade."

It was a parade, headed by the town band.

"Mebbe some sort uh posse," suggested Doc, uneasily groping for his gun.

"I reckon not," grinned Duck. "I'd make a guess that news uh your home-comin' kinda leaked out. Yo're the first uh the boys tuh git back. Chinook aims tuh kinda let yuh know yo're home."

It was a motley crowd that surged along in the wake of the band. Some were on horseback, shooting at the sky; others on foot; a few in machines, adding klaxons to the general noise — business men, gamblers, cowhands, saloon men. They led three horses with empty saddles decorated with bunting. And up in the lead of the parade rode the sheriff. That his presence might not be misconstrued, he carried a banner on which was painted in large red letters:

"*Welcome Home!*"

"So that's why you wanted Dick's saddle yesterday," Bob accused Slim. Pecos bent a keen eye on Buck. He had missed Lance's saddle that morning.

"As we didn't know where Doc's hull was," explained Buck, "the folks aroun' here kinda pooled in an' got him a rig. The saddle-maker made it fer first prize at the Fourth last year. The gent that won it soaked it when he went into the army. We got the sheriff to fix the parade. We aimed tuh have the band cached in the baggage-room, but Pecos headed the sheriff off, thinkin' he was after you boys. The way he talked, them old charges is dropped. Here comes the parade."

There was handshaking and back-slapping, and the three returned soldiers were boosted into their saddles and made to ride to the hotel, where long tables were laid with fitting decorations.

There was one man among the crowd that Lance greeted warmly. It was the heavy-paunched bartender from the Last Chance.

The banquet lasted into the afternoon. There were drinks and speeches and home-cooked food.

"An' to think," said Doc, a fat cigar

jammed into his teeth, "that we was nigh to hangin' Champ when we left this country."

"What tickles me most," Lance told Doc and Teton, "is the change in old Dick. He hasn't been two feet away from his dad since he landed."

"Promise me, Lance," whispered Teton, "that you'll tell me all about finding your mother. When is she coming here?"

"When she can get away," said Lance. "She has a hospital filled with wounded men. The skipper's going back as soon as the demobbing is finished. He'll bring her here. Gee, Tonnie, she's wonderful!"

"Her letters are more than wonderful."

"I didn't know she wrote you."

"There's a lot that you men don't know," smiled Teton mysteriously.

Jim Kirby and his women-folks went home in the flivver. The others rode horseback through the gray winter twilight, Pecos and Doc and Buck and Slim breaking trail through the drifts — Dick and Bob riding behind. The hills were white, the wind bleak and cold, but to the three returned soldiers it seemed just wonderfully quiet and peaceful. It was Montana. It was Home.

Because nothing should mar that homecoming of the three soldiers, no mention was made of the storm of disaster now threatening the two cow outfits. Nor was there, in the attitude of Bob Kirby, any hint of the bitter disappointment that had been his lot as the man who stayed home. But Lance knew, and as they rode side by side he reached over and gripped Bob Kirby's hand.

"Bob, old boy, we all savvy. It took guts to do what you've done. I hope you haven't been bothered with any fool notions about not enlisting."

"We couldn't all go, Lance. I'd be lyin' like hell if I said I don't envy you and Dick. It was shore tough to stick sometimes. Buck and Slim hated it as bad as I did. But even the draft board turned them down. Buck's eyes is bad, so they said, and Slim has a bum valve in his heart or something. But nobody ever called us slackers. Say, you three birds must have seen the scrap first-hand. Tell a man about it."

"Tell him about bringin' Doc back, Dick," suggested Lance with that twisted smile of his, "then Bob'll savvy why we don't care to remember."

Dick told about how he had found Doc, more dead than alive, shackled to a dead German, how Doc, out of a fog of horror and insanity, had carried, in his tortured brain, information that would have been of untold value save for the fact that the war had come to an end. Bob listened in awed silence.

"No wonder he's been decorated," said Bob softly.

Chapter XXXII

One incident occurred during that homeward ride. In the gathering dusk they met four riders. Lance and Dick recognized Lon Jimson. Also they noticed that Pecos and Buck separated so that the four men passed between them. Also Slim dropped behind so that the men must pass between him and Bob Kirby. The men had passed without speaking. But Lon Jimson's slit eyes had scrutinized the three army overcoats and the faces of the three men that wore the soldier clothes.

"I see the coyotes haven't got Jimson yet," said Dick.

"No. Jimson is the new stock inspector."

"What?" gasped Lance and Dick in unison.

"Jack Parsons had him appointed. The other three are working for Parsons."

"I noticed they packed saddle guns," said Lance.

"Uh-huh," agreed Bob with feigned indifference. "Likewise," put in Dick, "I see that you boys all go well heeled. Something brewing, Bob?"

"You'd just as well know, I reckon," said

Bob grimly. "Parsons has been building up his spread. Formed a company and bought up two or three outfits along the river. Their riders are scattered all over the country. For all we've ridden night and day, we keep losing stock. Our fences are cut, haystacks burned, and our horses run off. The Bench-K and the Circle Seven are broke. We're running on our bootstraps now. Jimson, of course, is working in with these damn cow-thieves. The sheriff is with us, but what can a few of us do against a hundred of these night-ridin' coyotes."

"So that's what Pecos meant in his letter," said Lance grimly. "Well, Bob, there's three more men on our side now. Two or three other boys from our outfit want to go back to punching cows. I reckon we'll give Parsons a scrap that will be a scrap. Eh, Dick?"

"You said it, Sailor."

"The question is," said Bob, "what will we use for money? The Bench-K owes Lance fifteen thousand dollars."

"Which don't matter a damn and you know it. Shall we clean up on this bird, Dick?"

"And the Circle Seven is as busted as we are," Bob went on. "Our credit is bent to the busting point. And we're bucking an outfit worth a million, if they're worth a cent. They're buying up land that the dryland farmers starved to death trying to cultivate. Ben Fisk and the bank have been grabbing up those deserted homesteads for a song. They have a crew of shrewd lawyers to tell them what to do. They play inside the law always."

"How about the fence-cutting and rustling?" put in Lance. "That was law-breaking when I left here."

"The question is to catch 'em at it. We're lucky not to have our home ranches burned down. Have to keep men on guard there all the time. Zack Tanner had the Circle Seven barn soaked with kerosene when Sultan killed him. He admitted the arson business before he died. . . . Implicated the others, but he croaked before Pecos and Jim could get a written confession from him."

"Tanner was alive when they found him, then?" asked Lance.

"Yes." Bob shot Lance a quick glance as he lit a cigarette in the gathering darkness. "He talked a lot. He died yellow. I reckon he figured he'd get a better break where he was goin', if he told what he knew. Just Jim and Pecos were there. Something he said sure hit Jim hard. He begun practicing shooting with his left hand. He's sure good, too. I think he aims to kill Lon Jimson some day. Pecos told me to keep 'em separated if I could. We've got to keep Jim from shooting Jimson. Jimson being stock inspector, they'd give Jim life. If Jim'd talk, I'd feel better. But he won't say why he's so bent on killin' Jimson."

Lance rode in silence. He knew why Jim Kirby had learned to shoot left-handed. Later that night, at the Circle Seven ranch, Pecos confirmed his suspicions.

"It was Lon Jimson that was after Teton that evenin' of the blizzard. Zack spilled it all. I had hell keepin' Jim from goin' after Lon then an' there. We gotta stop it some way if I have tuh shoot Jimson personally."

"No, Pecos," said Lance tonelessly, "I reckon that job falls to me. Don't worry, I'll not make a fool play of it. I'm not a kid any more. I'll try to talk to Jim. Pecos, we're going to lick this Parsons combine and do a neat job of it."

Dick and Bob had gone home. Pecos and Lance were alone in the big living-room.

They built up the fire in the fireplace and smoked as they thawed the chill from their bones. Doc came in with more wood.

"We're busted, kid," said Pecos. "I reckon I'm a plumb failure as a cow boss. I ran fifty-fifty with the Bench-K like you said an' both outfits is down tuh bedrock now."

"How many men have we?"

"Six. We need twice that many. But we can't hire cowhands fer nothin' a month an' beans."

"That's where you're wrong," grinned Lance. "Inside of a week we'll have a full crew. Eh, Doc?"

"I'll tell a man. An' every man uh them is a fightin' fool."

"If we win, they get paid double. If we lose, they lose. But those troopers don't savvy the meaning of that word 'lose.' "

Lance went to his room after a while. Pecos and Doc occupied another room. As Pecos prepared for bed, Doc found pencil and writing-paper.

"Pecos," he asked abruptly, after he had spent several minutes gnawing the end of the pencil, "ever have any dealin's by mail with she-dukes?"

"She-whos?"

"Earls an' what nots, lords, dukes, counts — she 'uns."

"Barrin' a few shootin' scrapes, a pasear er so at hoss-rustlin', an' runnin' wet hosses down on the Rio Grande," said Pecos haughtily, "I've led a respectable life. I ain't never fergot I was ol' man Hall's boy. No, sir. I seen a movin' pitcher uh one uh these she-dukes oncet. Theda Bara played it, wearin' a dress that fit like a rattlesnake's hide, with damn little front an' no back to it — held up by one gallus acrost her shoulder. A poem went with it . . . suthin' about a rag an' a bone an' a hunk uh hair. Look here, Doc, you ain't gone an got yorese'f snarled up in no she-duke's spider-web, have yuh?"

"What you don't know about nobility is shore a-plenty, Pecos. I kin see where you ain't gonna be much help to a man. Got a dictionary handy?"

"I got the last copy uh the 'Drover's Journal,' a book by a feller named Mark Something, 'Huckleberry Finn,' an' the new almanac."

Doc shook his head. The pencil was moistened and, being an indelible pencil, began the epistle with a vivid purple, "Deer Miz Burke, *alias* Lady Mansfield: I take my pen in hand to drop you a few lines. [Here the purplish hue faded dismally.] Like I promised to do so, I am leting you no the shape things is in her at the Circle-7. They are up agin er bad. Flat broke. Like you was afraid of, remember as per our talk? The sheriff lets on to be plum friendly but I never seen the John Law yet that would not bare watchin. They met us with a brass band and fed us up good at the Chinook House. We shore et and the kid made a speech that was rotten. So did me and Dick. This Parsons gent has made considerable snake tracks sinse we was gone, and it looks like somebody would haf to make a bunch quitter out of him and his outfit. But that will be easy as taller on a boot fer us. The wurst is not havin money fer runnin expenses. Just like you sed. It is shore cold here. Hopin this finds you the same. YRS. DOC FOGARTY."

Pecos had been snoring for an hour when Doc sealed the envelope and addressed it. Then with the air of a man who has successfully survived a trying ordeal, he lit a cigarette and prepared for bed. His disrobing was a matter of few moments. Spiral puttees were unwound, shoes and breeches removed, and the cigarette stub pinched out. Then the lamp was extinguished and Pecos was prodded over to one side of the double bed.

"Go makin' a practice uh that snorin'," Doc muttered at the audibly slumbering Pecos, "an' yuh'll sleep with a sock in yore mouth."

Five minutes later the snoring became a dual melody.

Chapter XXXIII

"This is the sort uh weather," announced Pecos, as he thawed the brownish icicles from his mustache, "that makes a feller wonder what he done with his summer's wages." He unbuckled his overshoes and kicked out of a pair of Angora wool chaps. He and Doc and Lance had been in the saddle since dawn. It was now after dark and they grinned at the hot food and the warmth of the cherry-red stove in the Mansfield living-room. A Rochester lamp sent a yellow glow about the room. A grate fire crackled. Before the fire was a huge leather chair. Its occupant was hidden, save for a pair of feet encased in tan army boots. Upon close observation one might detect an artificial stiffness to one of those booted legs. The boot fitted too well. Instead of army breeches, the man wore British-tailored Jodhpur riding-pants.

Pecos scowled at the feet. Lance and Doc exchanged startled glances. The man in the chair smoked away at a cigar, the smoke curling from the unseen lips.

"Well, I'm a son-of-a-gun," muttered Pecos. "Who's that?"

"Might be Parsons," suggested Doc, winking at Lance.

"Or some dude officer," added Lance. "Jump him out, Pecos."

But Pecos was not to be thus trapped. Instead he strode over and shoved a hand toward the occupant of the chair.

"I'm bettin' two-bits you're Burke."

"And you're Pecos," came from the chair. "Excuse me for not rising, but my store leg is unhinged. I'm damn glad to meet you, Pecos."

Lance and Doc rounded the chair and shook hands with Burke. Burke's artificial leg, with its boot, lay on a footstool.

"Sounds goofy, but the toes of that lost leg hurt like hell. Cold weather does it."

"I got a bottle uh snake-bite tonic that'll he'p 'er, Cap'n," grinned Pecos, stalking to the cellaret.

"Now what brings you here all of a sudden, skipper?" asked Lance. "We've only been back a week. Didn't expect you for a while yet."

"Just on my way to San Francisco. Thought I'd drop off on the way and see how things are going."

"Oh, we're getting along all right," lied Lance. "Cold, ain't it?"

"Glad you're making it okay, kid. Yeah,

cold as hell." Pecos came back with a bottle and glasses.

"How you fixed for feed, Lance?"

"We'll make it." Lance did not add that they had lost so many cattle that their hay would now feed the remnant of the Circle Seven and Bench-K herds.

The Chinaman called them to supper. When they again were lazing about, tobacco smoke clouding the air, Burke once more felt Lance out about his financial condition. But Lance had made up his mind to fight this through without Burke's assistance. The idea of taking money from Burke, his stepfather now, seemed somehow weak and spineless.

"I'll admit we're bucking a hard game, skipper. The Parsons combine have done their best to freeze us out. But we'll winter what stuff we have left. I'm sending for half a dozen of the boys to help us out. I'll manage to pay 'em off if I have to pay 'em in calves. There may be a scrap or two if Parsons cuts any more fences, and a few initiations into the Tar and Feather Society will sort of dampen their zest for burning haystacks. I don't look for any casualties. We'll just give 'em the bum's rush out of the country. When I cut Jack Parsons's sign, I'll work him over by hand. It'll sort of disappoint the boys when I let 'em find out they aren't to kill a few skunks. But this must be played without any shooting if possible."

"I'll drop in on you again on my way back from the coast, kid. Hope you can swing this all right. If you need dough, I've put plenty to your credit in the bank at Helena. Draw till you hit the bottom of it."

"You're a real pal, skipper. Don't think I'm ungrateful. But I went into this against Judge Truman's advice and I'm going to play my string out. If I go flooey, it'll be just too bad. Have another cigar."

Burke left for town the next day. Lance rode with him to the Kirby ranch, where Maw Kirby fed them fried chicken. Big Jim and Burke got on famously.

"Yeah, them gone toes uh yourn will hurt fer a long time. Same with this hand I lost. Shore odd. Usta git kinda chilblains that itched somethin' fierce. . . . Have some more chicken. You ain't eatin' enough tuh fatten a bird." Burke had eaten chicken until he felt on the verge of bursting.

"And," Teton added, "I'll be thinking you don't like my biscuits."

"Yeah," said Burke, "I've proved I didn't like biscuits. I ate six; that's all."

When he rode along the road to town, Burke felt happier than a king inheriting a new kingdom. He liked these people and their open-hearted hospitality.

He caught the train for Helena. For all his haste to reach San Francisco he spent a week in Montana's capital. Although he was still in the army and now held the rank of major, he wore civilian clothes. His week was spent mostly at the Montana Club, where he met a number of men. Among these was Captain Jack Parsons.

"Captain Parsons," said the banker who introduced Burke, "I want you to shake hands with Mr. Burke of New York. Mr. Burke has cattle interests in California. He's interested in polo ponies."

"Indeed! Selling or buying, Mr. Burke?"

"Both. I hear you have a few colts that might make polo ponies."

"Five," announced Parsons. "They're being schooled now at Pasadena. I'll give you a card to my stable boss. Look 'em over when you get to the coast. How about a little drink?"

They had several. Parsons, warmed by the liquor and prospects of a sale, insisted that Burke dine with him. Burke accepted. There were more drinks. Burke caught a late train for the coast. Now and then he chuckled softly to himself. In his pocket was a bill of sale for five polo ponies.

Parsons took Burke's check for five thousand dollars to the bank the following morning.

"Sorry, Mr. Parsons," said the cashier, "but Mr. Burke has stopped payment on this check."

"What the devil is the idea?" snapped Parsons. "I sold him some horses — gave him a bill of sale. The man is either a crook or he's crazy."

"Mr. Burke is not a crook," smiled the banker, "nor have I ever thought him in the least demented. I've known him for twenty-five years. I fancy, Mr. Parsons, that there has been some mistake somewhere."

Parsons scowled blackly. He had fancied that Burke was quite drunk when they closed the deal. Perhaps, sobered, Burke had wired the banker to stop the check. For Burke had paid a big price for half-broken ponies.

"When did Burke stop payment on this check?"

"Let me see. It was two days ago, Mr. Parsons."

"Damn it, man, I hadn't met Burke two days ago. The check was made out last night!"

"Then I would surmise," said the banker coldly, "that Mr. Burke anticipated the meeting — also the check. Good morning, Mr. Parsons."

Jack Parsons was visibly upset as he left the bank. He scented a trap. The burden of guilt rested heavily on his mind, for those five horses were stolen — colts out of the stallion Sultan. He sent a long wire to his stable foreman at Pasadena. The reply came that afternoon.

"Moving ponies to Arizona. You know me, Jack. It will take more than a bill of sale to get these geldings." It was signed Bill Ryan.

"Now, Mister Slicker Burke," smiled Parsons, "it's your move. And there are some boys in Deer Lodge for passing bad checks." He poured himself a drink from the bottle in his club locker. But even the good whisky could not deaden Parsons's qualms of fear. What the devil was this Burke fellow's game? Who was Burke? He sought out several men with whom he had seen Burke talking — club members, men of solid finance.

"Burke? Why he's a New York millionaire. Best sort of rating with Dun and Bradstreet. Eh? Crooked? Hardly. Didn't need to be crooked. Had a card to the club from the Governor of Montana."

"Well," mused Parsons, "he won't get

those ponies. But what the hell's his game?"

But there was no reply to that haunting question. There was to be a reply some day. And that day was not distant.

Chapter XXXIV

A Chinook wind was cutting the drifts. The whine of its warm blast called men out of the bunk-houses. It was St. Valentine's day. Lance pulled his horse to a halt at the Kirby gate. Teton met him with a gay smile. The pack of hounds following Lance almost knocked her down in their boisterous greeting.

"Come on, Tonnie. Get your horse. A camp-tender from Olson's sheep outfit came by early this morning. Wolves got into one of his bands last night and killed about fifty sheep. We may get a chase out of 'em." Teton nodded, eyes bright with excitement. Lance saddled Midnight and they rode away in high spirits, for a wolf chase is bound to be jammed with thrills.

The older dogs trailed behind the horses, but the big pups roamed on ahead, chasing an occasional rabbit, their tongues lolling, puppy eyes bright with joy.

"The big chumps," grinned Lance. "If we jump a wolf, they'll be too played out with rabbit-chasing to get near the brute. It'll be up to Brin and Bridget and Don and Sparticus. Bridget's disgusted with her kids."

For so it seemed. When the long-legged, panting pups returned with moist caresses, their mother turned away her shaggy head and ignored them.

They kept to the ridges. The older dogs kept sharp lookout. They ran by sight rather than by scent, and little they missed as they trailed along behind the two horses.

They found the sheep. The three men were stripping pelts from the ripped carcasses. All about them, staining the melting snow, was grim evidence of the wanton cruelty of the wolves.

The Swede herder told them he thought there must be three of the wolves. Lance picked up the stale tracks in a coulée half a mile beyond.

"They're headed for the Bad Lands, Tonnie. Hope they're full. That'll mean they'll coulée-up and sleep. And they'll be slowed down by full bellies. Bet we get 'em. Gosh, those three gray devils could sure kill a lot of calves and colts this spring. That's all we need to finish us. Come on."

They had gone five miles when big Brin swung past them, Bridget at his heels. A mile away a black spot moved across a snow bank.

"Atta Brin! Get 'em, sons!" called Lance. The pack streaked past, lean bodies fairly skimming across the ground. The big pups, not in the least understanding what it was all about, lumbered behind, yipping a little with excitement. . . . The race was on.

Brin ran like a streak, Bridget alongside him. A mouse-colored greyhound named Spinner shot past the two lead hounds. Lance and Teton rode at a run, reckless with the fever of the race.

Midnight floundered through a drifted coulée, wetting Teton with snow. Lance saw that horse and rider were safe, then raced on.

"Head for the next coulée!" he called back. Up ahead, Spinner was shortening the distance between him and the running wolf. Foot by foot the fleet greyhound gained on the killer. He was at the wolf's flank now, now alongside. A gray shape flung into the air, then lit running.

"Spinner flopped 'im!"

Again the greyhound turned the wolf over but did not attempt to hold the big gray beast. Spinner, when younger, had once limped for many weeks with a ripped shoulder. Now the swift racing dog was too wise to do battle with the bulkier wolf. Again he flopped the wolf, who halted, snarling and snapping, to kill this tormenter. But it was big Brin who met the wolf's attack. Brin, who was part Dane, and whose bulk was equal to that of the wolf.

Wolf and dog reared, met with white teeth bared, then rolled over and over in the snow. Brin's powerful jaws were locked in the wolf's neck, just below the ear. A shaggy shape ripped in; Bridget, her punishing jaws snapping at the wolf's flank. Sparticus and Blue circled the fight, enjoying an occasional slash. Ruffs stiff, eyes red, white teeth snapping, the pups and a comical, slow-gaited Airedale came up now. The Airedale halted, brown eyes alight, wire hair bristling. Then he went into it and was lost in the mêlée. A pup catapulted into the fray, emerged with a yip and a little three-cornered tear in his shoulder; then, with puppy rage, charged more warily.

They had the wolf stretched out when Lance got there. Brin was worrying at the wolf's torn throat. The Airedale and Bridget and Spinner ripped savagely at the twitching carcass of the dead killer. The chase was over. Teton shuddered and rode away. "I'll wait over here. Never could get hardened to this part of it. I'm always hoping the wolf will get away."

"I used to be that way," admitted Lance. "It didn't seem sportin' as Dad used to say, for a pack to pull down one wolf. But I saw a

310

pup or two ripped something fierce and lost sympathy. Then I rode up on five wolves after a colt one day. They were circling the colt. The mare was fighting with all four feet and her teeth for her baby. They were trying to hamstring the colt. I was lucky enough to get two with my six-shooter. Now I don't feel any qualms about killing Mister Gray-wolf."

The pups now began charging excitedly at the bloody gray body. The older dogs, with the exception of Brin, now lay in the snow, panting, their work completed. But Brin still lay crouched, his jaws clamped on the torn gray throat — growling softly, not bothering the foolish pups who fought the dead wolf with ruffs bristling.

"Let's go," said Lance. "No time to bother skinning him. The pelt's spoiled, anyhow. And there's two more wolves between us and the Missouri River. Come, dogs!"

But it was almost dusk and they were thirty miles from home when they caught the second wolf. Moreover, they were on Jack Parsons's range. They could, from the ridge where they now sat their horses, see the corrals and buildings of the Parsons home ranch. Lance brought out his binoculars.

"We'll see if anyone's moving around down there," he laughed. He was jesting, but there was a grim twist to his smile. Since six of Lance's army buddies had begun riding the range, no more fences had been cut, no more haystacks destroyed.

"Nobody in sight," Lance reported, his glasses searching the ranch. "Smoke coming from the cook cabin, though. Whoa, there's some cattle coming toward the ranch — riders with 'em."

"I can see that without glasses," added Teton.

"Eight, nine, twelve men. About forty head of cattle. They're puttin' 'em in the shed. Well I'll be doggoned!" He whistled softly. Presently he lowered the glasses and turned to Teton.

"At least six head of those cows are Circle Seven cows. I've shoveled hay to 'em too often to forget their markings. Anyhow, Pecos gave me some long, hard lessons in remembering oddly marked cattle. I'd know those six head anywhere. And there's more than those six, bet on that."

"Look, Lance — coming!" She pointed along the ridge. Four riders were coming toward them. Lance focused his glasses on the distant riders.

"Lon Jimson, Jack Parsons, and two

strangers. They've sighted us, too. They're half a mile away." He put the glasses back in their leather case on his saddle and jerked out his .45. He had finished the second wolf with a bullet. Now he ejected the empty shell and filled the chamber with a fresh cartridge. Also he shoved a cartridge into the sixth chamber, usually left empty under the hammer. Teton watched him, a little frightened. Lance was smiling crookedly, his eyes on the approaching four riders.

"What are you going to do, Lance?"

"Nothing, I hope. We'd avoid meeting them if we could, but this ridge is our only way back out of the Bad Lands. Got a gun on you?"

"A thirty-eight Colt's police pistol."

"Keep it handy. I don't know what sort of play they'll make. But if they get me, you quit the flats. Shoot at anybody that follows you. If they halt me, you ride on and keep riding."

"But I won't run away and . . ."

"You'll run, Tonnie. Streak it for the ranch. You can only make things worse by staying."

Chapter XXXV

They rode to meet the four men. The ridge was narrow. On either side was a frozen adobe, melted at the top to a slimy mud that sloped abruptly on either side. In order to pass, they must almost brush stirrups with the four riders, riding abreast.

But plainly Parsons had no intention of letting the two pass without first halting them. The dogs, weary and indifferent to the riders, trailed behind Lance and Teton.

"One shot and Brin will jump something. A horse's tail, like as not. Pecos has 'em ruined. Then the pack will join in. It'll be a great mêlée if anybody shoots, that's all." They rode on, side by side.

"Mind you keep on riding if they don't stop you, Tonnie."

"All right." Her voice was calm enough.

The four men halted when Lance and Teton came up. The four horses completely blocked the trail. Parsons swept off his hat with mocking gallantry. The others leered at Lance and the girl.

"This is an unexpected pleasure, Miss Kirby. Greetings," he ignored Lance, save with his eyes.

"The pleasure is all yours, Mr. Parsons," Teton smiled frigidly.

"Since you are so interested in seeing what goes on down at my ranch," Parsons suggested, "I shall take great pleasure in offering you the opportunity of a closer inspection. And them I'm going to ask for some sort of explanation concerning the trespassing on my range. I have signs posted warning trespassers."

"Some other time, thanks," returned Teton coldly. "We're late now. Let us pass, please." She edged Midnight forward. Jimson shoved his horse in front of her mount, halting her with a leering grin.

"Miss Kirby asked to pass," said Lance, his voice shaking a little. "I reckon you didn't notice I was along *this time,* Jimson. You know what I'm getting at. So do some other folks. Zack talked some. Under this wolf pelt that's across my saddle pommel is a gun. It's covering you now, Jimson. It's about to go off and when it does, you'll be deader than this wolf hide. Let the lady pass."

"Stay where you are, Jimson," snapped Parsons. "I got the idiot covered."

"But my gun's cocked," smiled Lance. "Lon'll be dead before I quit my saddle. You're delaying us, Jimson. Pull aside. I've

315

told myself that I'll either run you out of the country, Jimson, or kill you. Take your choice of postponing the journey or getting killed now. Pull aside."

Lon Jimson saw the gun under the wolf pelt jut forward. With a sickly grin he let Teton ride past.

"Yore jawin' won't save my hide, Jack Parsons," growled the man. "I know when tuh lay down a pair uh deuces."

"That's the best thing you do, Jimson, is lay down. It's the cur in you." Parsons was white with anger. His hand tugged nervously at his gun. Jimson eyed his employer with an ugly sneer. Lance sat his horse, smiling at the pair. He was giving Teton a chance to get clear. She was pushing Midnight to a lope now. Lance gripped his gun and waited, determined to go down fighting.

"Damn you, Parsons," growled Jimson, "that ain't no way tuh talk to a man as has done as I done by yuh. There's suthin' you don't know about that made me let that gal through. . . . Between me'n the Kirbys."

Parsons turned to Lance, a calculating glitter in his eyes.

"Do you know of any reason why I shouldn't kill you, Mansfield? I have three witnesses that will go on the stand and swear I shot in self-defense."

316

"Will they, though? One witness might stand pat. Two is a bigger risk. But, no three men of their type will hang together. You're a good enough crook to know that. There'll be a prosecuting attorney at Helena that will make monkeys of them. No, Parsons, you can't kill me here and get away with it. Jimson hates your guts. The other two will share Jimson's fear that you will murder them because they know too much. So they'll either testify the truth or shoot you in the back.

"That's one reason you won't murder me here. There's a second reason riding on that black gelding. She'll swear you waylaid us and her testimony will go larther than the combined words of three such paid dogs as these. She's riding a horse that will outtravel anything in this country and she's now out of rifle range.

"Reason number three is this: My gat now is pointed square at your belly, Parsons, and I'd rather pull this trigger than see Santa Claus. I'll kill you like a dog in one holy minute if you don't get under way. These hounds are trained to pull down anything I shoot at. They'll tear you to ribbons while you're dying. Now, while my gun's pointed at your guts, tell these three birds to travel along. When they've gone, I'll let you follow. I'll kill you some day, perhaps. Maybe to-day. I'm holding a pat hand, Parsons. Six lead aces. If you feel lucky, start the game. . . . I'll finish it."

"Go ahead, Jack," taunted Lon Jimson. "Let's see the brand uh yore toughness. You was shore eager fer Lon tuh see how good this jasper kin shoot. Now you try 'im. Don't let 'im bluff yuh, Parsons." Lon Jimson grinned at the other two men, who grinned back. They had no particular love for Jack Parsons. Theirs was the natural curiosity of their breed. Would Parsons call Mansfield's pat hand? Was Parsons that game?

Had Lance kept silent now, probably Parsons would have weakened. But Lance, playing a desperate game of one against four guns, sought to further dissuade Parsons from murder.

"I'm only sorry that my skipper ain't here. He's the man that's going to keep you from grabbing the Circle Seven and the Bench-K. Burke's got the . . ."

"Who?" Parsons snapped the question, a new glint in his slit eyes.

"Burke. Know him?" Lance wondered if the two had ever met.

"New York?" snarled Parsons. "And California?"

"And of the A.E.F. He queered your arresting me in France."

"Damn me for a thin-brained fool! So that's the Burke? Your backer, eh? Then he can bury your carcass when he finds . . ."

Parsons suddenly spurred his horse, shooting at the same time. But Lance was waiting for such a move. His bullet ripped through the flesh of Parsons's upper arm. He had shot to kill, but his aim was spoiled. Parsons's gun spun through the air.

Lance yelled, "Atta Brin!" and jumped his horse into Lon Jimson's mount. Jimson's bullet sang past Lance's face. The dogs were at the horses now, swinging on to the terrified animals' tails. Four horses piled in a tangle, pitching, kicking. Lance lay along his mount's neck and jabbed his spurs home. Over his shoulder he saw Jimson thrown into the snarl of hoofs, dogs, and mud. Parsons was thrown clear and was crawling toward his gun. Lance raced along the ridge, whistling shrilly for the hounds to follow. Then he shot in the air. Brin heard the shot and raced after his master, the other dogs following.

A couple of miles farther on Lance caught up with Teton. She was badly frightened, but brave enough to force a smile.

"Those shots, Lance! Honey! I was afraid they'd . . ."

They rode stirrup touching stirrup. Lance reached out an arm and pulled her toward him. "Gee, Tonnie, I love you. I've always loved you, I reckon."

"And there's never been a minute when I didn't love you," she laughed gently, almost timidly, as he kissed her again.

"And to think," she said as they rode along, holding hands, "it's St. Valentine's day."

"Is it?"

"*Is* it? Where's your chivalry, pardner? There was the place where you should have swallowed your surprise and, lying like a gentleman, pretended that you knew all along."

"You'll marry me right away, Tonnie?"

"When your mother comes, I will. I'll run the Bench-K iron on you and there'll be one maverick less on this range. It's time you were claimed."

"Hogtied with the preacher's knot," grinned Lance. "Hope I don't have to push a plow to support you."

"Just so some one don't take a shot at you and you wind up by pushing up the wild flowers."

"I don't look for trouble."

"Trouble may hunt you, though. Lance, I'm afraid of those men. Afraid for you and my dad and brothers."

"I don't think Parsons will start much." But if Lance could have seen the group at the Parsons ranch, he might have thought along different lines — for Jack Parsons, white with pain and fury, was planning war.

Chapter XXXVI

Back at the ranch, Lance told Pecos of the cattle he had seen at the Parsons's ranch.

"But," said Pecos, in answer to Lance's suggestion that they ride down there in a body and claim their cattle, "them cows is a long time gone by now if Parsons thinks you spotted 'em. What a fool play you made, takin' Teton down that direction."

"I know it. Didn't realize we were that far. But I sure spoiled Parsons's gun arm for a few weeks. I don't know what kept me from killing him. I sure meant to at the time. I'm glad now I didn't. The hounds saved my bacon, bless 'em. Where's Doc?"

"Doc pulled out about noon. We got word that Parsons had a warrant sworn out for him as one of Dutch Henry's old gang. Doc's takin' to the rough country fer a spell. There's a bran-new deputy in the bunkhouse now waitin' fer Doc tuh show up. I told him Doc might be in any minute."

"Doc went alone?" scowled Lance.

"Plumb alone. Didn't want no company. He seemed tuh get a kick outa runnin' off into the hills."

It was nearing midnight. Lance had taken

Teton home, then ridden on to the Circle Seven. Lance was eating as he talked to Pecos. Suddenly the door opened and Bob Kirby stepped in nodding a brief greeting. Bob's face was grave, his eyes troubled.

"Jim pulled out to-night after Teton got home," he announced in a hard, flat tone. "He listened to her tell about meeting Parsons and Jimson — sat there smoking calm and thoughtful, but he didn't fool me. So when the folks had gone to bed, I watched Jim. He's taken to sleeping out in the barn loft lately on account of fires being set. I put out my light and watched the barn door. There's a pretty good moon to-night. Directly I saw him lead out his horse and ride off, I woke Dick and then rode over here. What's eatin' at Jim, anyhow?"

"He's gone tuh kill Lon Jimson, Bob," said Lance. "I wish I'd killed Lon when the play came right to-day. But I didn't. Now Jim's gone to do the job."

"But why?" questioned Bob. "What's Lon Jimson done that calls for a killing?"

Lance explained. Dick burst into the room, but half-clothed and a heavy cartridge belt about his hips.

"Looks like Jim's kinda touched off the dynamite, boys," said Pecos.

"If I'd known what I know now," said

Bob Kirby a little unsteadily, "I'd have killed Jimson long ago."

"That's what I should have done, Bob," gritted Lance. "I knew it all the time."

"And to think," put in Dick, "that I herded with that damn skunk when I stayed at Parsons's place. Pecos, what'll we do now? You're the oldest head at the game."

"Wake up the boys in the bunk-house." said Pecos grimly, reaching for his gun belt. "Fetch that deputy along if he'll come. Then we're goin' tuh head Jim an' pay this Parsons spread a visit. Dick, we kin use that information you give me about them hidden corrals. The time has come. We're gonna feed a bait uh lead pizen to them cow-thieves. Wish the sheriff was here, but his deputy'll do."

"Doc Fogarty will be off us for life for not letting him in at the showdown," said Dick. "But it can't be helped."

Lance roused the men at the bunk-house. The deputy scowled uncertainly but pulled on his boots and hat.

"You're positive about those cattle, Mansfield?"

"Absolutely. Dick Kirby knows about some hidden corrals they use. Jimson and Zack Tanner built 'em back in a box cañon. They don't know that Dick ever found 'em." Lance rolled a cigarette and grinned wryly.

"One man had better stay here at the ranch. Can't afford to leave the place unguarded. I know it's tough lines on the man that loses out on the fun, but if Parsons thought this ranch was unguarded, he'd send a man to burn us out. Better draw lots."

It fell to Pickott to stay. "All I hope is that some birds will try to smoke me out," he said. "Me'n the Chink will make believers out o' them, and I don't mean perhaps."

Pickott swallowed his disappointment as he watched the others ride away. Then he built up the grate fire in the living room and turned on the Victrola. Sleep was out of the question. He was still playing records when a high-powered car roared up to the door. Pickott stepped out on the veranda, a .45 in each hand.

"Don't shoot!" called a crisp voice from the rear seat. "You might hit somebody."

"Captain Burke!" gasped Pickott.

"And wife," added Burke, scrambling out and reaching a fur-mittened hand to some one swathed in bearskin robes. "What's the idea of the cordial Colt's welcome, Pickott?"

Pickott explained briefly and in the

manner of a soldier reporting. Burke turned to the two men in the front seat.

"Shut 'er off. Cover the radiator and come in. We're about in time, by the looks of things. Cold, Janet?"

"No, not cold. But worried."

They went into the living-room. Pickott found the Chinese cook chattering about the kitchen.

"Throw together a lot of coffee with whiskers on it, Charlie. We got company. A lady in the party. Savvy?"

"You betcha, savvy. Alleesame hot time chop-chop ketchem hamanegg double-time damn pronto. My name not Charlie. Alleesame callem Ah Hell. Be bossyman kitchen. Cowboy vamoose. Savvy?"

Pickott beat a retreat to the living-room. "The cook reports that his name is Ah Hell and that breakfast is coming up, Captain."

Somewhere a bell jangled harshly. "Telephone," explained Pickott, and went to answer it. "First time it's worked in a week. They run the line along the horse-pasture fence and when a bull rubs a post down, the line goes on the hummer." He picked the receiver from the hook. "Howdy! Hello! Yeah. Who! No, they done left, Miss Kirby, but hold the line." He turned to Burke. "It's Teton Kirby, askin' for Bob and Dick and her dad."

"I'll talk to her," said Burke. He took the phone.

"This is Burke. Yes. . . . I sure did bring her. . . . Great! . . . I'm shoving off for the Parsons place in a jiffy. I'll stop any fireworks, believe me. It'll disappoint the boys, but killing folks went out of vogue when the Armistice was declared. Those wild hyenas don't know the war's over. Don't fret that pretty head of yours another minute. And Janet will be tickled to death to see you. Bring your mother and those papers I mailed you from California. And don't worry. I'll stop this range war right now. Your damn tootin'. Have the gang back for lunch. G'bye. See you about noon. Bundle up; it's colder'n hell."

"Such language," protested Janet.

"Was I cussin' again? Sorry, dear. It slipped out." He turned to the two men who had ridden in the front seat.

"Either of you boys know the road to Parsons's ranch?"

"I think I can find it," said the big man who had driven. "I was there once or twice, you know — buying cattle."

"Good," Burke chuckled. The two men smiled a little. Each of the two men might have been business men. They were well-groomed, spare of speech, unobtrusive of manner. But Pickott's quick scrutiny had seen the badges under their coats and the shoulder holsters under their armpits.

"Fly cops," he mentally labeled them.

"Is the road to Parsons's ranch passable, Pickott?"

"It's rough an' you'll need chains."

"We have chains on all four wheels. You'd as well come along with us."

"I was told to stay here as guard, Captain," came Pickott's reluctant admission.

"There's a car behind us with three men besides the driver. They'll be guard enough." Burke grinned and the two officers smiled thinly.

"Then I'm your pilot, skipper."

Chapter XXXVII

They gulped down black coffee and a hasty breakfast. Janet Burke seemed a little sad, but smiled bravely enough whenever Burke looked her way. He knew that she felt more than a little upset, here in this house that had been Tom Mansfield's home. He shared something of that same discomfort.

Burke had never allowed her to unbury her past. Always he had kissed the words from her lips.

"Janet, I love you. Nothing you or anyone can say could make me think you'd ever done anything wrong. It's dead, that past of yours — dead and best forgotten. I know you loved Tom Mansfield once when you were just a kid. I know that I'm the only man that ever really won your real love. And don't let yourself think that Tom Mansfield killed himself because of you. He wasn't that breed of weakling."

When the others were in the car, Burke held her in his arms, there by the grate fire.

"I hate like the devil to leave you here, dear. But the Kirbys will be here in a little while. Only by nipping this thing in the bud can I prevent a bad scrap."

"I'll be all right, dear," she told him. "I'm glad I had the courage to come here. I feel somehow different about it all. As if Tom understood everything and was wishing me happiness. Sounds foolish, but I feel that he expected me to come here someday, to find my son. That sounds silly, does it not? Now you must go, dear. I won't be afraid, really. Quite the contrary, I rather wish to be alone for a little while." She kissed him warmly and he joined his companions. The powerful motor roared and the car swung into the moonlit night.

When they had gone, Janet stood staring thoughtfully into the fire. Ah Hell padded about softly, eager to serve this beautiful lady. Better than anyone, this aged Chinaman had known Tom Mansfield. Behind the opaque brightness of his brown eyes lay the wisdom of his race. When the table was cleared he put a fresh log on the fire.

Janet walked to the bookshelves that lined the walls. Many of those books had been in India when she was Tom Mansfield's wife. Her eyes swept the long lines of expensive bindings. Mansfield loved his books and kept them carefully, in an orderly fashion: Dickens here, Thackeray there, Burns, Chaucer, Keats — Kipling in crimson binding. She had given him the Kipling set for his birthday. She had often sat through the evening reading aloud from "Kim," when Tom was sober enough to listen. She had been reading aloud from "Kim" that last evening at Rangoon as they idled away an hour before they left for the officer's dance. Tom had drunk heavily that day. Otherwise he would not have so forgotten himself as to knock down a young officer for making harmless love to his wife. The young officer always made those silly love declarations to any woman who would listen. It was a joke among the other officers. No one had ever taken Lieutenant Harry Stanley seriously. . . . He invariably came around the next morning and apologized, and stayed for lunch perhaps, or a whisky and soda.

Janet, until that night, had always kept clear of Harry Stanley's silly speeches. But she had gone out on the veranda with a headache, and the young cub officer had found her. It was dark. It is doubtful if the young ass knew who the woman in the porch swing really was. He was on his knees pouring forth an intoxicated plea of devotion when Tom Mansfield stalked up out of the shadows.

The scene had been a painful one. Tom, drunker than usual, Stanley lying there on the veranda, battered and horribly bloody. Tom Mansfield, heedless of the crowd that gathered, openly, hotly, insanely branding Janet, his young wife — much younger than himself — with the red brand of infidelity; words that might be easily regretted but never forgotten; words that would keep the tongues of gossip wagging in India and Great Britain for many a day. For Janet Mansfield had come from the theatrical world and had been accepted only because she was Tom Mansfield's wife. Add to that the unmistakable fact that she was the most attractive woman in the Indian army. The wives of other officers, women who had accepted this Stanley chap's maudlin love-making with a cigarette and a smile of amused tolerance, now were more than eager to brand this particular incident as something sinister and unclean.

It was old Sir James Mansfield, Tom's uncle, colonel and post commander, who silenced Tom with a growled order, then sent him to his quarters under arrest. Then that white-haired old gentleman and officer had left with Janet. She passed the battery of accusing ayes with high-held chin, but her heart was as ice within her. They never saw her again at Rangoon. Sir James had put her aboard a steamer that night and she had left India forever.

Major Tom Mansfield had left soon afterward. Sir James had accepted his resignation from the army.

Upon the advice of Sir James, Janet had filed suit for divorce. Lance, then aged five, had been cared for by a governess at Sir James's home. Janet came every day to see him.

Then came the divorce trial. To the consternation of Sir James and the utter terror and grief-stricken horror of Janet, Tom Mansfield was given custody of his son. He sailed that night for America and had taken Lance with him. He had vanished as completely as if he had died. And in time, gossip grew weary of the scandal of it all. Janet hid her grief with the skill of an actress. Out of the wreckage stood the tall, white-haired figure of Sir James, her one friend.

And now she had come to the house where Tom had come with his son, his whisky, and the bitter blackness of his memories. There were his books, his pipes, his fire into which he had stared, night after night — drinking, remembering — ripped and stabbed by pride, by love, by remorse. There, in this house of memory, had he died by his own hand, driven by just what motives he alone knew to ending his life with his own gun. Behind him he had left his house in order. He had left without the gesture of farewell.

The Chinaman poked the fire into a blaze. Lady Janet's hand was icy cold as she reached for the crimson-bound copy of "Kim." Tom had once called it "our book." She did not see the eyes of Ah Hell watching. She did not see the smile flit across his parchment face as she lifted the book from its place.

Fearfully she opened the book. Rather it came open at a page marked with a leather book-mark. A sheet of thick note-paper with the Mansfield crest lay there. That sheet of paper carried an undated message in Tom Mansfield's handwriting. To Janet, it was a message. To anyone else it was simply the scribbling of some one who had found a bit of pleasing verse and copied it:

I built a chimney for a comrade old;
I did the service not for hope or hire.
And then I traveled on in winter's cold,
Yet all the day I glowed beside the
fire.

It was one of Edwin Markham's poems. The book was significantly marked at the page where Janet had left off reading that night so many years ago. As if the man, in passing, knew that some day she would find the book and open it.

Ah Hell padded his way into the kitchen. Had he seen Tom Mansfield, that night before he died, pen those lines on the note-paper and, selecting this crimson-bound book, carefully place it where the leather marker parted the pages? Had Ah Hell, with his sphinx-like understanding, read its meaning? Ah Hell alone could tell the answer to that riddle, and one might better ask of a rock its age and expect reply.

With the book and its message in her hands, Janet knelt and prayed for the man who had so wronged her prayed for Tom Mansfield who had built this home and was too afraid, or too proud, to ask her to share it. She had gone on hoping that she would someday find it, knowing that she would find it in her heart to forgive.

When Teton came, Janet met her with a gay smile.

Chapter XXXVIII

The crimson flashes of guns ripped a gray dawn. Brimstone Burke, roundly cursing a stalled motor, heard the faint echo of gunfire.

"Almost there and this blankety-danged motor coughs like a sick cow and dies off. I'd hoof it, only this damned peg leg of mine is an anchor."

"It's two miles to Parsons's place," grumbled Pickott. "Hell of a note, gettin' this far, then goin' lame. Never did trust these machines."

They grouped about the lifted hood with that hopeful hopelessness of men with a machine that is perfect, yet does not respond. There is nothing quite so dead as a dead motor — especially an expensive one.

And two miles away a battle was beginning. Men squatted behind woodpiles, rocks, and corrals, squinting along carbine barrels. In the buildings other men, men who were warm and better sheltered, joked, cursed, and gulped hot coffee as they jerked gun levers. Jack Parsons strode up and down the long bunk-house, his bandaged arm in a silken sling, smoking and lashing his men with words.

"Why the devil don't you terriers charge those men out there! I pay you to fight and you hole up like a bunch of coyotes."

"We'll lick 'em our own way, eh, boys?" snarled a giant Texan who was the recognized leader of Parsons's hired fighting men. "Us boys savvies our game without no advice. If you're rarin' tuh bust out that door, I don't see no bars on it tuh stop yuh, Jack. We might shoot straighter if we had a shot uh redeye."

A shot from outside whined through the window. Parsons ducked. The big Texan chuckled softly. The cabins nestled in the cañon. On either side sloped steep ridges. Save for a scattered growth of scrub pines, an occasional boulder, the ridges afforded no shelter for the attacking party. So they had crept down into the cañon, among the corrals and sheds, scattering like quail.

They had planned to surprise the Parsons faction, but a trick of fate had ruined the bit of strategy. A gun had been accidentally discharged. The alarmed men inside the bunkhouse had met their rush with a ready fire that sent the attacking party to quick shelter. What had been intended for a surprise attack had now become a siege.

Pecos and his men had missed Jim Kirby. Not a trace of the big cow-man had been seen.

"Mebby," said Pecos, "we passed him in the dark. He mighta heard us comin' an', mistakin' us fer Parsons's outfit, took to the brush as we rode past."

"Mebby so." Bob Kirby's voice lacked conviction. "But if they got Jim, may God have mercy on 'em. They'll git none from me an' Dick."

"When one uh them easy-goin', level-headed cusses like Bob Kirby gits on the prod," Pecos told Lance as the two shared the shelter of a haystack, "they're shore hell on wheels. No stoppin' 'em till they drop dead. Then a man can't be too sure they won't keep shootin'."

Bob and Dick Kirby lay behind the corral branding-chute.

"What do you reckon become of Jim, Dick?"

"Wish I could make a decent guess, Bob. He's after Lon Jimson. He either got Jimson or was killed a-tryin'. I don't think we ever caught up with him. He was ridin' Wart-hog. Wart-hog would uh nickered the minute he sighted us er caught our scent."

"But if he'd jumped out Lon, the rest uh the Parsons gang would uh bin millin' around instead uh sleepin' when we come off the slope." Bob took a snap-shot at the cabin window. "Damn this Injun-fightin'. It's as excitin' as a ice-cream social. Cold, too."

"We're doin' no good peckin' away at that cabin. They got grub an' a fire. We got a cold wind an' empty bellies. Can't win much layin' here. If we charge in the daylight, they'll cut us down in our tracks. Feel like takin' a little stroll, Bob?"

"Stroll? I don't get yuh, Dick."

"Them hidden corrals is about half an hour's stiff walk. I think Jim knew about 'em. He mighta had a hunch he'd find Jimson there."

"Then let's go. Can't do much good here." They crept along the log corral, dodged across an open space, and slipped up the cañon that was graying with the coming of daylight.

They had been hitting a stiff gait over the uneven ground for fifteen minutes when a gruff voice bit the silence.

"Reach fer the clouds, Polecats!"

"All right, Jim," called Dick. "Don't go shootin' yore family!"

"Great gosh!" Jim Kirby stepped into the trail, a long-barreled .45 swinging in his hand. "What you kids doin' here?"

"Huntin' you, dang it."

"Figgered ol' Jim was gittin' too old tuh take care uh hisse'f, eh? But I'm right glad tuh see you boys. Need some help movin' some cattle uh ourn that Parsons has hid up the cañon. What's the shootin' about? I figgered when I found them three gents dead at the corals, the Parsons outfit had split an' was fightin' 'er out."

"Three men dead at the corrals?"

"Lon Jimson an' two more," said big Jim grimly. "I was just slippin' fer home when I heard you two puffin' along up the trail. God! Listen!"

A terrific roar, crashing, echoing, came up the cañon. . . . A volley of shots. . . . A terrific crash. . . . Then silence.

"Hell's busted," grunted Dick. "Come on!" He raced back along the crooked trail, Bob and Jim Kirby at his heels.

A high-powered, foreign-made motor had suddenly come to life.

"I thought it was that dang gas-line all along. The —"

"Get in," snapped Burke, taking the wheel. "Hang on. We're leaving Cheyenne!" He slid in the gears and the big car leaped forward. Burke ripped into high gear and opened the throttle. Ahead lay the road down the ridge, rutty, slippery, treacherous. Pickott, in the front seat beside Burke, shouted in his ear.

"Road drops down sudden off the ridge. Bad slant."

"Gotcha!" Burke flung the word through set jaws. The headlights suddenly showed a yawning black chasm ahead. Burke, gripping the wheel, slammed on brakes that squealed shrilly. A brake rod snapped. Ping! The big black car gave a sickening lurch, righted somehow, and dipped over the black edge, motor backfiring like a machine-gun. Like some shiny, fire-eyed monster it catapulted down the slope, spitting fire, roaring, shrieking. At the wheel Burke sat with lips bared in a ghastly grin. The machine hit level ground, throttle wide open. Lurching like a thing gone mad, it sped across uneven ground, the headlights picking up the bunk-house dead ahead.

Pecos, Lance, and the others saw the machine, like a stampeding horse, headed straight for the door of the bunk-house.

"Come on, men! It's Burke!"

The machine, with a terrific crash, ripped away the door of the log bunk-house. Glass from the shattered windshield and headlights sprayed the men in the car. The huge car, brakes locked, throttle jammed,

341

seemed to leap forward through the mass of wrecked door. It skidded sideways, side-wiping men and furniture. Steam burst hissingly from a torn radiator. Then the skidding car lurched sideways, buckled, and overturned, throwing all but Burke clear.

Red flames shot up from the ignited gas tank.

Jack Parsons lay sprawled on the floor, an ugly gash oozing blood into his eyes. Two crippled men crawled for the doorway in silent fright.

Flames crackled. The big Texan gunman stood white-faced, hypnotized.

"At 'em, men!" gritted Lance, entering the place on a run. "Take prisoners. Snappy, damn it. Lend a hand here, a couple of you. Somebody's under that damn car. God, it's the skipper!"

Willing hands risked the flames, heaving at the burning car. Lance pulled Burke clear. The two officers who had accompanied Pickott and Burke, together with the deputy sheriff from Lance's party, were herding sullenly docile prisoners outside the burning building.

Lance carried Burke out, for the erstwhile driver of the racing car was partly stunned, his face ripped and bloody where the flying glass had struck him. Pickott's face was a mass of cuts also.

The three Kirbys pulled up, breathless. "What the hell, Bill!"

Parsons stood, swaying a little, his eyes on one of Burke's law officers.

"I always had a hunch, Ryan, that there was some rat in you. I was a fool to let you handle those ponies at Pasadena. God, how I hate a fly cop!" He turned to the big Texan.

"You boys keep your traps shut, get that?" Parsons felt gingerly of his wounded arm. "We have an attorney that will clear us of anything. Build me a smoke, Big 'Un. Ryan, if you come near me, I'll kick the belly off you. I'm going with you without bracelets."

Flames from the burning cabin lit up the scene. Burke, lying on the ground, suddenly sat bolt upright, blinking a little.

"Take it easy, skipper," cautioned Lance.

Burke grinned crookedly, his eyes on Parsons, who returned the scrutiny coldly.

"We meet again, Parsons. You don't seem happy." Burke chuckled, then got to his feet, testing his artificial leg.

"I was afraid the blamed thing had gone haywire on me. The old hinge works all right now, though. But I'll never trust it again. Not by a long shot."

"Gosh, skipper, you sure spit in the devil's eye comin' off that slope," said Pickott. "Next time I ride with you, I walk."

"One feather stuck on behind an' you'd bin flyin'," said Pecos. Burke nodded, his gaze on the burning bunk-house that was consuming the wreck of an expensive car.

"This leg." He again tried the offending member. "Can't trust it. Dang thing balked on me and I couldn't pull it off the foot throttle. We came off the top of the hill with that fool cork leg holding 'er wide open. You didn't think I did that devil's slide on purpose, did you? Hardly. Then the brakes locked and I knew we'd somersault. So I pushed her nose into Parsons's house. My only regret is that old Doc Fogarty couldn't have been along. Where is Doc, anyhow?"

But blank silence answered. Burke did not repeat the question.

It was daylight now. Preparations for departure were under way. Bob Kirby told Pecos, Lance, and Burke of the three dead men at the hidden corral.

"I'm afraid," said Lance quietly, "that Doc must have been Injuning around, and when they spotted him he shot it out with 'em. They'd hardly hear the shooting here. Perhaps old Doc is hit. Those three were all good shots. They wouldn't be getting shot at without doing some lead-throwing. Let's go see what it looks like in daylight. Dick and Bob and I'll go."

Chapter XXXIX

Filled with foreboding, Lance rode up the cañon, Dick and Bob following.

There, near the corral and shed that was filled with frightened cattle, they found the three dead men. A quick examination of their guns showed that they had fought for their lives.

Lance tried calling, but no reply came to his hails. Half an hour later they followed a blood-spattered trail to a clump of boulders. There lay Doc Fogarty in a crouching heap, a Winchester in his lap, a hatful of cartridges beside him.

"God, he's dead!" muttered Dick. "Went out a-fightin' too."

Lance bent over the huddled man. "Get some water, Dick."

"You mean he's —"

"He's bleeding like a stuck pig. Dead men don't bleed like that. Hurry, Dick!"

Dick brought a hatful of water from a near-by spring. Lance sat, naked to the waist, ripping his undershirt into bandages. Bob did likewise.

"He's got four holes in him, but none of 'em's fatal, near as I know, unless he bleeds to death. A tourniquet here and another on that leg and we'll get it checked. He's breathing."

They checked the flow of blood, bandaged the wounds, and gently carried Doc to level ground.

"We'll need a stretcher to move him. Gosh, the old boy's coming alive. Lay still, Doc, old-timer."

"All right." Doc tried to smile. "Am I croakin', kid?"

"Not unless somebody comes along and hangs you, you ain't."

"They shot hell outa me, Champ."

"But you're not dying, Doc. Not by a long shot."

"Dunno about that, kid. I feel shore weakish. Ain't got much tuh lose, noways. Jest a maverick, kid. No home ner kinfolks."

"So," growled Lance, "you're goin' to turn yellow, eh? Gonna quit like a dog, eh? A sheep lays down an' dies with a cut on his leg. It's the first time I ever knew you had sheep guts, Doc Fogarty. After all the trouble us boys have taken, you turn your face to the wall and die like a damned sheep, eh?"

A twinkle came into Doc's eyes. He recalled that day in the hospital when he had taunted Lance Mansfield. "You win, kid. I

reckon I gotta live now tuh show yuh I prac-
tise my own preachin', eh?" He grinned and
reached for Dick's cigarette.

"They'll hang me yet if I ain't keerful,"
said Doc. "But get word tuh Jim Kirby that
Lon Jimson is dead. He'll savvy, I killed him
a-purpose. Follered him here from the
cabin. Then them other two cut in an' buys
chips in the game. Tell Jim I got Lon. He'll
savvy."

A grimace of pain twisted Doc's face. His
eyes closed. Lance took the cigarette from
his bared teeth.

"Is he dead, Lance?"

"Ever see a corpse breathe like that? He's
a long ways from dead. Takes more than a
few bullets to kill that warhorse." Lance
winked at Bob and Dick. He had a feeling
that Doc heard and understood what was
going on around him. Doc nursed a secret
pride about being tough. They made a litter
of a blanket and carried Doc down the
cañon to the ranch buildings.

"Dick and I are staying with Doc," Lance
told Burke. "Get a doctor down as soon as
possible."

"I'm on my way fer one right now,"
snapped Pickott.

"Doc'll be in shape to be moved to the
Circle Seven in a week," said Burke.

"Meanwhile, don't feel that you're eating an enemy's grub. I own a big interest in this place."

"You do like hell!" sneered Parsons. "This belongs to the Parsons Land and Cattle Company."

"And the stockholders of that company," nodded Burke blandly, "are in my employ, my friend. They bought in with my money. I'm the man who owns all the stock save yours. Those men are now waiting for you at the Circle Seven. We're holding a stockholders' meeting. You're going to tell us the how-come of some crooked deals you've pulled. That bill of sale for those stolen ponies will cook your goose, my slick hombre. Then there are those Circle Seven and Bench-K cattle in Wyoming. You didn't know your Wyoming foreman was another United States deputy marshal, the same as Ryan. Those cattle go back to their owners. You go to the pen. These men trail with you. A man that makes snake tracks should cover them more cleverly, Parsons." Burke turned to Lance and the Kirbys.

"For a girl, Teton Kirby is a great business man," he said. "Thank her for helping me put this over. She's kept me posted the past year. Whoever said that a woman can't keep a secret never met Jim Kirby's daughter. She learned enough from Parsons one night at a dance to get a line on him. She kept her eye on Ben Fisk, the land-grabber. Fisk tried to prove that Tom Mansfield committed suicide. None of you knew that, not even Parsons — nobody but Teton and I and a gentleman from China known as Ah Hell. Seems that Teton had a hunch Ah Hell knew more than he let on. Her hunch was right. So when Ah Hell went to Helena, he called at the insurance office. Teton went with him.

"Tom Mansfield did not commit suicide. He contemplated it, yes. Then changed his mind. I have Ah Hell's word for it, and that Chinaman would rather have his tongue cut out than voice a lie. Yes, gents, Tom Mansfield, for some reason, changed his mind. He was unloading his gun when the thing went off accidentally. Talk about the irony of fate!

"Now if somebody will stake me to a cayuse that's broke to pack a man with a wooden leg, I'll be getting Parsons to the Circle Seven for the directors' meeting. Once he is out of the company, I hope to organize a pool outfit. Almost have to pool the Circle Seven, Bench-K, and Quarter-Circle Z to straighten out all the stolen stuff.

"Lance, Jim Kirby and sons — think

you'd like to pool in with me? You'd better. My erstwhile partner and manager Parsons has been stealing you blind. I've wintered half your cattle. Do you gents want to form the Circle Seven Pool?"

"With you puttin' up the money?" growled Jim Kirby.

"And you the experience," put in Burke. "Nobody's going to lose a dime. We'll all make money. Hell, you can't back out. Teton's my sidekick and general manager. Better start in a fence crew pulling down the line-fences between the places. Doc can run this end of it when he gets able to ride again."

"I dodged enough sheriffs down in these hills to shore know the country," said Doc, who lay on Jack Parsons's bed. "Say, I just killed three men. One of 'em was Lon Jimson, who was wearin' a stock inspector's badge. Mebby so I wain't what yuh might call at liberty tuh jigger a cow spread?"

"Jimson's badge," said United States Marshal Ryan, "don't weigh much. We let him get appointed to give Parsons enough rope to hang them all. And there may be a reward on the other two. I'll look 'em over. As for any old charges against you, Fogarty, your war record balances the sheet. It's what you do from now on that counts."

"You say I'm gonna be the main rod down here, Brimstone?" quizzed Doc. "Holdin' a real foreman, straw-boss, seegar-smokin' position uh more-er-less-general manager?"

"That hits 'er, Doc."

"With hirin' an' firin' privilege?"

"Sure thing. Hire 'em and fire 'em to your heart's content."

"Never did hire nobody — ner fire nobody. It's always bin a kinda dream ambition uh mine to do it. There's a list I got made out in my mind. Gents I'm gonna hire at top wages, then fire 'em next day. Jimson an' Tanner headed the list, but they're past firin'." Doc lay back, a contented smile on his mouth.

"Buck an' Slim'll be shore hot under the collar," said Pecos, "when they find out what they missed." He had been exploring the house that was Jack Parsons's living quarters. From his hip pocket he pulled a large silver flask and set it beside Doc's bed. . . .

"Yep, them two jaspers'll have big fits an' little uns, losin' out on this party. Lance, you got a mother an' gal waitin' fer to see yuh. Me, I ain't got nobody but Sultan an' some houn' pups. I'm stayin' with Doc an' this snake-bite medicine I dug up. There's mebbe more somewheres, when me'n Doc annihilates this dram. Me'n Dick kin ride herd on Doc."

So Lance, eager to see his mother and Teton, rode up the ridge with Jim Kirby and Burke and Bob. The officers took care of the prisoners.

Two men came behind with the bodies of Jimson and the two hired killers in a spring wagon.

"Brimstone," said Jim Kirby, addressing Burke by the name that was to be his cow-country title, "Maw an' me an' Teton an' the boys won't never fergit what —"

"Unless you want an imitation of a one-legged man licking a one-armed man, pull in your ears and light a smoke. Look yonder. A robin. Looks like the winter's gone."

"You an' Chinook hit us about the same time," grinned Jim Kirby. And had the old cow-man tried, he could not have expressed Burke's welcome more aptly.

As their horses climbed the trail, home-ward-bound, the words of a cowboy's song came drifting through the scrub pines:

"Parson, I'm a maverick, just runnin'
loose an' grazin' . . ."

We hope you have enjoyed this Large Print book. Other Thorndike, Wheeler or Chivers Press Large Print books are available at your library or directly from the publishers.

For more information about current and upcoming titles, please call or write, without obligation, to:

Publisher
Thorndike Press
295 Kennedy Memorial Drive
Waterville, ME 04901
Tel. (800) 223-1244

Or visit our Web site at:
www.thomson.com/thorndike
www.thomson.com/wheeler

OR

Chivers Large Print
published by BBC Audiobooks Ltd
St James House, The Square
Lower Bristol Road
Bath BA2 3BH
England
Tel. +44(0) 800 136919
email: bbcaudiobooks@bbc.co.uk
www.bbcaudiobooks.co.uk

All our Large Print titles are designed for easy reading, and all our books are made to last.